ONE SWEET LOVE

One Sweet Love

MEGAN BYRD

ARDENVILLE PRESS

To Mom,
I love you.

1

MARCH

Julie

WHEN I'M SURE the chocolate mixture is the perfect consistency, I pour it into the waiting clover-shaped molds on the counter in front of me. I gently shake the molds to get rid of any air bubbles, wipe the excess chocolate from the top of each, and one-by-one carry them to the cooling fridge to set up for a few minutes. In the meantime, I turn my attention to making more of this month's specialty truffle, affectionately nicknamed Pot of Gold. The not-so-secret ingredient is Bailey's Irish Cream.

The phone rings, jolting me from my rhythm of rolling balls of chocolate and placing them on the conveyor belt. It rings again and I stick my head through the doorway leading from the kitchen to the main part of the floor. Emily, part-time employee and my best friend, is serving a customer and the line of people waiting to be helped stretches halfway across the store. The phone rings again and I rush over to it, peeling the chocolate-coated gloves from my hands and tossing them in the trash can.

A whirring sound starts up behind me and I turn to find the

conveyor belt inching the truffle centers toward the chocolate enrober's waterfall of liquid dark chocolate. Dashing back over to the machine, I flip the lever to turn it off, then take a calming breath before answering the call. "Little Shop of Sugar, this is Julie. How may I help you?"

"Do you make wedding cakes?"

"No, sorry. I can provide tiers of truffles, if you're open to a non-cake dessert option."

It's quiet on the phone and I wonder if the person's hung up, but then the voice comes through. "No, we want to cut a cake. Thanks, though."

After washing my hands and putting on a new pair of disposable gloves, I return to the big bowl of truffle mixture. I scoop some out with a melon baller and then roll it into a perfect ball between my palms. Most people probably wouldn't take the time for this last step, but I pride myself on having uniform globes of truffles in my store. I set it on the conveyor belt next to me, smiling at the perfect rows of half-made confections. Something trickles down my forehead from under my hat and I brush it away with my wrist. My elbow hits the melon baller, which falls off the counter, taking the bowl with it. The scoop clatters against the floor and the bowl lands with a splat, chocolate-side down.

My head drops back, and a groan of frustration erupts from my belly. After giving myself a few seconds to pout, I bend down and pick up the bowl, tossing the melon baller in the sink. Thankfully, I'd already gotten most of the chocolate onto the conveyor belt, so the mess is minimal. Still, it means I'll have to make another batch of truffle centers tomorrow. I scrape the remains of the bowl into the trash, deposit the bowl in the sink, then clean up the floor.

The phone rings again, but Emily must pick it up because it only rings twice. I turn on the machine and watch the conveyor belt carry the balls through the sheet of liquid chocolate, looking silky and delicious on the other side. When the shells are firm, I dust them with edible gold powder and carefully affix a green shamrock made of chocolate to the top with tweezers. When they're finished, I set them all on a wax paper-lined tray and transfer them to the walk-in fridge right next to a tray of Blackouts distinguished by the dark chocolate swirl design adorning their dark chocolate shells. I survey the rows of truffles, pleased with the day's work.

After washing dishes and cleaning up the kitchen, I head out to the main floor to see if Emily needs help with customers, but the shop's empty. No wonder. I've worked past closing time. Emily comes through the other doorway with a broom and dustpan. I hold out my hand.

"Here, let me take that."

Emily hugs the broom handle to her chest. "Nope, you've been hard at it all day."

"So have you."

She sets the dustpan behind the counter, then walks to the corner near the door and starts sweeping. "I've just been helping customers. You've been doing the heavy lifting. Head on home."

"You know I can't do that. I'll stay and keep you company, even if you won't let me help."

Emily shrugs a shoulder. She's familiar with how stubborn I am. "Suit yourself. Hey, I fielded more calls from people looking for wedding cakes today. You really should add that to your services. I bet we'd get a lot of truffle orders along with it. Many people have multiple desserts at weddings these days."

Leaning against the wall, my arms crossed over my chest, I shake my head even though Emily's facing away from me. "We've discussed this. I know it has great potential, but I'm barely treading water with my current responsibilities. I can't even consider adding anything else."

"I know you're doing the best you can. Hiring additional help would ease your load a little, but what you really need is someone who can help you out on the managerial side."

Emily gives me a stern look, and I give her one right back. "You turned down my offer of a promotion to business manager, or have you forgotten?"

She scoffs. "Have *you* forgotten I don't have the experience, nor do I want that level of responsibility? I'm happy working with customers."

My shoulders sag. My body feels heavy, and it's hitting me how tired I am. "No, I remember. I'll think about it." I don't know how much longer I can survive like this. *But Uncle Bill did it alone.* Thanks, brain. I know. Maybe he made a mistake giving me the business. This isn't the first time I've had this thought, but it's become more pervasive as the store's success has grown.

I turn our conversation to lighter subjects, and by the time the shop's cleaned up, we're both laughing. Emily gives me a hug before grabbing her purse and heading home. I do one last check around the store, then lock up and walk to my apartment.

When I open the door, Sadie nearly knocks me over in greeting, her tail whapping hard against the wall. My heart lifts at her enthusiasm for my return. Everyone should have a dog. There's nothing that makes me feel better than seeing her mouth open in that doggy grin I love so much. I grab her leash, and we head outside to the park. After a couple loops, Sadie's ready to head back home. I fill her food and water bowls, then choose a container of leftovers from the fridge, not even bothering to see what's inside.

Settling myself on the couch, I pop open the lid and smile tiredly when I see it's taco night. They're gone in a flash and I have to force myself to get back up, put on pajamas, and brush my teeth before I crash onto my bed, knowing tomorrow will be just as taxing as today.

Owning a business is an exhausting and lonely endeavor, but I have Sadie, who's as faithful as can be. That'll have to be enough for now.

2

Jayson

AFTER ANOTHER LONG day at the office, I'm happy to be home where I can watch television and unwind. My work helping families grow through adoption is busy but rewarding. So much better than some of the other days dealing with divorces. Thankfully, Aunt Alicia seems to sense how much I enjoy bringing families together and has increased that part of my workload. Coming in through the garage, I toss my keys into the bowl on the kitchen counter, then open the fridge. My box of leftover Chinese food is missing, but there's still Italian. I empty the cardboard container onto a plate and warm it up in the microwave. While it heats, I chug a glass of water and refill it again.

When the microwave beeps, I grab my plate and some silverware and head out to the living room. I stop short when I discover two heads sticking up from the sofa. My shoulders sag, knowing that I won't be watching mindless shows tonight. *You can do it, Jayson. Make small talk and then jet when your food's gone.*

"Hey Britt. Neil." I set my plate on the coffee table and drop into a chair, not missing the plates already there with evidence of my missing fried rice and General Tso's chicken.

My sister's boyfriend lifts his chin in acknowledgment, but keeps his eyes on the screen. Britt picks up the remote and mutes the basketball game they're watching. At least they were actually watching it and not making out on my couch. I've lost count the number of times I've walked in on that exact situation. No one wants to see their baby sister kissing another person.

"Hey, Jay. How was your day?" she says.

I take a bite of my chicken parmesan and then breathe out of my mouth when the molten cheese burns the roof of my mouth. After successfully choking down the food, I cut up the rest of the chicken into bite-size pieces so it can cool. I twirl some spaghetti on my fork and test a strand with my tongue. Satisfied that I won't get second-degree burns, I shove the fork into my mouth. The food is good, but not amazing like what I've gotten at Gli Amanti. I need to go there again soon. Maybe if the firm wins another high-profile case, my aunt will take me.

Britt's looking at me expectantly and I realize I haven't answered her yet. I quickly chew my food so I can answer. "Busy, obviously. How about you?"

"Pretty good. We booked another wedding today, so now all of our summer Saturdays are officially full."

"That's great!"

We turn our attention to the game, and Britt turns the volume back on. I can't help but notice how cozy Britt and Neil look on the couch. Neil's arm cradles Britt's back, hugging her to him. Britt's legs are slung across Neil's lap and her head rests against his shoulder. A twinge of longing shoots through me. Don't get me wrong, I'm happy for my sister, but maybe I'm ready for some happiness of my own.

Work's great, but I've allowed it to take up more than its fair share of my days. That I'm eating leftovers on a Friday night with my sister and her boyfriend is proof I need to think about changing something up. But where would I meet someone? Certainly not the office. And the courthouse isn't a viable option either. Definitely not at basketball. The only women there are players' girlfriends. So that leaves me with either the restaurants where I pick up food or joining a dating app. Neither of those sound appealing to me. I'll figure something out. First things first, I have to stop working late, so I have time available to go on a date.

My eyes catch on Britt's and Neil's hands intertwined together and my heart twists. *Maybe if I admit I'm ready for a relationship, it'll happen.* I don't want to broadcast my loneliness to the world just yet, but I can allow myself to be open to the possibility. It's a start, albeit a tiny one.

Neil turns his face and places a tender kiss on top of Britt's head and I'm done. I can't watch this sweet lovefest anymore or I'm going to feel like an even bigger loser. I scarf the rest of my dinner and stand up.

"I think I'll turn in. Enjoy the rest of your evening."

Yes, I realize I just said I was going to bed at—I look at the time on the microwave—nine o'clock on a Friday. I'm only twenty-eight. Too young to be acting like a retired person. Starting tomorrow, I'm going to look for opportunities to talk to women I'm not related to. I'm a decent-looking guy with a good job. I even own my home. Yes, my sister lives with me, but that's not permanent. *Look out, women of Asheville. I'm ready to mingle.*

3

APRIL

Julie

I SWEAR UNDER my breath, worried I'm going to be late. I enjoy being late as much as I like solicitors trying to sell me new, energy-efficient windows for the store—a building I don't own. The pace of my sweeping picks up as I plead with the floor to magically divest itself of dirt. Why did I agree to attend the meeting, knowing I can't physically be in two places at once? Why am I so stupid sometimes?

"Hey Julie, are you okay?" Emily stands behind the counter, watching me with concern.

"Yeah, I'm fine. Just trying to get the store cleaned up so I can head over to Rachel's book club."

"Doesn't that start in two minutes?"

My shoulders slouch as I loosen my death grip on the broom handle. I feel like I'm constantly failing these days. "Yes, it does."

Emily steps around the counter and holds out her hand. "I'll finish closing the store for you. Get out of here and have fun."

I shake my head, clutching the broom handle to my chest. "I

can't make you do that, Em. I'm sure you have your own plans for the evening."

Emily tsks. "Julie, I've worked here for two years now. I know what needs to be done. You gave me a key. Let me use it."

I hesitate, and she fixes me with a frustrated scowl.

"What happened to the store when you went to Charlie's wedding?"

My brows pinch together as I try to remember what happened last January. "Um, nothing?"

"That's right. I handled everything just fine while you were in New York and I will be just as responsible while you're across the street."

I duck my head, properly chastised. If I can't trust my best friend, who can I trust? It's not right to thrust my own doubts and insecurities on her. She's as responsible as they come. She shouldn't have to deal with my self-made messes. "I feel bad passing my responsibilities on to you."

"I can handle things tonight. Trust me."

Her words pierce my conscience. Emily is well aware of my trust issues. Sometimes I'm amazed at her patience with me. I angle the broom handle toward her, and she takes it with a smile.

"There ya go. Not too hard, right? Now, you really better go. You are officially late and, if I'm not mistaken, you're in charge of dessert."

"You're right! I still have to put truffles into a container. Rachel's going to regret inviting me to her group."

"I've got you covered." Emily walks behind the counter and then sets two gold boxes on top of the chocolates display.

My shoulders sink with relief. "You're a lifesaver, Em. What would I do without you?"

She shrugs. "You'd work even harder than you already do, probably. Which is why you need a business manager."

"We're back on that again, huh? My uncle didn't need a

business manager, and he did just fine."

"Did he also have no life apart from the store?"

I stop to consider that. "Um, I don't know. He wasn't married, so he didn't have a family to spend time with. But neither do I, so I guess I'm good. Besides, I *have* a social life. I'm going to a book club, or haven't you heard?"

Emily sighs. "There's more to life than work, Julie. And, I'd like to point out, you haven't actually *gone* to a book club meeting yet. In fact, you're going to miss the one tonight if you keep arguing with me."

I startle. "Oh, right." Hurrying behind the counter, I grab my purse and the chocolate boxes, and head toward the door. "Thanks for your help tonight. I owe you."

"No, you don't. Just go have some fun and relax. I've got everything covered here."

I half smile, half grimace. "I'll do my best."

Backing out of the front door, my eyes light up when I hear the merry tinkle of the bells. I love that sound. The bells have been above the door for as long as I can remember. All my childhood memories of the Little Shop of Sugar involve the airy tinkle and my uncle's huge grin, which went all the way to his eyes. There's a pang of sadness as I remember Uncle Bill. How has it already been four years since his death?

Out on the sidewalk in front of the store, I suck in a deep breath and let it out slowly. I've worked so hard to make sure his business continues to thrive. All I want to do is make him proud and prove I deserve the confidence he had in me. I think he'd be happy with how things are going, but also have to admit that the store has taken over my whole life. I barely have time for my dog. Maybe I really should figure out how to add some more non-work activities to my schedule for that balance I've heard is so important. I can start right now by joining Rachel and her friends at Page Turner Books.

Straightening my back and shoulders, I head for the

crosswalk. After looking both ways for cars, I step out into the street just as I feel my phone buzz in my purse. Is it Rachel wondering where I am or Emily with a question? I glance back at the store and can just make out Emily holding the broom. Something slams into my left side, wrenching the boxes out of my hand. My purse slides off my shoulder, its contents spilling all over the street. A moment later, something cold and wet hits my chest and trickles down my shirt. My eyes widen in surprise and I yelp.

Looking down, a large brown stain covers most of my cream-colored blouse. Trails of dark liquid run down the legs of my black slacks, some pooling in my shoes. My gaze snags on a pair of immaculate black Oxfords about a foot in front of me. My eyes rove up gray tailored suit pants and a matching jacket with a crisp white dress shirt and sleek black tie. None of which have brown stains on them, I note. My eyes continue up, my head raising to reach the face of this tall human being. He sports a short, neatly trimmed beard and mustache and a brush cut fade. His eyes look like onyx against his medium brown skin. My gaze catches briefly on his full, parted lips. I blink away the feeling of attraction and shiver as a slight breeze reminds me I'm half-soaked through with an unknown liquid that is definitely sticky and smells strongly like coffee.

Narrowing my gaze, I stick a hand on my hip, waiting for some sort of excuse or explanation. The man just stares, frozen. I continue to glare at him.

He shakes his head, blinking quickly. "I'm so, so sorry. I didn't see you there. I was trying to text and walk, which, as you can see, was not the best idea."

My ire ebbs when I remember I hadn't exactly been paying full attention to where I was going myself. Any remaining feelings of ill will continue to dissipate until the next words leave his mouth.

"But, I mean, didn't you see me coming? Couldn't you have

gotten out of the way? Now I have to go buy another coffee."

Heat shoots to my face, and I release any thought of claiming partial fault in the fiasco. "Ex—*cuse* me? Could *I* have gotten out of *your* way?" *Who does he think he is, king of the sidewalk?* "How did *you* earn sidewalk priority?"

The man's eyebrows shoot up his forehead and he rocks back on his heels. "No, that's not what I meant—"

"And who cares about you having to spend another five dollars on a beverage?" *By the looks of that suit, it shouldn't be an issue.* "You, however, have *ruined* my outfit and I'm late for a meeting. I guess I'll have to hope they aren't too big on first impressions, as I can only imagine what this will make on them." I wave my hands up and down my body for emphasis.

My glare stays strong throughout my rant, daring him to say something else insulting or condescending. He holds his hands up like shields. "I didn't mean to ruin your outfit or make you late for a meeting. I was distracted and I apologize. Let me pay for your dry cleaning. Send me the bill, or let me buy you a replacement."

He reaches into his pocket and extends a business card to me. I eye it skeptically before taking it from his fingers. "Jayson Thompson, Attorney." That explains his holier-than-though attitude and fancy clothes.

He shuffles his shoes and shoves his hands into his pockets. "That's me. And you are...?"

"Still late for a meeting." Pocketing the card, I search the ground for my dropped items. One box of chocolate is at my feet. I bend down and pick it up, shoving all the small things from my purse back inside. Turning to look for the rest of my stuff, I'm once again staring at those expensive leather shoes. Glancing up, I find the other box and my book, one of the things dislodged from my purse, in Jayson's hands. I can't help but notice his nails are short and neat. Does he get manicures? Probably.

He hands them back, nodding at the stack of items in my hand. "*A Man Called Ove*, huh? Good book."

"Yeah, I thought so. At first, I wasn't sure what to think, but Backman's way of writing a character where he reveals information over time really won me over to the guy's side."

Jayson nods, his serious expression evening out to something resembling a smile. "And I think—"

"I'm still late for my meeting. I'd say 'nice to meet you,' but, well..." My hand motions to my wet clothes.

He closes his mouth and nods. I think that's the end of it, but then his appealing mouth opens again. Not that I was looking at it and imagining what it might feel like against mine or anything. Nope, definitely not.

"Again, I'm sorry. Let me know what I owe you."

I pluck the soaked shirt away from my skin and grimace at the way it peels away. There was a lot of sugar in that iced coffee. Raising my chin, I maneuver around Jayson, heading toward my destination. I fight the urge to glance back one last time.

4

Jayson

AFTER MAKING SURE the woman makes it safely across the street, I turn back around and survey the mess. I pick up the empty cup, lid, and straw, tossing it in a nearby trash can. I feel awful about ruining her shirt, especially since she has an important meeting. Hopefully, she'll take me up on my offer of paying for her dry cleaning. Maybe then I'll learn her name. I close my eyes and picture her wavy brown hair and her brilliant emerald green eyes that flashed like lightning at me. A few freckles were visible before her cheeks flamed in anger. While I don't know what she looks like without iced coffee splashed across her front, the wet shirt highlighted her gorgeous, curvy figure. I can't believe I was so rude to her, but I must admire her ability to give it right back. It's not every day you run into such an intriguing woman.

When I open my eyes again, there's no trace of my fiery foe. Retracing my steps to Hill of Beans, I join the order line for the second time in fifteen minutes. I pull my phone out and sigh when I see it's nearly seven-thirty. I'm going to be working late again tonight. So much for changing my habits. When I reach the register, I order another iced coffee and add a latte for myself. On impulse, I also pick up a small box of chocolates near the register. The gold lid stirs something in my memory, but I can't quite put a finger on it. Perhaps the chocolate and caffeine will help me push through the fatigue I'm feeling. When my order's ready, I grab the cups and head back to the office.

Inside the conference room, Aunt Alicia's pouring over a bunch of documents spread out across the table. She looks up at me. I put the cup in her hand when she reaches out expectantly. She takes a long pull on the straw. "Ah, that's the stuff."

"You're welcome. I ran into someone, which caused a delay."

Her face lights with interest. "Anyone I know?"

I shake my head. "No. It wasn't anyone I know either. I literally ran into someone."

She chuckles. "That sounds embarrassing."

Yep. Definitely embarrassing. But maybe also a little exciting. I don't think I've seen the woman before, but if she had a meeting, she might be local. I'll have to keep my eyes open for the spunky brunette. "It was. I spilled your coffee on them and possibly ruined their shirt."

"Did you offer to make amends?"

Experience tells me her question is actually a statement. She knows I was raised to do everything in my power to rectify a situation. "Of course, Auntie. But I don't know if she'll take me up on it. She was pretty upset."

Her head snaps up. I can see by her smile she thinks there's more to the story, but her response is casual. "She was probably just embarrassed."

I shrug, not wanting to give anything away. "Maybe. Anyway, how's it looking?" I gesture toward the table, hoping the distraction will close this conversation topic.

"It looks like we'll be okay, but I need to make sure we have everything lined up. Drake Johnson is representing the other side and you know how meticulous he is. We can't afford to miss anything or have anything out of order."

"Very true." I take a drink of my coffee, only then remembering the truffles in my pocket. I open the lid and pop one in my mouth. The rich chocolate flavor on my tongue overwhelms me. My eyes close while I savor the taste. This is good. Superb, even.

"Everything alright, Jayson?"

When I open my eyes, my aunt is studying me, her head tilted and forehead scrunched up. "I'm fine. These truffles are delicious. Have one."

She chooses one from the box in my hand. When she takes a bite, her hum of delight makes me grin. "Mmm, these are good. Where'd you get them?"

"I picked them up at Hill of Beans."

The shiny gold lid is void of a logo, so I lift the white box bottom and peer underneath. A sticker affixed to the bottom lists the name and address of the store. "It's from Little Shop of Sugar on Haywood Street."

"I think I've seen that place. Brown and white striped awning and a neon sign?"

"I think you're right."

"I'll definitely be stopping in there soon."

"Maybe I will, too."

5

Julie

WHEN I OPEN the door to Page Turner Books, the loud mechanical "ding-dong" startles me. I turn the lock as Rachel instructed, then walk down the main aisle toward the back of the store. The pleasing aroma of freshly brewed coffee draws me through the maze of bookshelves and toward a light at the end of a hallway.

Loud chatter fills my ears as I approach the door leading to a brightly lit room. I pause at the threshold, taking in the scene. Rachel's talking animatedly to a woman with bright pink, short, spiky hair. Three other women are over by the coffeepot. One looks like the quintessential grandmother with permed gray hair, black slacks, and a flower print shirt. Another wears dark jeans and a red sweater, her straight white hair hanging halfway down her back. The third woman sports a blunt brown bob and chic green-rimmed glasses, dressed in khaki pants and a light blue sweater set.

Rachel turns my way and smiles when we lock eyes. She claps her hands together, garnering the attention of the room. "Ladies, my future sister-in-law is joining us this evening! Please make her feel welcome. Come on in, Julie."

I step fully into the room and walk toward Rachel. Her eyes widen as she takes in my disastrous appearance. "Oh, Julie. Do you need a towel?"

I smile wanly. "Yes, a towel would be great. Or maybe a restart button for the past few minutes."

Rachel hurries over to a set of lockers on the far wall, opening a door, and pulling out a towel. "Here. I'll walk you to the bathroom down the hall and then find a clean shirt for you to wear."

Gratitude bubbles in my chest at her consideration. It eases some of my annoyance and frustration. "That would be wonderful. What should I do with dessert?"

I hold up the boxes of chocolate, and Rachel passes them to the woman with the pink hair. "Anna, would you get these set up for us? Dig in, and we'll be back in a few minutes."

Inside the bathroom, I study my reflection in the mirror. My shirt is practically see-through and clinging in a way that highlights my chest. My cheeks flush in embarrassment. Ugh, the lawyer probably noticed, too. No wonder he'd frozen. At least it's my nice bra. I peel my shirt off and run the towel over my torso. Stepping out of my shoes, I pick them up and tip them toward the sink, watching brown liquid drip out of the heels. Then I grab a few tissues off the sink to remove any remaining moisture.

The bathroom door opens and Rachel enters carrying a green t-shirt and a plastic bag. "You can stick your wet shirt in here."

"Thanks." Each act of kindness Rachel shows me makes me like her more. I'm so glad she's the one my brother's marrying. I pull the shirt over my head, remove my hair from the neck, and turn back to the mirror. I read it and smirk. "All the cool kids are reading, huh?"

Rachel chuckles. "All the shirts in our store are book-themed. I hope that's okay."

"It's wonderful. I need some levity after having iced coffee spilled all over me. In fact, perhaps I should start selling chocolate-themed clothing in my store."

Rachel nods. "I'd buy a shirt that says 'Chocoholic' on it. That's a coffee stain? I didn't think you liked iced coffee."

"I don't. Some jerk ran into me and spilled his coffee."

"Ah. I'm sorry. Are you still up for joining our group this evening? I understand if you'd rather just go home."

The thought tempts me, but I'm already here, so I might as well stay. "I think I'm good. I can't wait to meet these Book Babes you've talked so much about."

Rachel grins. "Great. Let's do it."

When we return to the meeting room, the other women are sitting in chairs arranged in a circle holding small plates of truffles. Their conversation comes to a halt, and all eyes turn my way. Rachel ushers me over to the refreshments table and hands me a plate, but I stop her with my hand. "I eat enough of these at work," I whisper.

"Lucky," she whispers back, before placing two truffles on her plate. She leads me over to the circle and I sit down between Rachel and the woman with the glasses.

"Now that we're all arranged," Rachel says, "let's share a little about ourselves to help Julie feel more comfortable. I'll go first and then Anna, you go next, and we'll continue around the circle with Julie finishing up. Sound good?"

Heads nod. "Excellent. I'm Rachel, obviously. My first novel comes out this year, and I'm working on a storyline for the second one. I'm engaged to Tom and we're getting married in two months." She nudges the pink-haired woman. "Your turn."

"I'm Anna. Deb invited me to this group." She motions to the grandmotherly woman next to her. "I'm single and work at Pack Library. I've lived in Asheville for seven years and love hiking and kayaking." She swings her gaze to Deb, who gives me a warm smile.

"My name's Deb. I'm a widow with two grown children and

three grandchildren. I used to be a florist but am now retired, and have lived in Asheville for nearly twenty-five years. And, I just wanted to say that I remember your uncle from small business meetings we used to attend together. I'm sorry for your loss, hon."

Tears spring to my eyes at the mention of Bill. I blink to hold them back while considering whether to talk to her after group and find out what she remembers about him. Deb nods to the woman next to her with the straight white hair.

"I'm Lori, one of the founding members of Book Babes with Deb and Rachel. Gerwing Family Dentistry is where I work as a dental hygienist. Although I'm married, I'm obsessed with Colin Firth and have seen all his movies, though *Pride & Prejudice* is my favorite."

The woman with the glasses turns to me. "Hi, I'm Susan. I'm a stay-at-home mom of three boys, two already in college and one who's a junior in high school. My husband, Roger, is an accountant. In my free time, I volunteer at the animal shelter."

Susan turns her gaze to me, and I take a breath. "Hi, I'm Julie, owner of Little Shop of Sugar across the street and soon-to-be sister-in-law of Rachel." I smile at Rachel. "I've lived here since I was eighteen, about fourteen years. We used to visit my uncle in the summers, so I was already familiar with the area. I have a dog named Sadie." I pause, trying to come up with another interesting fact about my life, but draw a blank. "I guess that's it."

"Alright," Rachel says, clapping her hands. "Now that we've made introductions and have eaten some of Julie's delectable confections, let's dive into the discussion of *A Man Called Ove*. Deb, what was your overall impression of the story?"

When the meeting's over, I stay behind to help Rachel straighten up. I tackle the refreshment table while she stacks chairs.

"That was fun," I say, feeling energized after interacting with new people.

"Yes, it was. I'm so glad you could join us."

"Thanks for the invitation. It was nice to get out and do something with other people for a change."

Rachel places the last chair on top of the others. "Do you think you'll come back next month?"

"I haven't read *A Room with a View* and the description sounds intriguing. If I'm not too busy, I'll plan to be here."

Rachel claps her hands together, bouncing on her toes. "Excellent. I'm so glad to hear that."

"Your group was passionate about tonight's book."

Rachel smiles. "Yes, they're a very spirited bunch. I appreciate your help with cleanup."

"You're welcome. Do you want to take the leftover chocolates home? There's an Ancient Treasure and a couple of Blackouts. You and Tom can share."

"You know I never turn down your truffles. Thanks so much!"

"Thank Tom for walking Sadie for me. I feel like I'm neglecting her these days. The store's been so demanding. I don't know how to change things to give her more attention."

Rachel dismisses my guilt with a wave of her hand. "Oh, he loves it. He and Sadie have so much fun at the park. I don't think he considers it an inconvenience."

"That's good to hear. How's he been doing with less travel?"

Rachel tilts her hand back and forth in a so-so motion. "So far, so good. I can tell it's been weird for him not going anywhere for a couple of months and I know he's missing seeing Jeff, but they'll come to town for the wedding, so he doesn't have to wait too much longer."

"Yeah, it's a big change for Tom. For you, too. How are you doing with him being around all the time?"

"I love it."

We smile at each other for a few seconds before a thought pops in to my head. "I'm in charge of dessert for your wedding, but is there anything else you need me to do as a bridesmaid?"

Rachel reaches over and squeezes my shoulder. "That's so kind of you to ask, but I think we've got everything handled. I'm so glad we found such a lovely venue."

I grin. "Yes. And one that holds history for you two."

Rachel's cheeks color and her eyes sparkle. "I know. The memories may be my favorite part of our location. Oh! My sister's hosting a shower for me next month at my apartment. I'll send you the details, but I hope you'll be able to come."

"I'll put it on my calendar." Which gives me an idea. "Would you send me the email addresses of the Book Babes? I'd like to get everyone's input on which truffles I should bring next time."

"Oh, you don't have to do that. I'm more than happy to come by and pay for them."

"I'm glad to do it. Besides, it'll make sure I show up." I give her a conspiratorial wink.

Rachel smiles. "You don't have to twist *my* arm. I'm a sucker for your truffles, and I'd love for you to keep joining us."

"Then it's settled."

"And we're all done here, too. Time to head home."

I pick up my purse and hand the chocolates to Rachel. When we reach the front door, Rachel pulls me into a hug, then sets off down the street toward her home. I turn and walk in the opposite direction toward my apartment, already looking forward to relaxing a bit before bed.

6

Julie

"I'M HEADED OUT to grab a smoothie while it's quiet in here." I glance at Emily when I exit the office, slinging my purse over my shoulder. "Would you like one?"

Her eyes brighten. "Sure. I'll take a Strawberry Blast. Thanks." She might love the smoothies from Hill of Beans more than I do.

"You got it. I'll be back in about fifteen minutes, depending on the line."

The door chimes merrily when I exit, eliciting an automatic smile from me. I head down the street to the right, making two left turns before opening the door to Hill of Beans. The line is three people deep, which gives me time to figure out what I want.

The man in front of me is so tall his head blocks the menu board from my view. He's wearing a well-tailored navy suit and impeccable brown leather dress shoes. The entire outfit screams money. My stomach sinks when I realize who it is. *Oh no, it's the lawyer who spilled his coffee on me. I really don't want to deal with a self-absorbed guy right now.* I consider bolting, but am really craving a smoothie. Besides, I should be fairly incognito with my hair hidden under a hat. For extra assurance, I slide my sunglasses off the brim and over my eyes. *Perhaps he's too engaged with his phone to even glance my way.*

When it's my turn at the counter, I place my order, careful to keep my face angled away from him, pretending to be engrossed in the display case of muffins and cookies, but still keeping the lawyer in my peripheral vision.

"Um, excuse me?"

There's a tap on my shoulder. My mind scrambles for a plausible excuse not to respond, but comes up empty. I look up, making my face as blank as possible. "Yes?"

"Do we know each other?"

He hasn't put it together yet. Technically, we haven't met because I never gave him my name. Time to play coy. When I speak, I pitch my voice high to throw him off. "I don't think so. Maybe I have one of those faces." I'm wearing my store uniform of khaki pants and navy polo, which shouldn't give him any clues.

He shakes his head, leaning closer to study me. I take a step back, sweat prickling the back of my neck, but not before I get a whiff of his cologne. It's one thing to be attractive, which any woman with a pulse would notice about this man. But why does he have to smell so good, too? It's almost enough to knock down my defenses. But I know how disastrous it was the last time I fell for a hot guy who smelled delectable. Fool me once, and all that.

"No, that's not it. Have you been to court recently?"

I furrow my brow and press my lips together, feeling affronted. I prepare to give him a verbal dressing down, but the barista halts me by calling Jayson's name and setting two drinks on the counter—one hot and one iced coffee. Reflexively, I take another step away from him. He's not spilling on me today.

He picks up the drinks and hits me with a piercing gaze. My face warms under his scrutiny and I tug the bill of my hat lower.

"A Strawberry Blast and an Orange Dream for Julie."

Thank goodness for the barista. I give Jayson a wide berth as I step up to the counter and retrieve my order. When I turn,

Jayson's still watching me. I head toward the door. His long legs beat me there and he holds it open for me. Is he a boy scout too, besides being an unusually tall, very handsome, and well-dressed lawyer? Avoiding eye contact, I duck my head. "Thanks."

I turn left, retracing my steps back to the store. When I turn right, there's a chuckle behind me. I pick up the pace, hoping to put some distance between us. A rumble of laughter sounds behind me after I take another right back onto Haywood Street. I spin around. Jayson's grinning, humor in his eyes. Annoyance sparks inside. I lower my head in a glare before realizing the effect's probably muted by the sunglasses covering my eyes. To get the point across, I lower my voice to a growl. "Are you following me?"

He stops in his tracks, a stunned look on his face. "Aha!" he says. "You're the woman I ran into the other week." He looks around and points at the crosswalk up the hill. "Right over there, as a matter of fact."

My eyes skitter over the scene of the crime and back to Jayson. *Thanks for the reminder of that embarrassing moment.* Time to cut and run. I shrug and turn toward the front door of my store.

"Wait," he calls. I don't turn around, but hear quick footfalls as he catches up to me. "Please." Jayson steps in front of me. "You didn't contact me. What happened to your shirt?"

The earnestness of his voice surprises me. He actually seems genuine in his concern, something I'm not used to from charming men like him. "It was ruined. I had to throw it out."

"Please let me pay for a replacement." His face crumples with remorse. That emotion is even rarer to me than concern. Then I remember he's an attorney and wonder if he's just a good actor.

I wave my hand and step to the side so I can get around him. "Don't worry about it. It wasn't very expensive."

He moves with me, successfully blocking my way forward. "I hope your clients were gracious about the situation."

My face heats at his words. Should I tell him the truth and let him off the hook? Nah, it's none of his business. "Luckily, they were."

Jayson's shoulders drop, and he releases a heavy breath. "Oh, that's good news. Look, um, Julie is it?"

He knows my name now. Great. I simply nod.

He extends an arm like he's going to touch me, but then seems to notice the iced coffee in his hand and quickly pulls it back, a sheepish grin crossing his handsome face. "I really can't let the shirt fiasco go until I've made amends."

Amends, huh? My mind flits through ways to embarrass him—like tripping and accidentally spilling my smoothie on his dashing suit. But then I'd have to apologize, *and* I'd be out a smoothie. I'd rather just be done with him and this situation. "Look, everything is fine, so don't worry about it. You're forgiven. I have to get back to work now. I've already exceeded my break time."

Jayson takes a step back. "Oh, okay. Right. Enjoy your day and your smoothie."

I take a step forward, preparing to maneuver around Jayson, who's still blocking the front door, when I realize he's leaning toward me, his arms reaching toward me. Is he about to hug me? I quickly reverse directions, taking a giant step back. "What are you doing?"

Jayson's head snaps back and the rest of his body follows, his elbows pressing against his sides. "Uh, nothing! What were you doing?"

His awkwardness makes me smirk. It's almost endearing, and I have to shake that thought from my head before it sticks. "I was trying to go to work, but you're blocking the door."

He looks over his shoulder, seeming to realize where we are. "That's right," he says, nodding toward my shirt with the shop's logo. "You work at the candy store?"

I harrumph. "It's not a candy store, it's a confectionery."

Jayson's eyes sparkle in amusement. "Apologies for the

misnomer. The truffles from here are amazing. Though I suppose you already know that."

Why does his unintended comment please me so much? I have to fight back a smile. "I do."

"I guess I'll see you around. And I promise to do my best not to douse you with more beverages when I do."

He grins, but I keep my face blank, despite feeling the corner of my mouth twitch. After saluting with one of his drinks, he turns and heads up the street.

A mix of emotions stir inside. I'm both annoyed at him for calling my upscale shop a candy store and pleased by his enjoyment of my hard work. I shake my head and head inside, handing Emily her smoothie and finally taking a sip of my own. My shoulders drop and I close my eyes, delighting in the tangy orange flavor mixed with smooth vanilla.

"Is there a bee in your bonnet?"

I startle at Emily's words. "Excuse me?"

She holds her free hand up in front of her like she's trying to halt a charging bull and I realize my words came out sharper than I meant. "You looked angry when you came in." She cocks her head to the side. "But maybe pleased too? Is everything okay?"

I sigh, taking the sunglasses off my face. "Sorry, Em. Yes, everything's fine. I just saw someone I wasn't expecting."

Emily leans in closer to me. "Who was it?"

"Remember when I got soaked by an iced coffee?"

"Yes." Emily's eyes sparkle. "Did you see the same guy?"

I nod, taking a large gulp of my smoothie.

"Did he recognize you?"

"Yeah, he did. By my growly voice, apparently."

Emily laughs. "It is pretty surprising coming from you."

I narrow my eyes. "What are you saying?"

"You have a very distinct tone of voice when you're annoyed. And also a signature glare. I've definitely seen it a time or two. Like right now."

I force my face to relax into neutral and release a chuckle. "Yeah, I seem to have perfected it. He was in the coffee shop and followed me back to work."

Emily frowns, and I can see her protective instinct kick in. "He followed you?"

I place a calming hand on her arm. "Not exactly. He was heading back to work and our routes aligned."

"That sounds a little less creepy."

I stifle a laugh. "Sorry if I worried you. I guess I got overdramatic in my storytelling."

"So what did he say?"

"He offered to pay for the damage."

Emily tilts her head and studies me. "But you didn't let him, did you?"

I tilt my head, mirroring her posture. "Why would you say that?"

"Because I know you. You don't want any help unless it's absolutely necessary."

"Is it wrong to be strong and independent?"

"It is when you're actually struggling and someone's help could ease the weight you're stumbling under. You know, like hiring a manager."

I sigh. Em's like a dog with a bone regarding this subject. "We're back to this again, huh? Look, I'm managing. Don't worry about me."

Emily slowly releases a breath. "Fine, if you want to stay in denial, then so be it. I just care about you and want you to relax and have more fun. When's the last time we had a girls' night?"

I drop my shoulders, not realizing I had scrunched them up near my ears. Maybe I'm a little defensive about this topic. "I know you're being a good friend. You're right, we need to hang out more. I just really want to make this business a success by myself."

"It already is a success. We all know that. You're allowed to have a life outside of work. I don't think your Uncle Bill would mind."

I close my eyes and suck in a deep breath. Would he really be okay if I had more help? He didn't need any, but maybe I don't have the experience and education to run this business solo. I didn't go to college and study business like he did. "Maybe you're right. I'll think about it, okay?"

Emily smiles and nods. "Okay. By the way, this smoothie is delicious. Thanks!"

"You're welcome." A smiling couple with their fingers intertwined enters the store. I paste on a smile even while a zip of longing for companionship races through my chest.

7

Jayson

PEERING THROUGH THE window of Little Shop of Sugar, my eyes alight on a woman with turquoise hair. My gaze roams around the store interior, but no other staff is in sight. Is Julie working today? *I probably should have checked. Oh well, too late now.* Sighing, I pull the door open, careful not to upset the tray of beverages I'm carrying. A bell tinkles merrily above my head. I step over to the counter and bend slightly to peruse the contents of the case.

"May I help you?"

I straighten. The turquoise-haired clerk smiles at me. "Uh, yes. Is Julie working today?"

The clerk studies my face like she's trying to figure something out. "She is."

"Is it possible to speak with her?"

The clerk scans me from head to toe. There appears to be a glint of something in her eye, though I'm sure I haven't seen her before. It's hard to forget hair that bright. "Let me see if she's free. Just a sec."

She disappears through a doorway. I use the time to take in the store's interior. Besides the case of truffles, there are shelves of prepackaged gold-lidded boxes along with some impressive chocolate creations. Chocolate mountains, bicycles, bears, and flowers are displayed above the boxes. I move over to a case at the back of the room that showcases what's labeled as a Break Cake—a hollow chocolate shell shaped like a two-tiered wedding cake that can be filled with other edible things like candies or caramels. A small wooden mallet positioned next to it conjures images of a piñata, only this one's edible. What a neat concept.

"Looking for something special?"

I spin on my heels toward the voice. The tray in my hand wobbles at the quick movement and my free hand raises to steady it. I give Julie a cautious smile and almost laugh when her smile turns into a frown. I obviously made an excellent first impression. And apparently, the second one wasn't much better. My smile widens, hoping to diffuse some of the obvious tension in the room. "I was looking for you, so I suppose so."

The corner of her lip twitches and her cheeks flush, but she keeps a straight face. "Why did you want to see me?"

"I still feel bad about ruining your shirt." She sighs and rolls her eyes, but I won't be deterred from saying my piece. "Since you won't let me pay for it, I brought you a smoothie. Two smoothies, actually. I wasn't sure what you liked."

I hold out the tray containing two smoothies and coffees for me and my aunt. When she stays rooted to the spot, I close the distance and remove a cup from the tray. "Is this one yours?"

Julie eyes the orange-tinted cup in my hand. "Is it an Orange Dream?"

The reverent tone of her voice amuses me, but I hold in my reaction. I'm afraid she'd misinterpret the meaning of a chuckle and I'd be in hot water with her even more than I already am. Why does her opinion of me matter so much? I really just want to get rid of my debt and move on. Hopefully, this will do it. *Yeah, right, Jayson. You keep telling yourself it's not because she's beautiful and wants nothing to do with you.* "It is."

After the briefest of hesitations, she takes the cup from me, puts the straw to her mouth, and sips. "Thank you."

This feels like a small win. "You're welcome. What should I do with the Strawberry Blast?"

"I'll take it," says a voice behind me.

When I turn, the woman with turquoise hair waves. She walks over, takes the smoothie from the holder, and smiles. "Thanks. I'm Emily, by the way."

She offers her free hand and I shake it. "Jayson. Nice to meet you."

"What did we do to deserve such a sweet surprise?"

I glance at Julie, who appears focused on something over my shoulder. "I'm just trying to make amends for nearly ruining Julie's important meeting the other week."

"Oh yes, the *important meeting.*" Emily smirks at Julie, who flushes an attractive pink. What's that about? I try to get Julie to meet my gaze, but she's now studying the floor. The silence in the room stretches uncomfortably. I look up in desperation for a new conversation topic and notice a handful of banners hanging from the ceiling proclaiming awards the store's won for its chocolates. Huh. I thought they were good, but award-winning? Very impressive. Maybe I should comment on that.

"So, Jayson," Emily says, beating me to the punch and breaking the tension in the room. "Have you eaten anything from here? It's all pretty amazing."

I point to the banners overhead. "So I've discerned. I picked up a box at Hill of Beans and thought it was pretty good."

"You should get something while you're here. It's even better straight from our store."

"Sure. What do you recommend?"

"It all depends on what you like." She tilts her head and winks. Is she flirting with me? She's kind of cute, but way too short for me. She must be right at five feet tall. My six-foot-five inch frame demands someone no shorter than five-foot-six, otherwise I get a crick in my neck and a sore back from kissing. Ask me how I know. Besides, my eye has already snagged on someone who looks to be closer to five foot eight, definitely in the approved height range.

The bell sounds, drawing all of our attention to the door. A woman walks in, startled to find three sets of eyes staring at her.

"Julie," Emily says, "you help Jayson and I'll take the new customer." She gives me one more glance before focusing on the woman.

"So, uh, are you a milk or dark chocolate guy?"

Julie's voice startles me. I tear my gaze from the other side of the store and meet Julie's wary look. What's that about? Does she seriously dislike me just because I spilled coffee on her? She tilts her head and lifts a brow, reminding me she asked me a question.

"I like just about anything chocolate."

My response generates an eye roll. "Well, that doesn't really help."

I shrug. It's the truth. I'm not really a connoisseur of chocolate. Might as well ask an expert for help. "Which of the chocolates here is your favorite?"

Julie casts her gaze over the case of truffles. "I think our Sinful truffle is pretty good. It's a blend of four kinds of dark chocolate. But since you like coffee so much..." She points the straw of her cup at the drinks in my hand. "I'd suggest the Jitterbug since it has espresso in it."

My mind snags on the word "sinful." My eyes focus on Julie's face, zooming in on her perfectly pink lips. I wonder what they'd feel like against mine. Besides being obviously stubborn and very beautiful, she's got some sass I find alluring. Once again, I realize I'm taking too long to respond. "I like the names. How about I get two Jitterbugs and two Sinfuls?"

"Sure."

Julie wraps them up and hands the box to me, refusing to take my credit card despite my protests. See, stubborn like a mule. "Enjoy them and talk the store up to friends."

Speaking of the store, now I'm curious. "Do you know how long this store has been here?"

"Since 1986."

"Wow, that's quite a while. I'm surprised I've never been in here before."

Julie responds with a noncommittal shrug.

"I should probably get back to work. My boss is probably wondering where her coffee is. At least she likes iced coffee, so I don't have to worry about it getting cold."

"That was your boss's coffee that ended up on me?"

"Yeah. You sure I can't make it up to you?"

She dismisses me with her hand. "I'm sure."

"Okay. Thanks for the chocolate recommendation." I pretend to let it go, but I *will* pay my debt to her whether she likes it or not.

Since my hands are full, I use my hip to push the door open. I can't resist taking a quick look through the store window once I'm outside. The sight of Emily and Julie talking animatedly irks me. Why wasn't Julie like that when I was in the store? Why am I so bothered by Julie's cold shoulder? I'll just have to work a little harder to change her opinion of me, that's all. I don't need to make up for my mistake, because Julie gave me a pass, but things don't feel resolved in my mind.

The sun glances off the gold lid of the box in my hand. We're even more uneven now that she gave me chocolates on the house. I need to level the playing field again. My brain works overtime trying to find a solution the rest of the way back to the office. It only wanders once or twice to the memory of a certain brunette's enticing mouth.

8

Julie

MY BODY SWAYS side to side and I hum along to the song playing in my ear while making truffles, scooping out perfect spheres of mouth-watering chocolaty goodness and placing them on the conveyor belt of the Frichoc coating machine. I'll never not be thankful I convinced Bill to get one for the shop. Before the machine, he'd been hand-dipping each truffle. The addition of the machine sped up production without affecting quality and significantly improved our bottom line.

I'm so in the zone, I jump a foot when there's a tap on my shoulder. One hand flies to my drumming heart while the other removes one of my ear buds. Emily looks contrite. "So sorry to interrupt, Jules, but there's a phone call for you."

"Can you take a message?"

Emily shrugs. "The caller is insistent on talking to you."

I sigh, hating to be pulled from my groove. "Put it down over there. I need to take my gloves off."

Emily sets the phone on the counter and heads back out to the front. I take a deep breath to calm my fast-beating heart, and pick up the phone. "Little Shop of Sugar, this is Julie speaking."

"Hi Julie, this is Jayson Thompson."

My face scrunches as I try to place the name. I feel like I should know it. "I'm sorry. How do we know each other?"

A deep chuckle sounds in my ear, and I smile involuntarily. "I'm the coffee guy."

My smile vanishes and the lightness in my chest from his warm voice evaporates. *Oh, him.* "How can I help you?"

"I was wondering if I could take you to dinner tonight to make up for ruining your shirt."

I'm tempted to lie, but my conscience twinges at the thought. Reluctantly, I mentally flip through my calendar and am delighted to realize I really am already booked. "I'm busy tonight."

"Oh. Well, what about Friday, say six-thirty?"

Thank goodness for later store hours on the weekends. "I'm working late."

"Saturday?"

"Also working."

Jayson sighs, which makes me smile, slightly pleased I seem to exasperate him. "Well, when are you free?"

I roll my eyes. He's persistent, I'll give him that. "I close most nights. The earliest I can usually get away is seven fifteen or seven thirty."

"Can't your boss get someone else to close? It doesn't seem fair that he'd schedule you to close so much."

I'm oddly flattered at the note of annoyance in his voice. "*She* is a wonderful boss and I enjoy closing."

"Makes it hard to have a social life, though."

Now he sounds like Emily. And Tom. "I have the life I want, thank you very much." It strikes me that this might not be completely true, but I'm too worked up to dwell on my doubt at the moment or to admit this to a practical stranger.

"Whoa. I didn't mean to rile you up." His tone now sounds defensive. "Can you get someone to close for you one night next week so we can have dinner together? I'll set up a picnic on the sidewalk out front of the store, if that's what it takes."

The mental image of a sidewalk meal makes me cringe. People would gawk at us, which would be quite embarrassing. He's obviously not going to give up until he gets what he wants. The tenacity probably works well for him as a lawyer. "Fine. Let's say next Tuesday."

"Tuesday's great. Can I pick you up at your house?"

"Let's meet in front of the chocolate shop."

We hang up and I carry the phone back out to the front of the store.

"Who was it?" Emily says, curiosity lacing her voice.

"The guy who spilled coffee on me the other week."

"Smoothie guy?" Emily claps her hands together in delight. "What did he want?"

"To take me out to dinner tonight to make up for the incident. But I told him I couldn't go. Book club's tonight."

Emily fixes me with a skeptical look. "You'd rather talk about books with a bunch of women than have a romantic dinner with a hot guy? Come on, Julie."

I put my hands up defensively. "Whoa, whoa, whoa. No one said anything about romance and yes, I'd rather hang out with new friends. You should be happy I have something going on outside of work as much as you've been bugging me to get a life."

Emily rolls her eyes and waves away my argument. "Yes, yes. You know I'm happy you're getting out and socializing, but you should still let him take you out. Make him take you to that new sushi place around the corner. I hear it's amazing."

It loathes me to share this next part, but Em's my best friend and I *am* kind of dying to tell someone, even though it's not an actual date. Yes, Jayson is gorgeous, but I know all about model-hot guys and won't go down that road again. "I agreed to dinner next Tuesday, but we didn't decide on a place."

Emily squeals in delight. "Oh, yay! You have a date."

I shake my head. "Not a date. It's an apology dinner."

"With a gorgeous guy who likes you."

"He doesn't like me."

"How do you know he doesn't?"

I put a hand on my hip and pin her with steely eyes. "How do you know he does?"

Emily ticks her reasons off on her fingers like she was just waiting for me to ask. "One, he's gone out of his way trying to make up for dousing you with coffee. Most guys wouldn't have followed up even once after you declined the dry cleaning offer. Two, he remembered your drink order and brought you smoothies. Three, he's taking you to dinner."

I shrug, trying to dismiss her persuasive argument. "Maybe he's just a stand-up guy."

Emily stares at me in disbelief, then gives a disappointed shake of her head. "Think what you want."

"I will. By the way, can you close next Tuesday?"

"Of course. I'd do just about anything if it means you take a break from work and have some fun."

Just about anything? I open my mouth, but she stops me by sticking her hand in front of my face. "But I won't do that. We've already had this discussion. I don't want to manage the store."

I can't believe she quoted a Meatloaf song to me, but I can't blame her for not wanting more responsibility with the store. I nod, then return to our original subject. "Why is everyone so concerned about my social life?"

Emily huffs out a cynical laugh, crossing her arms over her chest. "Because it's obvious you don't have one. You need more balance, and I think this is a good start."

The phone rings again before I can think of a snarky retort. Emily picks it up and I can tell by her smile who's on the other line. Her husband calls her on his lunch break to check in. It's sickeningly sweet how in love they are. I obviously don't begrudge my friend her happy relationship, but it's a sharp reminder of how dismal my love life has been.

Not that I'm pining away for someone to love. I actually tried dating again after my divorce, but all the guys turned out to be duds. The men I met either had no intention of settling down with one person anytime soon or wanted me to stop working and stay home with the kids. Neither of those situations appealed to me. But then Uncle Bill got sick, I took on more responsibilities of the business, and there was no time or desire to have dinner with someone who couldn't respect me and my personal ambitions.

Still, every once in a while, I wistfully imagine someone's thinking of me when we're apart, and it's not a terrible thought. If only there was some way to have that without having to risk my heart. I sigh. It's been ten years since my ex trampled my heart. I thought time was supposed to heal all wounds, but this one still feels like a gaping hole in my chest. Seeing my friends and family pairing up should be evidence enough that not everyone is untrustworthy and destined to hurt me, but I don't know how to get over that emotional hurdle.

Emily's gotten me thinking more about testing the relationship waters again with her comments about Jayson and my nonexistent social life, but the chasm still feels so wide. Maybe dinner with Jayson can be a test date to see if perhaps it might be time to get back in the ocean. Before these thoughts tip me into mental paralysis, I opt for a mind reset. Replacing my ear buds in my ears, I select my "Woman Up" playlist, which is filled with angry, self-empowering songs. P!nk's "So What" plays and I take a minute to listen to the familiar tune before pushing away my feelings for now, washing my hands, grabbing new gloves, and refocusing on my work.

When I head across the street after Emily assures me she can handle everything, I catch myself looking for Jayson. *It's just so I can avoid being drowned in coffee again,* I assure myself. *Nothing more.* I make it into Page Turner Books unscathed. When I get to the back of the store, I hear the voices of the other women. I fix my face into a pleasant smile before walking into the room, making a beeline for the refreshment table where Rachel is setting out napkins and small paper plates. "Hey, Rachel."

"Julie!" She pulls me into a tight hug. When she releases me, I hand her the chocolates. "Thanks. I'll put these out. Go say hi to the gang."

Reluctantly, I join the small circle of women in the center of the room.

"Hey Julie," the pink-haired woman says.

"Anna, right?"

"That's me. How are you?"

"I made it here without receiving an iced coffee shower, so definitely better than last time."

Anna laughs. "Very true. Did you bring any new truffles for us to sample?"

"I brought one called Cherry Jubilee."

Anna crinkles her nose and frowns. "Does it contain liqueur and have a squishy cherry in the middle?"

I wrinkle my nose and shake my head. "No. I don't care for those either. If you like fresh cherries, you'll enjoy it."

"You're good at what you do, so I'll try it."

"I promise I won't be offended if it isn't your favorite. I'm working on a special white chocolate one for next month, but I don't want to give anything away just yet."

Anna's eyes sparkle. "Excellent. I love white chocolate."

"Alright ladies," Rachel calls from the refreshments table. "We're all set up. Grab a drink and some chocolate and let's get down to business. I'm so excited to talk with you all about *A Room with a View!*"

9

Jayson

MY CAR EASES to a stop in front of Little Shop of Sugar, but the sidewalk's empty. I'm on time. Where's Julie? I don't have her cell phone number, but I can try the store. It goes straight to voicemail, asking me to call back during business hours or leave a message. After a few minutes of waiting, I turn off the engine and get out. There's a light on in the store and I can see someone sweeping, but they're wearing a hat and their back is to me. I press my face up to the glass, but it doesn't help. The person turns to the side and now I can tell it's a woman, possibly Julie.

I rap my knuckles on the glass. The woman looks up from her sweeping and freezes when our eyes meet. I smile at Julie. When I wave, she walks to the front door, turns the lock, and pushes open the door. "Come in. I'm just about finished."

I frown. "I thought you were going to talk to your boss about someone else closing tonight."

"I did. Unfortunately, Emily called in sick with a stomach bug." Julie grimaces.

My nose wrinkles in sympathy. "Yuck, I'm sorry to hear that. There wasn't anyone else who could cover the shift?"

"We have a small staff. A lot of the clerks are college students who only work part time, and the boss doesn't trust them with the responsibility of closing. It's just me and Emily."

I'm affronted on Julie's behalf. If she had the day off, why didn't her boss fill in? "Couldn't your boss have come in? If she's so wonderful, why doesn't she cover for sick employees instead of calling in someone who had the time off?"

Julie half-laughs, half-sighs. "Because I *am* the boss."

I step back in surprise. "You?"

Julie scowls. "Yes, me. Why do you look so surprised? Do I not look like someone who can run a business?"

"Well... I uh..." I take a second to collect my thoughts. "The way you were talking in third person made it seem like you're just an employee."

She puts her hand on her hip, her frown deepening. Is it bad that I feel attraction for her right now? I didn't realize verbal sparring was such a turn on for me. "You're avoiding the question."

Her words return my thoughts to the topic at hand. "No, I'm not. It's just that this business has been here for a long time and you're not that old. It doesn't add up is all."

She tilts her head and studies me before nodding. "It's kind of a long story."

"Can you tell it to me at the restaurant? I don't want to be late for our reservation."

"I still have to finish sweeping and then I need to change clothes. It doesn't look like what I'm wearing is appropriate for dinner."

She gestures between us. I'm wearing my favorite navy suit. Julie's in khaki pants and a polo with the shop's logo on one side. She looks stunning to me. However, I don't want her to feel self-conscious at dinner.

"Why don't you go change and I'll finish sweeping."

Julie wrinkles her forehead. "Aren't you worried about getting dirty?"

I wave off her concern, reaching for the broom. "Nah, I'll be fine."

Julie shrugs. "Okay. The dustpan is over there. I've already gotten that part of the store." She points over at the shelves along the wall. "You can dump the dirt in the trash can behind the counter."

"Sounds good. Anything else that needs to be done?"

"Nope."

Julie turns on her heels and disappears through a doorway behind the far counter. I whistle to myself while I sweep. After I've thrown away the last bit of dirt, I survey the floor. Satisfied, I walk through the doorway Julie entered a few minutes ago, down a short hallway, and stop in front of a closed door with light shining underneath. I knock three times. "Where does the broom go?"

"In here," Julie says through the door.

I put my hand on the knob, but then pause. "Is it safe to enter?"

"Come in."

I open the door and step inside. My eyes catch on the show-stopping view in front of me. Julie's wearing a knee-length green dress that matches her eyes and tan leather sandals with ties that wrap halfway up her legs. Her hair cascades in waves down to her shoulder blades. She looks incredible. She brushes her hands down the sides of her dress and gives a self-conscious smile before pointing to the left. "There's a supply closet over there for the broom and dustpan."

I blink out of my stupor and move over to the closet, noticing how well organized the interior is. I have no trouble figuring out where the items in my hands go. After closing the door, I turn back to Julie, my eyes surveying her from head to toe for a second time. "You look amazing."

Color rises to Julie's cheeks. "Thanks. You look nice, too."

"Shall we go to dinner?"

Julie nods and leads me back to the front of the store, turning off lights as she goes. She grabs her purse, ushering me out the front door, and locks it behind us. I open the passenger door of my black Honda SUV and motion for her to get in. When she's situated, I get in on the other side and pull into traffic.

"I'm a little surprised by your car," Julie says.

Her statement intrigues me. Has she been thinking about me and what I drive? "Why's that?"

"I thought lawyers were supposed to drive impractical little red sports cars, not reliable SUVs."

One side of my mouth quirks up at her words. "Is that so? That wasn't mentioned in any of my law classes. Thanks for letting me know. I'll get right on that."

I look over at Julie and wink, eliciting a genuine smile from her. My insides warm at the achievement. I force my eyes back to the road, make a left, and then another quick right before pulling into a parking spot. "We're here."

Julie looks around. "Already? We could've walked here from the store."

"Maybe next time."

I grin at the surprised look on Julie's face at the implication of a second date. She must think this is a one-time thing, while I'm hoping maybe it's the beginning of many evenings together. I exit the car and rush around to the other side to open Julie's door.

"Thank you," she says.

"You're welcome." I turn and motion to the restaurant in front of us. "I hope you like Italian food." Even though I gesture for her to walk through the door ahead of me, Julie just stares at the name over the door, not moving from her spot on the sidewalk.

Concern and panic swirl in my gut. Did I do something wrong? "Uh oh. Don't tell me you're allergic to tomatoes or something."

"No."

I frown, worried by the flat tone of her voice. "What's wrong? Do we need to go somewhere else? We can. I honestly don't care where we eat."

"No, it's fine." She shakes her head slightly as if to clear it of some thought, then walks through the door. "I've heard this place is good but haven't been."

The knot in my stomach loosens a touch. "I think it's the best Italian place in town."

"That's some high praise."

When she smiles at me, I notice it doesn't reach her eyes. Did I offend her somehow? I sure hope not. I'd picked this place hoping to impress her. It doesn't seem to be working. Maybe things will turn around after we get some food. Otherwise, this is going to be a long, awkward evening.

10

Julie

GLI AMANTI? JAYSON *chose the most romantic Italian restaurant in* *town to take me to dinner? He's not looking for romance with me, is he?* Emily's obviously gotten into my head with her comments. He's probably just trying to be kind. I've heard this place is great from my brother, Tom, but haven't eaten here myself. It's not a place where one dines solo and I haven't been on a date in who knows how long. There's no way Xavier would have brought me here. It's much too classy for him, though he would call it *mainstream*, which is apparently the worst thing to be in his eyes. It turned out I was too mainstream for him as well.

I blink away the intruding thoughts and return my focus to the man sitting across from me in this plush, cloistered booth, tucked away from prying eyes. Jayson's eyes are looking over the menu, blissfully unaware of my troubled thoughts. He's been silent since we sat down. There's a heavy awkwardness blanketing our booth, and it's on me to diffuse it.

"So what's good here?" I ask, picking up the menu in front of me.

Jayson responds without lifting his eyes from the menu. "The chicken parmesan is amazing. I like it with the fettuccine alfredo. The cream sauce is so rich and flavorful."

Sounds way too heavy for me. My stomach hurts just thinking about that much food. "What about the pasta carbonara?"

"I haven't tried it, but I'm sure it's fantastic."

I nearly gasp at the prices on the menu. Probably another reason I've never been here. "Do you come here often?"

Jayson sets down his menu and meets my eye. The booth suddenly feels very intimate. "Actually, I've only been here twice, both times with my aunt."

He eats at fancy restaurants with his aunt? He must have a close-knit family. My heart twinges as thoughts of my uncle pop into my head. "Are you and your aunt close?"

Jayson nods, an amiable smile on his lips. Lips I definitely haven't been staring at from across the table. "Definitely. Otherwise it'd be hard working together every day."

"She's also an attorney?"

"Yes. She started Thompson & Associates. I joined a couple of years ago after I finished law school."

"Is your aunt the reason you became a lawyer?"

"Hello and welcome to Gli Amanti," a server says, setting two glasses of water down on the table. "My name is Wes, and I will be your server this evening. Would you like something else to drink?"

"Yes, two glasses of your house red," Jayson says, looking to me for affirmation. I nod.

The server nods and smiles. "Excellent, sir. And would you like to start with an appetizer?"

Jayson glances at me before returning his full attention to the server. "I'm not sure. Please give us a moment."

"Of course. I'll be back shortly with your wine." He bows slightly and glides away.

Jayson picks up the menu again. "How hungry are you? Would you be interested in splitting a caprese salad?"

My stomach growls in response and I put a hand over it, feeling self-conscious. "Sure, that sounds great."

Jayson smiles and sets the menu on the table. "Wonderful. And to answer your question, my aunt is part of the reason I became a lawyer. My dad's a lawyer, too. Though I started out studying economics in college before deciding to go to law school."

His forthrightness is refreshing. I used to have to drag answers out of Xavier. In hindsight, I should have been more concerned about his secretiveness. "Interesting. Why did you choose to work with your aunt and not your father?"

"He's a tax attorney, which I don't find interesting." Jayson mimes falling asleep, his mouth going slack and releasing a snore. When he opens his eyes and grins at me, my heart lurches. I didn't expect a lawyer to be so playful. I force myself to focus on what he says next rather than the confusing emotions swirling in my chest. "My aunt practices family law, which I enjoy much more."

"Does that mean you help with divorces and child custody issues?"

"Our firm specializes in adoptions, guardianships, and juvenile delinquency. We want to see kids find safe, loving homes and get back onto a good track for their lives. But, yes, we also deal with divorces and other unpleasant situations."

Wow, I did not expect that. Is this tall, muscular, model-gorgeous man actually a big softy? I sure hope not, because that could spell big trouble for me. "I'm sure adoption cases aren't always sunshine and roses, though."

Jayson lowers his eyes, his mouth turning down at the corners. "I haven't been at the firm very long, but my aunt has told me some stories that are absolutely heartbreaking."

My heart softens even more at his troubled look. I'm very tempted to reach out and touch his hand in sympathy, but am afraid he might get the wrong idea. *This is just an apology dinner, not an actual date*, I remind myself. Maybe I'm the one in danger of thinking this is something more. "Well, at least you and your aunt are helping to provide brighter futures for more kids."

Our server appears, setting down two wine glasses and a basket of garlic knots. "Have you decided on an appetizer?"

Jayson's smile returns. "We have. We'd like a caprese salad. And we'll put in the rest of our order as well."

"Very good, sir."

Jayson holds his hand out, palm up, toward me. "Go ahead."

I glance over the menu once more. "I'd like the pasta carbonara, please."

"Excellent choice," says Wes. "And for you, sir?"

"I'd like the chicken parmesan and fettuccine alfredo."

Wes takes our menus. "I'll put in your orders."

"Those smell amazing," I say, motioning to the bread.

"We can find out in a moment, but first I'd like to make a toast." Jayson holds his wine glass aloft.

I mimic his gesture, curious about what he'll say.

"To new friendships made in the most unorthodox of ways."

He clinks his glass against mine and winks before taking a sip. I quickly place my glass to my lips, hoping it will cover the blush on my cheeks. *He said friendship. Maybe he really is just making amends. It's probably for the best because this new side I'm seeing of him tonight makes it very tempting to consider something more, which scares me.* Swallowing down my thoughts along with the wine, I set down my glass and study Jayson. "It sounds like you and your aunt really value family and children. Are you close with the rest of your family?"

"Yeah, I'd say we're close. My older brother lives in Atlanta near my parents, and my little sister works here in Asheville. In fact, she and I live together."

Just like me and Tom. "Did you go to college in Georgia?"

"No, I went to Harvard."

His answer stuns me. I'm immediately self-conscious about my lack of higher education. I try to hide my discomfort with a joke. "Wow. I'm sitting across from a genius."

Jayson shakes his head and chuckles. "Not even close."

"Did you get both your undergrad and your law degree at Harvard?"

"Yes."

I tilt my head and raise an eyebrow. He just proved my point. Jayson gives a bemused sigh.

"Okay, yes, I did well in school," he concedes. "But I bet you could have gotten into Harvard if you wanted."

I shift in my seat, disliking the direction this conversation is going. I grab a garlic knot out of the basket and take a bite, trying to figure out how to change the subject without it being too obvious. "Are your brother and sister also lawyers?"

"No. My brother's an accountant and my sister's an event planner."

Wes appears out of nowhere and sets the salad in between us. "Do you need anything else?"

"No, we're fine, thank you," Jayson says, looking at me for confirmation.

When Wes heads to another table, Jayson pushes the plate toward me. I take a slice of tomato, mozzarella, and basil leaf, then slide it back toward him. When we both have food on our appetizer plates, Jayson cuts a piece of his salad, his mouth closing over the fork. He closes his eyes and hums in approval. I'm mesmerized by the pleased look on his face. My eyes snag on his enticing mouth. *Get a grip, Julie.* I focus my attention on creating a perfect bite of food. It hits my tongue in a tantalizing melody.

"So, Julie. We've talked plenty about me. I'd like to hear more about you."

I chew slowly to bide some time. "There's not much to know."

He waves away my pitiful excuse with his fork. "Of course there is. You own the chocolate shop. Tell me about that."

I delay with another bite of tomato, cheese, and basil drizzled with balsamic glaze, appreciating the melding of the flavors.

"Mmmm, good choice on the salad, Jayson."

"Thank you, but don't change the subject."

"I wasn't doing that." Of course I was. I should know better than to try to get anything past a lawyer. "There's not a lot to tell. My uncle opened the shop before I was born. We'd visit from California in the summers when I was growing up. He took me to work with him and taught me some of what he knew. When I graduated from high school, I didn't know what I wanted to do, so I came to work with him while I figured it out. It turned out I was really good at making chocolate and melding flavors, so I kept working there. About five years ago, my uncle was diagnosed with an aggressive form of cancer and passed away less than a year later."

Jayson's hand covers mine on top of the table. It's a reassuring blanket of warmth and comfort, but also inexplicably causes the back of my hand to tingle. "Oh, I'm so sorry, Julie."

"Thanks." I try to be discreet about breaking our physical contact, pulling my hand from under his to grab my knife and cut another piece of tomato. "Anyway, he didn't have a family of his own, so he left the store to me and I've been running it ever since."

"Wow. You've done a great job."

I shrug, ignoring the warmth his words ignite in my chest. "It's not a big deal. He's the one that started it from the ground up. I'm just keeping it running."

"I think you've done way more than just keeping it running."

"I'm only doing what needs to be done."

I focus my gaze on my dwindling salad, avoiding Jayson's eye and trying not to be bothered by the silence that falls over the table.

"So, is your family close?" Jayson says.

I twist my lips to the side. "I mean, we like each other, but we don't live near each other, so I'd say we're average closeness, maybe. We try to get together for the holidays, but I don't talk regularly with anyone except my younger brother Tom, and that's because he lives here."

"Where does everyone else live?"

"My parents are in Huntington Beach, California, though they lived here for a bit when my uncle got sick. My older brother, Charlie, lives in New York City with his wife, Serena. He's been there since he graduated from college. My other brother, Tom, has only been here permanently for a few months. Before that, he was pretty transient."

"What does he do?"

"He's a photographer. He used to follow the surfing circuit, but then he fell in love and decided he'd like to spend more time with his soon-to-be wife."

Jayson grins. "I'd hope he'd want to live with his wife."

I chuckle. "I honestly thought he'd never settle down, but you never can tell how love will change someone."

"That's true. Have you—"

Our food arriving interrupts Jayson's question. "Here we are," Wes says. "Would either of you like more wine?"

"I'm good," I say, smiling at Wes. Had Jayson been about to ask if I've ever been in love? That's definitely something I don't want to talk about, especially with someone I barely know.

"Same," Jayson says.

"Buon appetito." Wes leaves us with our entrées.

"Yours looks amazing," I say, hoping Jayson will forget about the love conversation.

"I'm sure it will be. You're welcome to try it if you'd like."

"Thanks, but I'm good."

We dig into our meals and the only sounds at the table for a few minutes are forks and knives on plates. Jayson catches my gaze and I tense up, waiting for him to complete his earlier question. What he says catches me off guard.

"Which of the truffles you make is your favorite?"

My shoulders relax and a genuine smile forms on my lips. Now *this* is a topic I can discuss comfortably for hours.

11

Jayson

MY BACK SETTLES deeper into the red leather booth and I groan in discomfort. "I definitely ate too much." Julie's eyes dance with amusement and there's a smirk on her face. "What?"

"What'd you expect after eating two whole entrées?"

"What're you talking about?"

"The fettuccine and chicken parmesan were both listed under dinner plates."

"How do you know that?"

Julie shrugs. "I read the menu. Is that what you always get when you eat here?"

I shake my head, a sheepish look crossing my face. "When I come here with my aunt, she orders family style, so we share everything. I just assumed the pasta was a side dish."

"I guess that kind of explains it."

"Why only kind of?"

"You didn't *have* to eat it all tonight. You could've boxed some up to eat later."

Her smug look doesn't rankle me as much as it should. It's because I'm enjoying this back-and-forth so much. "I could have, but you're wrong about me getting to eat it later."

"Why's that?"

Our server places a burgundy leather check presenter on the table between us. I grab it before Julie can react. I give the check a cursory glance, then place my credit card inside, handing it back to Wes.

"Do you need anything else?" Wes asks.

"No, thank you." I smile warmly.

After our server disappears, I fix my gaze on Julie. She'd asked me something, but now I can't remember. "What was that last question?"

"I asked why you couldn't eat the leftovers later."

"Because Britt would get to them first."

"Is Britt your girlfriend?"

I can't help feeling pleased that Julie's inquiring about my relationship status. Does this mean she might be interested in me? I'm flattered, but don't know her well. There's no denying she's gorgeous, but a relationship can't survive on physical attraction alone. There has to be an emotional connection as well. At least, that's what I've deduced from watching other relationships. I haven't ever been in love, so this is pure speculation. Still, the question gives me hope that something good could come from this dinner. I keep my expression even, hoping my face doesn't give away my thoughts. "No, my sister."

Her exhale is audible. Was she worried about my answer? "Your sister. Right. I'd already forgotten you were roommates."

Her words are the perfect excuse to turn the conversation back to her. "Do you have any roommates?"

"My brother is staying with me, but he'll be gone once he gets married next month. Then it'll be just me and Sadie."

"Who's Sadie?"

"My dog."

My scalp prickles with unease. "You have a dog?"

Julie smiles. "I do. A four-year-old black lab. She's the sweetest dog. I think, somehow, Tom has become her favorite human in the house."

She has a Labrador. Are those large dogs? I can't remember. Did she get it for protection? I'm sure a lot of single women get dogs to feel more secure. I suppose there's also the added factor of companionship. "Why do you say that?"

"I'm not home a lot because of work, so he takes her for walks and to play fetch at the park. I can't blame her. I feel bad I haven't been able to give her the attention she needs, so I'm thankful Tom's been around. Once he leaves, I'll have to hire a dog walker or something."

"Where's your brother moving to?"

Julie drinks the last of her wine. "Oh, he'll still be around. Just living with his wife instead of me."

There's a lull in the conversation. Before I can think of something to fill it with, Julie places her wrinkled cloth napkin on the table. "Anyway, I should be going. Work starts early for me tomorrow."

The check presenter is back on the table, returning sometime during our conversation. I remove my card, add a sizable tip, and sign the receipt. After closing the book, I stuff the extra receipt and credit card into my pocket. I stand and offer Julie my hand to help her out of the booth's deep bench. She accepts, placing her hand in mine, and a bolt of electricity runs up my arm. My eyes catch on her short, bare fingernails. I bet it's not practical in her line of work to wear polish or rings. It occurs to me I'm holding her hand longer than necessary and let go, giving her an embarrassed grin. I let her lead the way to the door and follow behind, admiring her legs. I look up in time to reach past her and push the front door open.

"Thanks for dinner, Jayson," Julie says once we're on the sidewalk.

"You're very welcome." I pat my stomach. "I shouldn't have

stuffed myself, but I just couldn't help it."

Julie smiles. "No, I get it. The food was amazing and I wouldn't want any of it to go to waste. Or to my sibling." Her smile looks teasing. Is she flirting with me?

"Exactly. You get it."

My hand plunges into my left suit pocket, searching for the key fob to unlock the car doors. I step around Julie and open the passenger door. "Shall I take you home?"

She hitches a thumb over her shoulder. "Actually, I'm walking distance from here."

"You are?"

"Yes. I made sure my apartment was close enough to walk to work, so I don't have to pay for parking if the weather's nice."

That's smart. Maybe I should have thought about that. Though there's no way I could afford a house like mine in this part of town. "That must be nice. My place is a twenty-minute drive from here, which isn't too bad, but it'd be great to walk to restaurants and shops."

"Why don't you move downtown?"

"It's more affordable where I am. Plus my sister's job is near the house and I'd rather she have the shorter commute."

"What a sweet big brother you are."

I shrug the compliment away, feigning a nonchalance I don't feel. "Well, you know. Other than my aunt and uncle, it's just her and me up here. Family comes first, you know?"

Julie nods, her face turning serious. "I do."

"Can I walk you home?"

She waves off my offer. "You don't have to do that."

"I know Asheville's pretty safe, but I'd feel better knowing you made it home okay."

She blushes and the stain on her cheeks makes her even more beautiful. "Well..."

"Or I could give you my number and you can text when

you're home." I grin, guessing which option she'll choose.

Julie opens her mouth and then closes it again. Her concerned expression makes me fear I'm being too aggressive. I backtrack. "Or whatever. I don't want to intrude, just trying to be a gentleman like my—"

Julie grabs my wrist, stopping my rambling when another zap of heat shoots up my arm. Julie also seems affected. Did she feel it too? She releases my wrist and looks away. "You can walk me home, but really, it's just around the corner."

"Thank you."

"This way," Julie says, avoiding my eye. She starts downhill away from the restaurant and I quickly catch up.

Coming toward us are a person and a dog. It's brown and muscular, and my mind conjures the image of a wolf. My body stiffens and I feel sweat break out on my forehead. I slide closer to the buildings on our right, but Julie's posture opens. "Hello, gorgeous," she says as they pass.

Glancing behind us, the duo keep moving at their leisurely pace. My shoulders drop and I release a slow exhale, wiping my brow.

Julie glances sideways at me. "Everything okay, Jayson?"

I shoot her a wobbly grin, hoping she can't hear my heart pounding. "Yeah, all good."

She waves her hand at a building coming up on our right. "This is me."

I laugh. "You weren't kidding about living close."

"Nope."

We stop in front of her building. "Thanks again for dinner, Jayson. You're off the hook for the coffee incident."

My eyes crinkle with amusement. "You call it the coffee incident, huh? I was calling it 'my night of complete humiliation in front of a beautiful woman.'"

I watch her face, registering her surprise, embarrassment, and possibly a hint of pleasure at being called beautiful. "Mine is less of a mouthful. Well, good night."

She turns away, but I'm not quite ready for this night to end. "I hope this isn't too forward of me, but could I give you a hug? My family loves to hug. It's how we say goodbye."

Julie's hesitant look tells me she's not sure whether she believes me. I hold up three fingers. "Scout's honor."

Her eyebrows shoot up. "So you *were* a Scout."

It's my turn to look confused. "I was. How did you know?"

She grins. "It was just a hunch. Okay, *one* hug." She holds up one finger for emphasis.

I take a step toward her and open my arms. Julie covers the last bit of space between us and raises her arms to my shoulders, then clasps her hands behind my neck. I wrap my arms around her lower back. My heart slows from its erratic pace to a leisurely beat. *Who knew hugging could be so relaxing? Or maybe it depends on who you're hugging.* I lower my face toward the top of her head and breathe in. "You smell like chocolate," I say.

Her chuckle rumbles against my torso. Her arms loosen around my neck much sooner than I'd like. I let go as well, taking a step back.

"I hope that's a good thing," she says, a smile on her lips.

"Oh it is," I reply. I realize I'm staring at her mouth and snap my gaze back up to her eyes.

"You smell pretty good yourself. What cologne do you wear?"

"The One Sport by Dolce & Gabanna."

"Sounds fancy."

I tug the lapels of my suit coat, and give her a teasing grin. "That's me."

Julie smirks, making my heart dance. "Night, Jayson."

After making sure Julie's in her apartment building with the door shut securely behind her, I head back to my car. That was an enjoyable evening, despite eating too much. Our conversation flowed well and there'd been some joking, even a little flirting.

Maybe I should spill coffee on attractive women more often. I shake my head at my lame joke. *Glad I didn't say that one out loud to Julie.*

I'd like to ask her out again, but she seems a little skittish about the idea of dating, and I don't want to scare her off. It might be more prudent to let her warm up to the idea. Which means it's on me to figure out another reason to spend more time with her that doesn't get her defenses up. I know about her family and where she works. And that she has a dog. My skin crawls at the thought. *Nothing to worry about now. I'll cross that bridge when I come to it.*

12

Julie

THE DOOR TO my apartment clicks shut and I drop my keys and purse onto the table in the hall. Sadie comes bounding happily into the room and presses her face against my thigh. I bend down to scratch Sadie's head and body, then move into the living room with Sadie right behind. Sitting down on the couch in the living room, I untie the laces of my sandals from around my calves.

I lean back against the couch and Sadie jumps up beside me, placing her head in my lap. I rub Sadie's head while mentally rehashing the dinner with Jayson. Was it a date? Or was it just a dinner undergirded with remorse?

It kind of felt like a date, especially with the hug at the end. It seemed like Jayson might be interested, especially with the comment about me smelling like chocolate. I also noticed his lingering gaze on my lips. I must admit, I was a little flirty with him, too. It's been a long time since I've gone out with a man, and never with one as attractive as Jayson. He's well over six feet tall with broad shoulders and a toned body, if his tailored suits are any indication of what they hide underneath. And I definitely felt solid muscle when I grabbed his arm.

He was probably just being nice. He's a good-looking lawyer. I'm sure he can date anyone he wants. I'm not a legacy lawyer or someone with an Ivy League education. There's no way he'd be interested in someone like me. Besides, how can I be sure he isn't another Xavier?

Even if Jayson isn't interested in me, I enjoyed the small taste of having a personal life. It's been ages since I've hung out with friends. It calls to mind Emily's suggestion of hiring someone else to help with the store, so I don't have to do everything. Right now, I don't have time to go out even if I wanted to. The store's always waiting, and I can't be out late on multiple nights each week. Not that I'm all that keen to step back into the dating waters, but a girls' night out sounds amazing.

It's been ten years since my divorce from Xavier was finalized and life is, admittedly, a little lonely. Tom's only staying with me for a few more weeks and then he'll be married and living happily ever after. I'm happy he's found someone after being dumped by his fiancée and losing his surfing career in the same year. If he can open himself up to love again, surely I can, too. Eventually.

Plus, I've been thinking about expanding the business into dessert catering. Agreeing to take care of the wedding cake for Tom's wedding is my way of testing the idea out. This new endeavor has already been a breath of fresh air for my creative spirit. But there's no way I can run the day-to-day business, online orders, and add weddings and social events all on my own. I definitely need help for all of that.

My mind snags on the word 'help,' and I feel a twinge of discomfort. I really don't enjoy asking for help. I grew up with the belief that to need help is failure, and I can't stand the thought of being a failure. Not that this is something my parents taught me. It's just something I unintentionally internalized at an early age. I need to talk to someone who can give me solid advice. It's early enough that I can call Mom and still get some decent sleep. I should probably also walk Sadie.

I get up from the couch and walk into my bedroom, exchanging my dress for a t-shirt and joggers. I slip my feet into a pair of flip-flops and head toward the front door. "Come on, Sadie girl."

Sadie trots in from the living room and I attach the leash to her collar. My keys and phone go into my pocket once I've locked the door, and we take the elevator down to the lobby. Out front, we turn right toward the park. I'm thankful for the streetlights lining the sidewalk. I shiver when the cool night air hits my bare arms, realizing I should have grabbed a jacket. It's spring, which means the nights are still chilly. Oh well. I let Sadie lead me on the familiar route to the park. Once we're on the walking trail, I dial Mom.

"Hi, Julie!"

I smile, warmed by my mother's voice. "Hi, Mom. What are you up to?"

"Just chopping some vegetables for dinner."

"I'm sorry to interrupt."

"You're never an interruption, dear. What's going on with you?"

My mom's gentle assurance calms my nerves. "I'm out walking Sadie before we turn in for bed."

"Are you still okay with your dad and I staying with you when we come out for the wedding? We're not kicking poor Tom out of his room, are we?"

"No. Tom's renting a house for the week to host Jeff and a couple of other surfing buddies. He's planning to show them the adventures to be had in the mountains."

Enough small talk. I need to just broach the subject.

"So, Mom. I've been thinking about hiring a business manager to help with everyday operations, but it feels kind of like cheating. I mean, Uncle Bill didn't have a business manager, right? He did everything by himself."

"Oh, sweetie. Bill had a manager. Don't you remember Brenda?"

"The name sounds familiar, but she wasn't there when I started working at the store."

"Brenda managed the business and office side of things until her husband was diagnosed with Alzheimer's. She stopped working at the store to help manage his care, and Bill was looking for her replacement when you asked to come work with him."

How did I not know this? Have I been working under erroneous assumptions all this time? "Does that mean I was the replacement office manager?"

Mom chuckles. "Kinda. I know he taught you all about running the business while you worked with him. That's why he was so confident about leaving it in your hands."

I'm quiet for a minute as I absorb this information. "What I'm hearing is that I'm not supposed to handle everything on my own."

"Of course not. I'm surprised you've been able to go this long without a manager."

Her gentle tone brings tears to my eyes. I cough to clear the sudden lump in my throat. "Well, honestly, I didn't know that was an option."

"Help is always an option. Depending on other people is not giving up or failing. I know trusting others can be tricky for you—"

I see where she's heading and change the subject before she brings up my ex. "It sure can, but I'm working on it."

"I know you've been let down in the past, but try not to let that keep you from getting help and support when you need it. Bill would want you to focus on the creative side of the business like he could because of you and Brenda."

I'd love to focus on the creative side of things. Maybe an office manager is just what I need. "You're right, Mom. Emily's been pushing me to hire more help. It's just hard for me to let go of complete control of the business. I want to make Uncle Bill proud of his decision to pass it on to me."

"He would be *so* proud of you, Julie. But he'd also want you to enjoy running it, not feel obligated or overwhelmed."

Her words strike a deep place in my heart. Do I feel obligated to keep it going just for Bill? I definitely feel overwhelmed. Things have to change or I'll be too burned out to really determine what I want. "Thanks, Mom. This has really been helpful."

"I'm glad. Your dad and I are both looking forward to seeing you. It'll be great to have everyone back together again. First Charlie and now Tom."

"Yeah. That's two weddings in two years for our family."

"Are you going to give us the trifecta?"

My eyes widen in shock. "What?!"

"I'm just teasing, Julie."

"Jeez, mom."

Her voice softens. "I know Xavier broke your heart and your trust, but you shouldn't let your history with him keep you from ever looking for companionship again."

"You're saying I shouldn't write everyone off because of one person. I get that, but right now I'm too busy with the store to even think about dating."

Unbidden, my mind flashes to Jayson's handsome face and gorgeous smile. I shake my head, realizing suddenly where I am. Sadie's led me back to the apartment. I was so focused on the conversation, I hadn't realized we were home again. "Mom, I need to go, but thanks for talking with me. I really appreciate it."

"You're welcome, sweetheart. We'll see you in two weeks."

Back in the apartment, I brush my teeth, change into pajamas, and snuggle under the covers. My mom's words swirl in my head. I'm glad I called and heard more about how Bill ran the business, but her prodding into my personal life was uncomfortable. I know she means well and is eager to join her friends in the Grandparent's Club, but she's barking up the wrong tree. Even if I found someone I'm willing to be vulnerable with, I still don't know if kids will ever be part of the equation. Especially with how busy I am with the store. Maybe having more staff to share the workload would change my mind, but that's all a bunch of hypotheticals. I don't have a business manager or a boyfriend at the moment, so who knows how things might work out?

Sadie jumps onto the bed and snuggles up next to me. I pat her side a few times before closing my eyes and willing my thoughts to settle so I can get some rest. The last thing to cross my mind before falling asleep is the feeling of being wrapped up in Jayson's strong arms.

13

MAY

Jayson

ENTRENCHED IN A mountain of paperwork in the conference room, a knock on the door interrupts my concentration. My aunt's standing in the doorway, giving me a stern look.

"Hi, Auntie Alicia. What can I do for you?"

"What are you still doing here?"

I gesture to the table in front of me. "Making sure we have everything in order for the Walkers' final hearing tomorrow. I want to ensure everything goes smoothly so they can finally, officially, call Tessa their daughter."

Her face relaxes into a bemused smile. "I'm sure everything will be fine. You're always so thorough and organized. Head home and finish up in the morning. It's nearly nine."

"Is it really that late?" I lean back in my chair, stretching my arms over my head and twisting my torso to release the kinks in my back. My stomach gurgles loudly.

"Pick up dinner on your way home and use the company card. You deserve it."

"Thanks." I survey the mess in front of me. "I suppose I can finish up tomorrow. Let me just get everything cleaned up."

She waves her hand. "Leave it. We both know you'll be the first one here in the morning."

"True." I cock my head to the side. "Why are you still here?"

My aunt's smile holds a hint of embarrassment. "Same as you, working on a case. Raymond called a few minutes ago, asking if he'd see me tonight."

I smile and stand up. Aunt Alicia and I are two apples from the same tree. "Let me grab my briefcase and I'll walk you to your car."

She wraps an arm around my waist when I reach her in the doorway. "Always a gentleman, my nephew."

I gently squeeze her in a side hug. "My mom would kill me if she ever heard differently."

She chuckles. "You're right about that."

The door to the garage squeaks closed, and I drop my keys into the bowl on the kitchen counter. I set the food down next to my keys and drop my briefcase against the wall.

"Do I smell lo mein?" a voice calls from the living room.

"And fried rice," I reply.

"Awesome! Bring it to the couch."

I shake my head even though Britt can't see me. "No. Tonight, we eat at the table like civilized human beings."

"Aww, come on, Jay. I'm in the middle of an episode of *The Bachelor*."

"Pause it."

There's a loud sigh. "Fiiiiiiine."

I open the bag and unload the takeout containers. Britt enters the kitchen, grabs two plates out of the cabinet, and helps me carry everything to the round butcher-block table. After a return trip for forks and drinks, we sit down next to each other.

"Thanks for dinner."

"Thank Aunt Alicia. She paid for it."

"Long day?"

"Yep. One of my clients has their final adoption hearing tomorrow, and I want to make sure there aren't any hiccups."

"Could there be a problem?"

I shake my head and grab a container, forking noodles onto my plate. "It's not likely, but I like to be thoroughly prepared. How was your day? Wedding season is gearing up, right?"

Britt portions out some fried rice, and we switch containers. "We have our first one of the season this Saturday. Which reminds me..."

She looks over at me with large doe-like eyes and I groan. I know what's coming. She only gives me that look when she needs something. I sigh in resignation, knowing I'll do everything in my power to help her out. "What?"

"Well, since it's May, we don't have our student help yet. I could really use some extra hands." She bats her eyelashes at me for extra sweetness.

I roll my eyes at her antics. "You know I'll help. What do you need me to do?"

She squeals and gives me a quick hug before settling back into her chair and picking up her fork. "Thanks, Jay. You're a lifesaver. Could you help set up the chairs for the ceremony?"

"Sure, no problem." That's not too bad. Last year, I had to wait on people during the reception, which is tiring, and thankless, work. I take a bite of food before realizing Britt has a guilty look on her face. I raise my eyebrows in question.

"And with the food service during the reception?"

I drop my head, but the answer is automatic. "Of course."

She spears some noodles, a sign her requests are complete,

but then pauses just as the fork reaches her lips. "Could you do one more thing for me?"

How could I have forgotten? "You want me to ask Carlos?"

Britt presses her palms together in a prayer pose, her forkful of noodles drooping over the back of her hands. "Yes, please. It would be such a big help. You both already know the routine. I don't know where else to find quality help in only two days."

I exhale, open my eyes, and nod. "You know I'd do anything for you. I'll talk to Carlos, but you're going to owe me for the short notice."

Britt smiles with relief. "Of course. Whatever you want."

"Whatever I want, huh? I'll have to think about that." I grin mischievously.

She narrows her eyes and frowns. "Uh oh. I don't like the sound of that."

"Come on, now. Have I ever embarrassed you?"

Britt rolls her eyes. "All the time."

"I'd better make this one extra memorable, then." Her concerned face makes me laugh.

With my mind working overtime on the perfect way to pay back Britt, I take a bite of my egg roll, the crunchy shell and flavorful interior hitting a pleasant spot. Repaying my sister will also hit a pleasant spot.

14

Julie

I TURN AT the sound of fabric rustling behind me. My eyes widen and I suck in a breath. "Rachel, you're stunning."

The top of her wedding dress is embroidered lace with crystals sewn into the design. It has thin shoulder straps and a slight V-neckline. The skirt is an A-line ball gown of tulle that makes it look like she's gliding along on a cloud. The diamond studs in her ears sparkle as much as the crystals on her bodice. She brushes the skirt with her hands, her cheeks pink with what I guess is a combination of pleasure and embarrassment. "Thanks."

Abbie walks over to her sister, carrying the veil. "Are you ready to put this on?"

"Yes. I still can't believe I'm getting married today!"

I grin. "I'm so happy for you. And Tom, of course."

Rachel squeezes my arm. "Soon I'll have two sisters."

She turns to face Abbie, who slides the veil's hair combs into the crown of her head. I look back and forth between them, amazed by their near identicalness. I knew Rachel had a twin, but hadn't met her before the rehearsal dinner last night when Abbie was wearing khakis and a blouse with her hair pulled back in a ponytail. Today, her hair is in the same updo as Rachel's and she's wearing a cerulean blue bridesmaid dress. Rachel's white dress is about the only thing keeping the two women straight in my head.

My phone buzzes on the table next to me. It's a text from Emily, who's setting up the dessert table in the reception hall. I'm struggling a bit with relinquishing control, but thankfully Em understands and indulges my high-strung tendencies.

Emily: Here's where we're at. We'll finish in plenty of time.

The attached photo shows the table set up with artfully arranged truffles. There's an open spot where the cake will sit. I check the time. Fifteen minutes until the ceremony, which means about forty-five minutes until guests will start heading over to the reception area for cocktails.

Julie: Don't forget to reserve some truffles for the cake.

Emily responds with the thumbs up emoji. While slightly reassuring, nervous energy continues to course through me. It won't be released until I can see the display in person. For distraction, I task myself with making sure everyone in the bridal suite looks flawless.

My feet cross the threshold, and I glance around. Yesterday, the room for the ceremony looked plain, with just the small stage at the front, where the officiant and wedding party stand, and rows of wooden chairs with white cushioned seats. Today, it's been transformed. There are two large flower arrangements filled with white peonies, lilies, and roses on the stage. Gauzy white fabric and twinkle lights swoop along all four walls. Small sprays of flowers dot every other row of chairs heading up the center aisle. It's simple, but lovely.

I consciously relax my grip on the bouquet in my hands and look down the aisle at Tom. He's trying to contain his smile, but failing spectacularly. His giddiness is palpable even from here. His groomsmen, Jeff and Charlie, look equally excited. I smile, straighten my shoulders, and begin the march down the aisle. When I reach the front, I nod at Tom before turning left to take my designated spot. Abbie walks the aisle next and joins me up front.

The doors at the back of the room close and the music changes. Everyone stands and turns around in anticipation of seeing the bride and her father. Everyone except me. My focus is on Tom, eager for that magical moment when he sees Rachel in her dress. I'm not disappointed. His eyes widen and his jaw drops before he collects himself and his lips curve up into a smile that could light up a small town.

Tears spring to my eyes and my heart swells with happiness for my younger brother. When he reaches up and swipes a finger under his eye, my own tears crest, forcing me to pull a tissue out of my pocket and deal with my own waterworks. *Thank goodness Rachel found bridesmaid dresses with pockets!* I tuck the tissue away just as Rachel and her father reach the end of the aisle.

The ceremony is simple but meaningful. Anna, one of the Book Babes members, sings about love that lasts a lifetime and there's a poem read about holding on to true love with all your might. By the time they get to the wedding vows, I've used all my tissues. Abbie discreetly passes me a handful from her own pockets.

"Rachel," Tom says. "I knew finding a woman with blue-green eyes that match the waters of Hawaii was something special. Not only are you beautiful, but you're smart, resilient, and so much fun. You challenge me and encourage me to be the best version of myself. I've loved our adventures together and look forward to many more. I love you and will be your biggest fan for as long as we both shall live."

My heart swells at the pure adoration on Tom's face. Here comes a river of tears again. I swipe a clean tissue under my eyes, glad I went with waterproof mascara today. Rachel pulls a piece of paper from the pocket of her wedding dress and unfolds it. She looks up at Tom.

"I wasn't sure I'd be able to remember everything without notes." She takes a deep breath. "Tom, I don't make a habit of embarrassing myself in front of good-looking guys, but lucky for me, all my gaffes endeared you to me. While I didn't initially appreciate your enthusiasm for my writing, I know now it came from your big heart. I don't think anyone's story is quite like ours, which means it might make excellent material for my next book."

The audience chuckles.

"Our love story has been unconventional, but I don't mind. I'm excited to see what the next chapter brings. You are my happily ever after."

After a collective "aww" from the crowd, the officiant moves on to the exchanging of rings.

My mind turns to my wedding ceremony a decade ago. It was a whirlwind affair. Xavier had proposed to me after six months of dating and said we should get married right away. I assumed it meant he was desperately in love with me and couldn't wait to join our lives together. Our friend officiated the wedding, and I asked my uncle to give me away. I found a simple white dress at a thrift store and we'd gotten married in a park under a tree on a weekday afternoon.

At the time, I was wholly infatuated with Xavier and didn't care about the pomp and circumstance of a big wedding, but now I wish we hadn't rushed everything. Maybe if we'd dated longer or gone through the process of planning a wedding, I'd have noticed a red flag or two. Of course, hindsight and all that, but I at least hope

I'm wiser now. Beware of the guy who seems too good to be true because he probably is.

I realize where my mind's gone and push the memories away. This is Rachel and Tom's day, and I'm thrilled for them. I refocus on them just in time for the first kiss and clap along with the audience. *May they have true love and happiness all the days of their lives together.*

The bride and groom start back down the aisle, hand in hand. Halfway to the door, Tom picks Rachel up in his arms and carries her the rest of the way. I laugh in surprised delight and my eyes tear up again. I'd once thought I had that kind of love. Is it too late to look for it again?

My older brother Charlie meets me at center aisle. I take his offered arm, and we walk down the aisle. When we exit the doors, Charlie hugs Tom and Rachel briefly, then heads back through the doors to continue his groomsman duties of escorting the mothers and grandmothers out of the room.

I hug my brother and new sister-in-law. "Congrats, you guys! That bride carrying stunt was a fun surprise. Did you plan that?"

Tom and Rachel lock eyes, and my gut twists at the envy I feel witnessing their loving look. "We'd talked about it at the rehearsal," Rachel says, "but Tom decided to go for it today."

"Well, done," Abbie says, high-fiving Tom.

"So what's next?" Tom's best man, Jeff, says.

"Next are pictures," Rachel says. "We'll do the wedding party and Tom's family first so Julie can head over to the reception hall and check on dessert."

I smile gratefully at Rachel. "Thanks. I've been worrying about it a little."

"Really? I hadn't been able to tell?" Rachel grins, and points down at my hands.

I've twisted the ribbon on my bouquet so tight my fingers are white from lost circulation. I grimace, unwind the ribbon, and shake out my hand. "Oops. I'm sorry. I just want it to be perfect for you two."

"Don't worry, Jules," Tom says. "We already know everything will taste amazing. And who cares how it looks?"

"I care," I say, shooting daggers at him. "This is an enormous opportunity. If it impresses people, maybe I can get more wedding dessert business. We all know how lucrative that can be."

Tom nods. "Then let's find the groomsmen and the photographer and get this show on the road!"

15

Jayson

THE NORMALLY PLAIN white walls of the reception hall at the Arboretum are draped with gauzy fabric today. Sprays of white and green flowers drape down them, making it feel like I'm in a garden. White wisteria vine garland hangs down from the exposed wooden beams, and paper lanterns intersperse with the garland, giving a soft glow to the room. The centerpieces on each table are gold-painted vases holding several large white peonies. Pretty without being gaudy. I've seen some outrageous decor over the years, but this is elegant.

I look closer at the table in front of me, trying to figure out what seems off. One knife has the blade facing out, and I turn it the other way so the place setting is identical to the rest of the table. I'm not sure why I take so much pride in something as small as finding errant cutlery. Perhaps it makes me feel like I have excellent attention to detail, a necessary skill for an attorney.

When I'm satisfied that the table is perfect, I turn and immediately notice a woman in a bright blue dress standing near the dessert table, her back to me. The fabric makes a deep V, showing off lots of skin. My eyes wander up to the rich brown hair twisted around on her head in a loose, curly knot. Small white flowers weave around the knot. The hairstyle gives me an unobstructed view of her long, graceful neck. When she plucks a small chocolate ball out of the container and adds it to the cake, everything falls into place. It's Julie! I was beginning to wonder if I had suddenly developed a thing for all brunettes, but maybe it's just this one.

Another woman in black slacks, a black blouse, and cotton candy pink hair appears from behind the table and holds out a container to Julie. I recognize her even though the last time I saw Emily, she had turquoise hair. *I didn't know Julie was a vendor here. Why haven't I seen her at a reception before?*

A bump to my shoulder interrupts my musing. I turn to find my buddy Carlos grinning at me. He wiggles his eyebrows. "I see you checking out the woman by the cake. She's pretty hot."

I cough. "What? Uh, yeah, I guess she's attractive." My noncommittal answer is unbelievable, even to my ears.

"Uh huh. You think I missed your eyes scanning her from head to toe and following her every move? But if you really aren't interested, I'll go talk to her."

"I know her." I scowl at Carlos, knowing he's trying to get a confession out of me.

Carlos scoffs. "Yeah, sure you do."

"No, really. We had dinner together not too long ago."

He still doesn't look convinced. "If you know her, go talk to her."

It's quite tempting, but loyalty to my sister keeps me from sprinting across the room. "We're working, remember?"

"It's not like your sister's going to fire us. Besides, no one's here yet. You're not scared, are you?"

I'm definitely not scared. But I might be a tad nervous, which is puzzling because I usually have no problem talking to women. *Pull yourself together, Jayson.* I roll my eyes. "Fine. I'll go talk to her."

"Atta boy." Carlos slaps me on the back, starting me in

motion toward the other side of the room.

I walk slowly, trying to figure out what to say when I'm face-to-face with Julie. *Fancy meeting you here? No, that's dumb. Long time no see? Also dumb. You look gorgeous? Too forward.* Before I settle on an opening line, I'm right behind her. *Just say something or you're going to look like a creeper.* "Hi, Julie."

She jumps, turning around slowly with wide eyes.

I take a step back, worried I'm crowding her. My eyes move from her face down to her toes before slowly roaming back up and settling on her face. She looks even more amazing up close. "I didn't mean to scare you."

Julie's gaze darts around the room. "Where did you come from?"

I motion to my white shirt and black slacks. "I'm working the reception today."

Her brow furrows like my words do not compute. "I thought you were a lawyer."

"I am."

"Then why do you need a second job?"

I grin. That's a valid observation. "I'm helping my sister. She's the event planner for the Arboretum."

"Brittina Thompson's your sister?"

I nod. "I don't recall seeing you at one of these events before. How long have you been one of Britt's vendors?"

She shakes her head. "I'm not. This is my brother's wedding. I'm doing this as a favor, though I'm considering branching into dessert catering. What do you think?"

She motions to the table behind her. The display is quite impressive. The cake is white with ribbons of fondant the same blue as the dress Julie's wearing. A few truffles dot the cake. Spread out across the table on small stands of various heights are waves of truffles in various shades of blue.

"It's like an ocean of truffles," I say, admiration lacing my voice.

Julie smiles widely and claps her hands. "Oh yay! That's exactly what I was going for."

"Well, you nailed it. I'm sure Britt will love it."

"Oh, I hope so. Is she around? I'd love for her to see it before people come and start taking things."

"I think she's in the kitchen. I'll find her and send her your way."

"Thanks, Jayson. I'm so nervous! I want everything to be perfect for Tom and Rachel."

Her vulnerability makes me want to gather her in my arms and whisper reassurances in her ear. The thought startles me at its vividness. *Whoa there, Jayson. That's a bit much for someone you hardly know.* Still, I can't ignore the desire to get closer to this woman. "You'll be fine. By the way, did you purposefully dress to match the cake?"

"Actually, I matched the cake with the dress. I'm one of the bridesmaids."

"Pulling double duty. Nice."

I flash Julie one last smile before walking to the kitchen, where I find my sister looking over her event list, probably making sure everything's on schedule.

"Hey Britt, the cake vendor wants you to see the display."

She doesn't look up. "Okay, I'll be right there."

"The tables are set. What else do you need us to do?"

"Can you and Carlos supervise the hors d'oeuvres table? The guests should arrive in a few minutes."

"Sure thing."

I enjoy watching people celebrate their love. I like all the smiling friends and family, the silly little traditions of clinking glasses to make the bride and groom kiss, and the first dance. Throughout the night, my eyes wander around the room in search of Julie. Jealousy lances through my chest when she laughs at something one of the groomsmen says.

"Would anyone like more champagne?" I say to the table before me, trying to refocus on the task at hand.

I fill the proffered glasses, emptying the bottle. While waiting for the bartender to hand me another one, I automatically turn and scan the room in search of a bright blue dress.

"Who are you looking for?"

I startle and look to my right. "Where did you come from?"

Britt grins. "I'm everywhere at these events, remember?"

"Sure."

She pats me on the back. "Everything's gone well tonight. Thanks again for your help."

"Not a problem. What'd you think of the cake vendor's display?"

"It was beautiful. She gave me her card in case I want to recommend her to wedding parties."

"Think you'll put her on the official vendor list?"

Britt scrunches her lips to the side while she ponders my question. "I don't know. I'll have to taste her desserts first. It may look amazing, but if it tastes terrible, then forget about it."

"I don't know about the cake, but the truffles are outstanding."

She frowns up at me. "And how do you know that?"

I chuckle at her concerned look. "Relax, I haven't been eating them tonight. The store's near my office and I've been in a time or two."

"Is that how you know the vendor?"

"What?"

"I saw you talking to her earlier. And don't think I haven't noticed you following her with your eyes all evening. Do you like her?"

She sounds suspiciously like Carlos. *Have they been talking about me behind my back?* If I admit the tiniest hint of attraction, I'll never hear the end of it. Best to play it cool right now. "We're acquaintances."

"Acquaintances who've been to dinner?"

I narrow my eyes, my suspicion confirmed. "You've been talking to Carlos."

She shrugs. "I just want to know what's up with my big brother."

I look down at my shoes, trying to keep my face and posture neutral. "Nothing's up. We know each other, but we're not friends or anything."

"Well, that's a shame, because I've noticed her checking you out, too."

My head snaps up, my eyes widening. "She has?" I wince as soon as the words leave my mouth. There's no way Britt missed the eagerness in my voice. So much for playing it cool.

"Ah-ha! I knew it. Jayson's got a crush. It's about time!"

"What are you talking about? Time for what?"

"Love!"

I scoff and hold my hands up in front of me. "Whoa whoa whoa. Love? You're putting the cart before the horse. I barely know her."

Britt grins, undeterred by my protest. "Yeah, but you *want* to get to know her. I can tell. And I'm happy for you. I don't know when I last saw you interested in someone. Probably high school."

"I dated in college."

"But no one serious, because you never brought anyone home."

"And who says I want anything serious?"

Britt lifts a shoulder. "I'm just saying you need to get out more. You work so much I was afraid you'd never make time for a relationship. If you see a romantic possibility, I say go for it!"

No use denying anything now. Her mind's made up. "Well, thanks for that, but it takes two to tango and Julie doesn't seem interested."

"Then change that. You can win over just about anyone if you try. I can put in a good word for you. Or tell her I'll add her to my vendor list if she goes out with you."

I make an X motion with my arms. "No, thanks, on both accounts. I can handle it on my own."

"Well, then, handle it, bro. Now, get back to work. I'm not paying you to chitchat."

"You're not paying me at all!"

16

JUNE

Julie

"THANKS SO MUCH for coming in, Trevor." I give him a genuine smile and hold out my hand. "I'll make a decision about the position in the next week."

"Thank you, Julie." He shakes my hand and leaves.

Emily emerges from the hallway, and I give her a sharp nod. "Three down, one to go. What time is our final interview?"

Emily glances up at the clock. "In about thirty minutes. I'm going to take my break and grab a smoothie. Do you want one?"

I can already taste the sweet creaminess of an Orange Dream. "A smoothie sounds amazing. Yes, please."

Emily grabs her purse, and I pull some bills out of my pocket. "It's on me. I really appreciate your help with the interviews."

Emily smiles. "No problem. I definitely want us to hire someone good, since we'll all have to work with them."

I shoot her a pointed look. "I still think *you'd* make an excellent business manager."

Emily tuts and rolls her eyes. "No thanks. I'm just in it to hang out with my bestie. Besides, if you hire someone, I won't feel so guilty about quitting when I have a baby."

My eyes bulge. "Are you pregnant?!"

Emily laughs. "No, not yet, but Daniel and I are thinking about trying in the next year or so."

My fear evaporates, replaced with excitement. I'm thrilled my best friend is thinking about having a baby. "Oh. Well, I'd hate to lose you, but I'd be excited to have a little Westing for Aunt Julie to spoil."

"That'll be fantastic, but Aunt Julie needs a business manager, so she'll have *time* to spoil Baby Westing."

I sigh. "You're right, I suppose. I don't want to feel tied to the store all the time. I love it, but sometimes it feels like a needy family member bent on spoiling my fun. It's weird thinking about giving a bunch of my responsibilities to another person."

Emily pats my shoulder and takes the money from me. "I'm sure, but if you keep going like you are now, you'll burn out and then what will happen with the business? I think you have some excellent candidates. Surely one will be a good fit. But if you want your smoothie, I need to get down to Hill of Beans pronto."

She makes some good points. I wave my hand at Emily. "You're right. Go."

❧

"You have an MBA from Harvard Business School," I say, looking over my notes.

"I just graduated last month," says Nikki Cooper.

"What brings you to Asheville?"

"My family lives in Atlanta, so I wanted to return to the south for work. Asheville's a vibrant, artsy city, which I like, and is driving distance from my family."

At the mention of Atlanta, my mind drifts to Jayson. He went to

Harvard, too. I bet they'd get along great. The thought prickles my neck unpleasantly. I look down at my paper to reorient myself. "Why are you interested in working here at Little Shop of Sugar?"

Nikki smiles. "I've thought about starting my own business but want to learn the lay of the land, so to speak. I figured working for a small business, especially one in the food industry, would help me decide if that's truly what I want."

My forehead crinkles in surprise. "What type of business are you thinking about?"

"I want to run a food truck."

"What kind of food would you offer?"

Nikki's hands gesture in the air as she gets into a subject that obviously means a lot to her. "Kenyan food. My grandparents are from Nairobi and I've grown up eating and loving the food. I'd love to introduce it to others."

I like her enthusiasm and that she's a dreamer. "I know nothing about Kenyan food. What are your favorites?"

Her eyes sparkle and I can't help but match her bright smile with one of my own. Joy is so infectious. "The most popular dish is called ugali, which is a cornmeal porridge. It tastes much better than it sounds. Sukuma wiki is essentially collard greens. Chipsi mayai is like a potato omelet. Pilau is also a popular dish of rice with meat or vegetables."

"That all sounds delicious."

"It certainly does," Emily says. "If you're thinking about owning a food truck, how long would you plan to work with us?"

"Yes, good question." I nod my thanks to Emily for getting the interview back on track.

Nikki takes a beat before answering. "I want to pay off my school loans and save enough money to buy everything I need for a food truck, so I don't think it'll happen for at least five years. Plus, I really want the hands-on experience of running a small business. I hope it'll help me decide if a food truck is just a dream or my passion."

She seems to have focus and a good head for business. I also appreciate her honesty about what she imagines for her future. You wouldn't believe the number of times I've heard people gush about chocolate just to get a job. "You'd certainly get a good look at the inner workings of a small food-related business here. If you work here, your responsibilities will be assessing and identifying new opportunities for growth in the market, recruiting and training new employees, making sure the business has sufficient resources such as personnel and supplies, ensuring we have all the insurances and permits up-to-date, and overseeing the budget. Obviously, I will help get you up to speed on everything. What questions do you have about these responsibilities?"

Nikki clasps her hands together in her lap. "I assume you have spreadsheets showing your current markets, budget, and supplies. You probably have a standard training manual for employees and a specific, organized place for the permits, licenses, and health inspections. Correct?"

I meet Emily's eye. We're both impressed. "Actually," I say, "I don't have a training manual, but definitely think that would be a big help. Then I wouldn't have to train each new employee like I'm currently doing. And I have a drawer for all of our important papers, but it could probably stand to be more organized. I can already see how beneficial you'd be to the business."

"It's pretty standard stuff. Did you go to business school?"

"No. That's one reason I'm looking for a business manager. What other questions do you have?"

"Are there specific hours you would need me to work?"

"It's a full-time position, but the store has weekend hours and is closed on Tuesdays, so your schedule wouldn't be the typical Monday through Friday, eight to five. You could work from home on days when we have plenty of staff to care for customers."

Nikki nods her understanding. The interview ends after a few more questions. I'm impressed by the variety of candidates we interviewed. Now to make a decision.

Emily and I sit down with our food at a table in Big Bob's Burger Barn. I take a bite of onion ring, delighted by the crispy breading and sweet onion tantalizing my tongue.

"I told you they're delicious," she says, a self-satisfied grin on her face.

"I'll never doubt you again. What did you think of our candidates?"

" Lindsey didn't seem enthusiastic about working in our store."

I nod, grateful for Emily's straight shooting. "I agree. Neither did Trevor."

"Candace definitely has potential. She's been a manager before at Ice Cream Emporium, which is also in the food industry."

"That's true." I take a bite of burger, sorting through the candidates in my head. "I'm kind of leaning toward Nikki, though."

"Why's that? She's fresh out of school with no real world experience."

I tilt my head side-to-side, acknowledging her point. "I know, but she seems hungry to learn our business and excel. Since she's a recent graduate, she probably knows the latest, best business practices. Her questions were very insightful and I think she could help tighten up that part of the business."

Emily takes a sip of her water before answering. "It *would* give you more freedom to focus on the creative side of the business, which you said you wanted."

"Hopefully, whoever I hire will open up that avenue for me."

"True. Did you see Nikki's reaction to the truffle you gave her?"

I chuckle. "Yeah. She definitely hasn't had our stuff before."

"Nope, but I bet she'll tell everyone she knows how good it is. I mean, she even bought a box before she left. None of the other candidates did that. In fact, Trevor said he didn't even like chocolate. Why would he apply to work here?"

"Who knows? I definitely want someone who can appreciate our product. If you were in charge, who would you hire?"

Emily takes a bite of her burger and chews while she considers her answer. "I think Candace and Nikki are definitely the top candidates post-interview. While I'm inclined to lean toward someone with related experience, they may be set in their ways of managing and not be open to learning what would work best here. I think I'd take my chances with the ambitious MBA grad. Even though we don't know how long we'll have her, I think she'll do great things for the business."

Her thoughts echo my own. It's so nice to have a friend who gives solid, wisdom-filled advice. Even when I take a while to follow it. "Thanks for being honest. I agree. I'll call Nikki tomorrow and offer her the position."

"Sounds great. Thanks for dinner, by the way."

"I have to keep my best employee happy, right?"

Emily gives me a sly look. "You know I'd work there just for free chocolate."

I grin back at her. "Is that so? I'd consider it, but I bet you could eat more in chocolate than you currently get paid."

She laughs. "You've got that right."

17

Jayson

ANSWERING EMAIL ON my walk to lunch, I send another response, before the sound of a bell snags my attention. I look up in time to avoid a group of people streaming through a doorway onto the sidewalk. The enticing aroma of chocolate wafts out behind the last customer. A peek in the window reveals I'm standing in front of Little Shop of Sugar. The memory of how beautiful Julie looked at her brother's wedding makes me smile.

I've thought about calling her multiple times to set up another dinner, but something's kept me from following through. Fear, probably. *Come on, Jayson. Don't let fear keep you from pursuing a relationship.* I'll stop in on my way back from lunch and pick up dessert. A flimsy but believable excuse. Decision made, I continue on to Dragon Sushi, my new favorite lunch place. Their Tipsy Tiger roll is amazing, as is the King Crab. My mouth salivates just thinking about them and I quicken my steps.

An hour later, I'm back in front of the chocolate shop, but with a belly that's complaining from too many sushi rolls. Totally worth it. I pull open the shop door and smile at the merry tinkling of the bell. I inhale the delicious scent of chocolate before queuing behind another customer and perusing the display case.

"May I help you?"

I look up into the warm, brown eyes of a stranger. She has tight, curly black hair and an open smile.

"Are you new?"

"I'm the business manager."

The news surprises me. Julie finally took the plunge. Good for her. Maybe this will work in my favor and I can convince her to go on a proper date with me. "Business manager, huh? I didn't think Julie'd do it."

"Are you and Julie friends?"

How can I answer honestly? "I suppose you'd call us acquaintances. Do you have an MBA?" The woman's face closes up and I realize how brash my question sounded. "That came out wrong. I wasn't trying to be rude."

The woman's shoulders relax, and her troubled expression fades. "No, it's okay. I actually just graduated from Harvard Business School."

"I went to Harvard too!"

A warm smile spreads across her face. "Oh yeah? What was your major?"

"Economics, but I also went to law school there."

"I studied economics, too."

It's always fun to meet a fellow nerd. "I've got a joke for you. What do you call the study of food-based market forces?"

She doesn't move or speak for a few seconds, and I wonder if she's actually trying to come up with an answer. Finally, she shrugs.

"Econom-nom-nomics!" I say, enthusiastic in my delivery.

Her groan and eye roll are the perfect reaction.

"Did you have Professor Harkema for macroeconomics?" I ask.

"I did. I was a little intimidated by him, especially when he told us he had a black belt in karate and won several tournaments."

I chuckle. "Yeah, I think he mentioned that fact in all his classes. Did you enjoy Cambridge?"

"It took time to adjust to Massachusetts. It's very different from Atlanta. A lot more snow."

"I'm from Atlanta, too. Welcome to Asheville. I'm Jayson, by the way. "

The woman stretches her hand across the counter, and we shake. "Nikki."

18

Julie

I HEAD OUT to the front of the store, stopping in my tracks when I spy Jayson standing at the counter. My heart speeds up, and a smile comes unbidden to my lips. He laughs and my eyes dart over to the person behind the counter. Jealousy pierces my chest when I realize my new employee's the reason for Jayson's wide grin. Surprised by the emotion, I don't realize my legs are carrying me quickly to the other side of the room until I'm right beside Nikki. "Jayson, hi." My voice is embarrassingly breathless.

When he smiles at me, my heart squeezes with pleasure. He's so good looking. Our eyes lock and my surroundings disappear as I focus on his face, noting the long dark eyelashes framing his umber eyes and the laugh lines radiating out from the corners.

"Hi, Julie. I see you've hired a business manager."

There's an unpleasant twinge in my gut, but I try to ignore it. "I have. Nikki's already been such a blessing to me."

"Glad to hear it."

The bells over the door tinkle.

"I'll help the new customer," Nikki says. "Nice to meet you, Jayson."

"Same," Jayson says.

I'm sure he's just being polite, but his kindness rankles me. *Maybe because I like him, but am too scared to admit it.* I tamp that thought down. "What brings you into the store today?"

"I was coming back from lunch and thought I'd pick up a sweet treat for dessert."

"What would you like?"

"I really liked the Jitterbug and Sinful truffles from last time, but I'd like to try something new."

I'm pleased he wants to sample more of my selection. "Since it's summer, we have the Beach Nut, which is a coconut and macadamia flavored truffle."

Jayson wrinkles his nose. "Not a big fan of coconut."

"The flavor or the texture?"

"Texture."

I nod, a small smile playing at my lips. "I know many people like you, but they still like the Beach Nut. It's coconut liqueur, not actual coconut."

"Meh. I'll still pass."

"Our Ancient Treasures truffle is fairly popular. It's got a bit of cayenne pepper to enhance the chocolate flavor."

Jayson perks up at the mention of spice. A new kernel of information about him that my brain stores away. "That sounds interesting. Okay, I'll take one of those, along with one of each of the ones I had before."

"Sure. I'm going to throw in a Beach Nut for free because I think you'd like it if you gave it a chance."

"Pretty confident in yourself, are you?"

"I *am* an award-winning chocolatier." I wink at him, and the saucy grin he throws back nearly makes my knees buckle.

"Oh, excuse me. I didn't realize I was talking to an expert."

"Now you know."

"I sure do." He rests his forearms on the counter and leans forward until our faces are only inches apart. My skin tingles at our proximity. "By the way, I'm glad you hired Nikki."

His words catch me off guard and jealousy pricks my heart anew. "Why's that?"

"Now you can take time to do other things you enjoy. You said you'd like to have time for things outside of work, right?"

My body relaxes, my lips curving up at the reminder of our dinner conversation. "Yes, that's true. What do you think I should do with my extra time?"

Jayson grins. "You came to the right person for advice. You should go out to dinner with a handsome, fun guy."

The realization that he's flirting with me sets off butterflies in my stomach. I try to make my voice sound teasing, hoping it translates. "Oh yeah? Do you know anyone like that?"

He furrows his brow and purses his lips in a mock scowl. "Uh, yeah, right here."

He motions up and down his body and my eyes follow his hands. How does he look so appealing in a business suit? Clothes cover everything but his face and hands, but still my body heats with desire. I swallow, returning my eyes to his face. "Oh, you?" My voice squeaks, and I cough to cover it up. "I suppose you might do."

The sparkle in his eyes shows me he's enjoying this back-and-forth teasing. He pushes off from the counter and I'm disappointed at the distance between us. He fishes his phone out of his pants pocket. "Yeah? I'll take it. What's your cell phone number? I'll check my schedule and call you."

I rattle off my number, and he types it into his phone. "Alright, I sent you a text so you'll know it's me. Now, I probably should pay for my chocolate and get back to work. My lunch break's been longer than normal today and I'm swamped with work."

I hand the box across the counter to Jayson. "On the house. Sorry to make you late."

"Oh, I'm not sorry. An opportunity to see you is well worth the stern look from my aunt."

The heated look he sends my way nearly has me melting into a puddle on the floor. I tilt my head down, trying to hide my ear-to-ear smile. "Well, anyway, enjoy and let me know what you think of the Beach Nut."

"Will do. I'll be in touch."

He hits me with one last devastating smile that makes my cheeks pink with pleasure. Once he's out of sight of the store windows, I turn toward a new customer, but don't miss the knowing smirk on Nikki's face.

19

Jayson

MY FINGERS DRUM on the table, my cell phone pressed to my ear, as I will Julie to pick up. After the sixth ring, I pull the phone away from my ear, but quickly press it back when I hear a breathless, "Hello?"

My already accelerated heart rate ratchets up another notch. "Hey, Julie. It's Jayson. Are you busy?"

"Yes, but for you I've got a minute. What can I do for you?"

Did she just insinuate she's willing to make time for me? It's a weird way to say she likes me, but I've noticed she guards her emotions. This could be a big admission for her. *Or maybe I'm reading more into it than I should.* Regardless, it gives me hope she'll agree to my proposition. "Are you free tonight to have dinner? I know it's a little last minute."

There's a long pause during which I swear my heart stops, my confidence evaporating like water on a hundred degree day.

"Um, yeah, sure, that'd be great."

I pump my fist in the air, grateful no one can see how uncool I'm acting. "Great. I'll pick you up at your store. What time do you finish up?"

"A little after seven."

"I'll be there at seven fifteen."

I hang up, grinning from ear to ear. That was easier than I thought. Now to figure out where we're going to eat.

My car glides to a stop out front of the store, and I hop out, excited for dinner with Julie. I open the back driver's side door, take off my suit coat, and lay it across the back seat. I also remove my tie and unbutton the top button of my blue dress shirt, before shutting the car door and walking around the back of the car and over to the front door of the store.

I tug on the handle, but it doesn't budge. I knock on the glass. Emily unlocks the door and lets me in. "What can I do for you, Jayson?"

"I'm here to pick up Julie for dinner."

Emily's brow furrows. "Are you sure? Tonight?"

The silence inside the store gives me a bad feeling. "Yeah, why?"

Emily gives me a sympathetic look. "Julie's at her book club. She left about half an hour ago."

My mind conjures various scenarios to explain what's happening right now. One, she was so busy at work that she was too distracted to really think through my invitation. Two, she said what she thought I wanted her to say, and intentionally stood me up. My stomach drops at the thought.

Did I read her wrong? She seemed pretty flirty with me the other day when I was in the store. Did I make too much out of her comment earlier today? There was a pretty big pause before she answered. Was she just humoring me? She seems like a straight shooter, so none of this makes sense to me.

A hand on my arm draws me out of my thoughts. I cringe at

Emily's pitying look. "Jayson, I'm sorry. We were slammed with customers this afternoon. I had to remind her about book club and force her out of the store so she wouldn't be late. I didn't know she had plans with you."

My lips press into a firm line. Maybe I should give Julie the benefit of the doubt. "She *did* sound busy when I called. I'm sure it's an honest mistake."

"I know she'll feel horrible when she realizes what happened."

"Well, there's no use worrying about it anymore. Though I do still have a reservation for Naranjas. Would you like to join me for dinner?"

"I love Naranjas! Unfortunately, my husband has dinner waiting for me at home."

I wish Emily a good evening and head outside to my car. I'm tempted to cancel the reservation, but I'm really craving their lobster macaroni and cheese so I make the drive, wondering what happened with Julie. She seemed harried when I called earlier. It was probably an honest mistake. I'll try to stop by tomorrow and see her. I'm afraid if I text her about it right now, I might come across as angry, which I'm not. Disappointed? Yes. I really just want to know the truth. If it turns out she dodged me on purpose because she's not interested, then I'll be able to tell from her body language. If she really was overwhelmed with work, then we can plan another dinner. I really hope it's the latter.

Inside the restaurant, I inform the hostess that I'm dining solo and she asks if I'd prefer to sit at the bar. I accept, happy that I'll at least have the bartender to talk to while I eat. Taking a seat, I order a beer. The coolness of the amber liquid feels good on my throat and my muscles relax.

The metallic clink of scraping chair legs draws my attention down the bar and I'm surprised when I recognize Julie's business manager. "Nikki, hey."

I raise my hand in greeting when she turns. Her forehead

creases and I realize she can't place me. "It's Jayson, Julie's friend."

Her face clears, and she gives me a polite smile. "Oh, yeah. Hi."

She orders a margarita, then looks at her phone. I guess she isn't in a chatty mood. I turn back to the bartender and put in my dinner order before pulling my phone out. My first instinct is to click on my inbox, but I'm really trying not to do any work after I leave the office. I sigh and slide it back into my pocket. I drum my fingers on the counter, trying to figure out how to distract myself until my food comes.

I glance around the room, counting the number of margaritas at the surrounding tables. Next I try to find every orange fruit in the room. I spot half a dozen in the wall decor. Do slices on glasses count as part or whole oranges? I roll my eyes at my pathetic attempts to keep my mind occupied, turn back to the bar, and pull out my phone again. This time I open the Crossy Road app and play as the slippy penguin.

A staff member sets a steaming bowl of lobster mac and cheese before me and I pocket my phone.

"Hey," a voice says, and I turn to where Nikki's staring incredulously at me. "Did we order the same thing?"

Sure enough, she has an identical bowl of yellow noodles and chunks of red and white lobster meat sitting in front of her. I smile. "It's my favorite. I rarely get anything else."

"That's good to hear because this is my first time here and I wasn't sure if I was making a colossal mistake."

I shake my head. "No, you're good. Enjoy."

I face the bar and unwrap my silverware from the napkin. The scrape of metal turns my head again.

"Do you mind if I sit closer?" Nikki says. "I wouldn't mind having some company while I eat."

I shrug. "Sure. It looked like you wanted to be alone earlier."

"It was just a long day. I'm still learning the business and figuring out how I can be an asset. But I get enough alone time at my new apartment since I don't really know anyone yet, so I thought I'd eat in proximity to others. I didn't expect to see a familiar face." She pauses. "But maybe you're here to eat alone. Am I cramping your style?"

"No, I'm happy for the company. I was supposed to have dinner with Julie, but I guess she forgot about her book club tonight."

Nikki frowns in sympathy. "That stinks, though Julie ran herself ragged today. She's trying to get a big order of truffles together for some fancy wedding this weekend and came into the store super early this morning. I doubt her mind's on anything else at the moment. If the event coordinators are pleased, it may open up a new avenue of business for the store."

That eases my worry about Julie intentionally ditching me. Haven't I gotten so absorbed in work that I've forgotten other things I was supposed to do? It happens to the best of us. Especially us workaholics. Still, I'll feel completely relieved when I hear it straight from her lips. I take a bite of my food, running through my brain for a new topic to discuss.

"So, how about those Braves?" I say.

Nikki gives me a weird look. I guess that *was* a bit random. I was trying to think of something neutral we could talk about and remembered our Atlanta connection.

"I wouldn't know. Never seen them."

"What?" My mouth hangs open, incredulous. "Are you seriously telling me you grew up in Atlanta and never, not once, went to a Braves game?"

Nikki shakes her head. "Nope. My family isn't really into baseball."

"Not even on the fourth of July to see fireworks?"

She shrugs and spears a bite of food with her fork. "We'd see them at Lenox Square Mall every year."

"Huh." I shake my head, unable to comprehend an Atlantan

who's never seen the Braves in person.

She narrows her eyes at me. "I'm sure there's some Atlanta tradition you've never done."

I smile and lean back, crossing my arms over my chest. "Try me."

"Have you run the Peachtree?"

"Twice."

Nikki rolls her eyes. "What about watching the Peach Drop on New Year's Eve?"

"Done it."

"Eaten at The Varsity."

"Like once a week in high school."

"What about The Vortex?"

"Both locations."

Nikki twists her lips to the side. Probably scrolling through her mental file of Atlanta knowledge. "Okay, smart guy. Did you ever ride the Pink Pig?"

My eyebrows shoot up. "The what?"

Nikki makes a tsking sound, the smile on her face growing wider. "Come on, Jayson, you've had to have heard of the Pink Pig."

She's got to be pulling my chain. Unless she's talking about a barbecue place, I can't imagine what it might be. "Does it have something to do with barbecue or the state fair?"

Nikki makes a buzzer sound. "Wrong. It's a monorail ride that runs during Christmas at Lenox. The attraction's been around since 1953."

I shake my head. "Nope, definitely not."

Nikki leans back in her seat and tilts her head to the side, her face screaming *told ya so*.

I smile. "Okay, you win. New question. What's something you'd want every guest to do when they visited you?"

"When the aquarium opened, that was my go-to attraction. I love the big window where you can stare at the whale sharks and rays for hours. It's so calming."

I nod and gather a forkful of noodles and lobster. "I like the aquarium too."

"Is that where you'd take guests?"

"Nah. I'd take them to the World of Coke. You can't taste sixty flavors of Coke products from around the world anywhere else. Plus, I love watching people try the Beverly."

Nikki chokes on the sip of margarita she's just taken. "No! You don't warn your guests off it?"

I can't help but laugh as I remember past visits with friends. "Nope. You should see the faces people make!"

Nikki shakes her head in mock disapproval, then shoots me a sly look. "Did you know you can also taste the Beverly at Epcot in Florida?"

I perk up, humored by her mischievousness. "You can?"

"Yep, in Future World at Club Cool."

I make a sour face. "Why?"

Nikki shrugs. "For the experience?"

I smack the counter with my hand. "See? You're proving my point."

She rolls her eyes and waves away my words. "Anyway. What are the touristy things to do with people here?"

I take her through my list of Asheville attractions while we eat our food.

Half an hour later, Nikki sets down her fork and pushes her bowl away. "This lobster mac and cheese is amazing, but I'm going to have to get a to-go box because I'm stuffed."

I grin at my empty bowl, then drink the last of my beer. "I told you it was good. Next time you come, definitely try the ceviche."

We pay our bills and head out front together.

"Thanks for keeping me company and sharing your knowledge of the city," Nikki says.

"Not a problem. Do you need a ride home?" I gesture to my car parked at the curb.

She waves me off. "No, I'm good."

"Okay. Guess I'll probably see you at the store."

I turn toward my car, but Nikki's voice stops me.

"Jayson? For what it's worth, I think Julie likes you."

I turn slowly, surprised by her words. "Why do you say that?"

She shrugs. "Just from watching her when you were in the other day. She's trying to hide it for some reason, but you seem like a nice guy, so I thought I'd say something."

"Thanks."

Driving home, I try to reconcile being stood up by Julie with Nikki's words. It doesn't quite add up, but it gives me hope I'm not imagining things.

20

Julie

MY GLOVED FINGERS are coated in chocolate from creating truffles when someone clears their throat behind me. I look over my shoulder to find Emily with her hands on her hips, her eyebrows raised in question. "You never responded to my texts."

I silently groan. Emily had blown up my phone with messages while I was at book club asking if I realized I'd stood Jayson up. However, I didn't read them until I woke up this morning. As soon as I saw them, my heart plummeted to my stomach. "I'm sorry. Book club went long, and I zonked after taking Sadie out. I didn't see your messages until this morning."

Her posture softens, arms dropping to her sides. "Did you really forget about your book club when Jayson asked you to dinner?"

I turn back to the table of truffles, my face heating with shame. I feel terrible for standing Jayson up last night. "It was a crazy day. I'm still trying to get all the truffles ready for the Bourgault wedding this weekend. I forgot I had book club until you reminded me it was time to go. By then, so much had happened that dinner wasn't even a glimmer of a thought in my brain. I texted an apology to Jayson this morning, but haven't heard back."

"You've been noticeably scatterbrained this week."

My shoulders round and I scuff a shoe against the floor. "Yeah, I'm sorry. I really thought hiring a manager would help me level up, but I still seem to be the same hot mess as before."

A hand on my shoulder lifts my head to Emily's concerned face. "Hey, don't beat yourself up. If Jayson's the stand-up guy I think he is, he'll understand. Besides, sure, you've hired someone, but you're also branching out in your business *and* expanding your social activities. You're adding a lot at once. A ball will get dropped every once in a while."

Releasing a frustrated breath, I shrug. "I still don't like it."

She lifts a shoulder and tilts her head to the side. "Well, if you're really concerned about Jayson, you can always make more of an effort to apologize. Go that extra mile, if you will."

I like her idea, but am not sure how to make that happen. I don't know enough about Jayson to customize an apology. Though he seems to like my truffles. I make a mental note to put together a box and hire a courier to take it over to his office. I can probably find his address online. Or on his business card, which is still in my purse. I was tempted to toss it when he first gave it to me, but resisted the impulse. "Thanks for the suggestion. What time is it?"

"Almost time to open. I'll make sure everything's straight out front. You keep working back here."

"Thanks. I've just got a couple dozen more to make. I'll be able to relax once I finish this part."

"I'm excited that you're doing another event. Perhaps this is the beginning of a booming wedding dessert business. Are you sure you don't need my help tomorrow?"

"No, I'll be fine. I'm not a bridesmaid this time."

After locking the front door behind the last customer of the day and cleaning the floor out front, I walk into the office and find Nikki at the desk. "I didn't realize you were still here."

Nikki glances up from the paperwork in front of her. "Just going over the employee training manual I'm working on. Can I go through it with you sometime next week to make sure I haven't forgotten anything?"

"Of course." She returns her gaze to the desk. I feel bad I haven't spent much time getting to know her. Since her orientation, work has kept me in the kitchen for the majority of every day. I shift my weight from foot to foot before clearing my throat. "Are you settling into Asheville okay? Need any restaurant recommendations or anything?"

"I'm doing okay, though it's tough not knowing anyone. Speaking of food, I ran into Jayson at Naranjas last night."

My gut twists with regret at standing Jayson up. He was taking me to Naranjas? That's one of my favorite places in the city. I love their coconut margaritas. Jayson sent a thank you text for the chocolates earlier, but nothing more. Worry that he's upset with me deepens the uncomfortable feelings swirling inside. I try not to let it show. "What did you think of the food?"

Nikki grins. "It was ah-may-zing. We both got the lobster mac and cheese."

My brow furrows. "Did you eat together?"

She nods. "We were both at the bar. It was nice reminiscing about Atlanta. He seems like a genuinely sweet guy."

My chest tightens with an unpleasant feeling. *Am I jealous that Nikki got to spend time with Jayson? Yes, yes, I am.* The strength of the emotion surprises me. It's been a long time since I've had this kind of reaction to a man. Maybe my heart's decided it's ready to get back in the game. If that's the case, I've really got to make sure things are right between us. I think he likes me, but Nikki is a smart, attractive, kind, and very likable person. If she and Jayson spend more time together, something could come from that. Do I want that to happen? No, I don't. I selfishly want to see where things might lead with Jayson. After the disaster that was my marriage, don't I deserve a second chance? But what does Jayson deserve? Someone who's reliable.

I realize I've been quiet a little too long. "Yeah, he is. Look, I know we haven't gotten much time together since you started. How about we go to lunch next week? You can ask me whatever questions you may have about the business and we can look over the manual as well."

She meets my gaze and smiles. "That sounds good."

"Good. I'm going to head out. Will you turn off the lights and lock up when you leave?" Letting someone other than Emily or myself lock up makes me nervous, but I hired her to help me with the business and I have to trust her or I'll never get the breathing room I desperately need.

"Sure."

I grab my purse off of the coat rack near the door and wave as I leave, but Nikki's focus is back on the papers in front of her. I force the green monster of jealousy down into my gut, reminding myself Nikki is helping me. She's not my competition. Jayson isn't even really mine, anyway. We've been to dinner once. *Could have been twice, if I hadn't been a flake yesterday. Maybe I'm not good enough for Jayson.* Where did that thought come from? It sounds like what I said to myself when things ended with Xavier. Time to recite the good things in my life to counteract my negative thoughts.

My business is thriving and even growing. I have a business manager who allows me to expand my business into additional creative ventures like weddings. I have the best dog in the world. Sadie's always happy to see me and quick to show affection.

The thought of my sweet dog makes me smile. I pick up my step, realizing Sadie's probably more than ready for another walk. I'd used my lunch break to exercise her, but that was over six hours ago.

There's a stab of guilt in my chest. I really need to find a dog walking service, so Sadie isn't cooped up in the apartment for most of the day. Am I being selfish keeping a dog I can't give as much love to as it deserves? It wasn't a problem when Tom was staying with me, but now he's living with his wife. I can tell Sadie misses the attention Tom gave her. I'm fantastic at failing those I love. *Maybe I should stay away from Jayson. I'd hate to hurt him more than I already have.*

When I open the door to my apartment, Sadie's standing by the door, leash in her mouth, her tail wagging fiercely. My guilt skyrockets. I pat the dog's head, take the leash, and attach it to her collar. "I know, girl. Sorry I'm late. Let's go for a walk."

Sadie trots down the sidewalk on the way to the park, and I sigh in frustration. My life is feeling even more out of control than ever, mainly from good things like work help and more business, but also due to increasing feelings of loneliness.

I, too, am feeling the space left by my brother's relocation. Sure, he's still in town, but he's married now. As is my best friend. I don't want to impose on them and their family time. Maybe I should date just for the opportunity to connect with others.

Jayson's face pops into my mind and my heart lifts. *Okay, body, I get it. I like Jayson.* Maybe if I see him face-to-face, I'll be straight with him and let him know I'm interested in spending more time with him. The idea of speaking my feelings out loud is terrifying, but it can't be worse than not finding out what could happen with the first man I've had real interest in since my divorce.

21

Jayson

WHEN I FINISH filling the water glasses at my table, I place the pitcher on the drink stand against the wall, then grab the one filled with sweet tea and return to the table. Carlos appears next to me and starts filling glasses with lemonade. "Did you see who's working today?" he says, inclining his head toward the other side of the room. "Isn't the dessert vendor your friend?"

My head whips up and over. There's a stunning off-white three-tiered cake with what looks like little braids running down all sides. A giant fake diamond serves as the cake topper. I look for truffles to confirm Carlos's assessment, but there are none. "Are you messing with me?"

Carlos puts a hand over his heart. "Nah, man. I promise I saw her."

I refocus my attention on setting up, but keep sneaking glances at the cake table. Soon, the wedding guests funnel in and I wander among them with appetizer trays. When the bride and groom enter, I glance again at the dessert table and am surprised to find it now filled with jewels in a range of colors—red rubies, dark blue sapphires, green emeralds, and purple amethysts. Is everything edible? Curiosity gets the better of me and I make my way across the room. It turns out the braids on the cake are tiny pearls. Large pearls are scattered among the gems. Up close, I can see they're made of chocolate, but from a distance, everything looked very real and very expensive. Whoever created this is amazing.

A tingle on the back of my neck has my eyes darting around the room, but don't see Julie anywhere. I meant to call her last night to thank her for the truffles she sent over, but ended up working until ten and by then it felt too late to contact her. I broke my rule of stopping work at seven, but the case goes up in front of a judge first thing Monday morning, and I figured working late on Friday was better than bringing it home and working over the weekend.

There are probably multiple businesses that make truffles for weddings, but Nikki said Julie was consumed with an order for a fancy wedding. And the crystal vases with sky-high flower centerpieces make this feel like a high-class event. After one more search of the room and no sight of the beautiful chocolatier, I return to the kitchen, set down the empty appetizer tray, and prepare for the dinner portion of the reception.

After clearing the glasses from one table into a gray plastic tub, I move on to the next one. When the tub is full, I carry it into the kitchen and grab an empty one. Carlos and I pass just outside the kitchen door.

"Hey Jay, I just saw your friend at the cake table."

I give him a skeptical look. "Fool me once, Vega."

"I'm serious."

I keep walking, moving toward a table still piled with glasses and dessert plates. Something catches my eye and I turn in the direction of the dessert table. A woman in black with brown hair in a low bun is boxing up the rest of the cake. My heart thuds in my chest when she turns to the side and brushes a stray hair behind her ear. Before another thought forms in my brain, my feet are already carrying me in her direction. "Hey, Julie."

Julie turns. "Jayson. Hi."

"Fancy meeting you here."

She smiles and crosses her arms over her chest. "Yeah, I guess."

"Do you know the couple who got married tonight?"

"No. The bride saw our wedding cake advertisement in our store and asked if we could do a cake with just two weeks' notice."

"Whoa, that's fast."

She nods, dropping her arms from in front of her body. "Yeah. Apparently, the first cake decorator she'd booked had a family emergency."

I gesture to the mostly empty table. "I never would have guessed this was a rush job. Everything looked incredible."

"Thanks. I should probably finish packing up and get out of here."

I'm not ready to stop talking to Julie so soon, so I blurt out the first thing that comes to mind. "The truffles you sent over yesterday were amazing. Just what I needed to power through a late night at the office."

It elicits a smile from her. "You're welcome. Thanks for being so understanding about my slip up. I'm really sorry to have missed Naranjas. And the company."

My brow furrows in confusion. "How did you know about Naranjas?"

Her smile slips a little. "Nikki told me she saw you there."

"Yeah. Your new manager is really nice." When her lips flatten out, I grasp for something to say that might return the smile. "So is her boss."

"Yeah?"

My attempt works, and I smile. "Yeah."

She meets my gaze, and something in her expression has me leaning toward her. It's on the tip of my tongue to ask for a dinner do over, when someone steps into my periphery. Julie and I break off eye contact at the same time.

Britt smiles at me before turning to face Julie. "Julie, just the person I wanted to see."

"Hi, Brittina. How can I help you?"

"Please, call me Britt. Harlowe raved about your cake. She was ecstatic you captured her vision perfectly. She said she's going to be recommending you to all her friends."

Julie beams and I can't help grinning along with her. "That's wonderful news. Thanks for the feedback."

"I'd like to add you to the Arboretum's list of preferred vendors."

"I'd love that. Thank you, Britt. I'm so excited."

"Great! Well, I'll leave you to it." My sister sends a curious look my way as she leaves.

I hike a thumb over my shoulder. "I guess that's my cue to get back to work."

"Yeah, I suppose so."

She gives me a genuine smile, which zips straight to my chest. Before I get distracted again, I toss out, "Let's connect next week and maybe try dinner again."

Her eyebrows raise, and then she nods. "Yeah, I'd like that."

I return to cleaning up the reception hall, but can't help sneaking looks at Julie until she's gone. Heading out to my vehicle when the place is spick and span, Carlos bumps me with his shoulder.

"Hey, man. How'd things go with your girl? I saw you two talking earlier."

"Now she's my girl, huh? We're really just friends."

Carlos gives me a roguish grin. "Do you mind if I ask her out, then? She's pretty cute."

I glare at him. "Don't even think about it."
He laughs. "Yeah, that's what I thought."

22

Julie

"HOW DID THE wedding go on Saturday?"

I look over my shoulder, surprised to see Nikki standing in the doorway. She usually arrives around nine, so seeing her at seven-thirty in the morning is a surprise. Maybe she needs to leave early today, which is fine. I set down the truffle ball in my hand and turn to face her. "Fantastic. The couple loved their dessert table, and the Arboretum event coordinator offered to add me to their list of preferred vendors."

"Julie, that's awesome!"

"I know! And it might not have happened without your help."

She gives me a puzzled look. "What'd I do?"

"Not worrying about the business side is really helping my creativity. I'm getting more ideas and feel like the quality of my output is increasing."

"That has nothing to do with me. Your truffles were pretty fantastic before I got here."

I wave a chocolate-covered gloved hand at her. "You know what I mean. I've created four new truffle flavor profiles since you started. Before that, I was lucky to get that many in an entire year."

Nikki smiles. "Well, thanks, boss. I'm learning a lot working here and definitely enjoy the free chocolate perk."

"So glad to hear."

The store phone rings. "I'll get it. You keep doing your thing." She motions to the truffles in front of me, then turns on her heels and heads out to the front of the store. The phone rings once more and then I hear her chipper voice as she answers.

The ringing phone reminds me of the last time I answered a call at work. It was Jayson asking me to dinner. Guilt at my forgetfulness wells up. *Jayson forgave you and said he wanted a redo.* The reminder makes me smile. I'd like to see him again, but I'd prefer it to be something with less pressure than dinner. *What about coffee?* I can spare half an hour to spend time with Jayson. Decision made, I pull off my gloves and retrieve my cell phone from the counter next to the sink, typing out a message before I can talk myself out of it.

Julie: Hey Jayson. Can I take you for coffee? Let me know when you have a spare half hour and we can meet at Hill of Beans.

There's no immediate reply, so I put my phone in the back pocket of my pants, wash my hands, and grab a new set of gloves. Returning to the truffle table, I get back to work.

The phone pings in my pocket and breaks my concentration. The pleasant hum of conversation floating in through the doorway and the occasional tinkle of the bell over the doorway make excellent background music for creating truffles. I blink my eyes a few times and glance up at the clock, startled to find that it's nearly one o'clock. Have I really been working for almost five hours? A glance at the surrounding tables piled with truffles confirms it.

I remove my gloves before reaching for my phone.

Jayson: I can meet in fifteen minutes if that works for you, but can we grab a burger or something? I need to eat lunch.

My stomach growls in response.

Julie: Sure. How about I see you at B4?
Jayson: It's a date.

My heart zings around my chest at his words. *Calm down. It's just an expression. Though, obviously, I'm open to having more dates with Jayson.*

I remove my apron and hang it on a hook, then walk behind the store counter past Emily, who's fully engaged with a customer, through the other doorway, and down to the office. Nikki looks up from the desk when I enter.

"I'm heading out for a quick lunch at B4. Do you want me to bring you back something?"

"Before what?"

I forget Nikki's new in town. "Oh, sorry. Big Bob's Burger Barn. Locals call it B4 for short."

"No, thanks. I already ate."

"Okay. I should be back in about forty-five minutes."

I remove my purse from a desk drawer and head out into the sunshine. The humidity greets me like a slap in the face. I walk down the block, make a right and then a left, reaching the restaurant in about four minutes. I consider waiting outside for Jayson, but my shirt is already sticking to my back with sweat, so I head inside for the glorious air conditioning. I pick up a plastic order sheet and tick off my selections with a dry erase marker.

"An onion ring fan, I see."

Startled, my head whips up. "Jayson! I didn't hear you come in."

He smiles. "Sorry about that. It's a hot one out there."

I give Jayson a proper look. He's ditched his usual jacket and tie. His white dress shirt is unbuttoned at the collar and his sleeves are rolled up to his elbows. My eyes catch on his muscled forearms. Why do I find that so attractive? I quickly drag my eyes back up to his face. His gorgeous face with the oh-so-kissable lips. *Focus, Julie. This is only your second date. It's too soon to maul the sexy lawyer.* "What are you going to get?"

"My usual. The Deluxe with extra onions and an order of onion rings."

I scrunch my nose. "Raw onions. Yuck."

"I think they're delicious."

I shrug. "You do you." It's not like I'm going to be kissing him anytime soon or anything. There I go, thinking about his mouth again.

We place our orders and sit down at a table.

"Was there something you wanted to talk about?" Jayson says, cutting right to the chase. He must need to get in, eat, and get out.

"Not really. Just wanted to spend some time with you. Get to know you a little better." My cheeks heat at the confession.

There's a sparkle in his eye. "Oh yeah? I like that. What do you want to know?"

My mind goes blank and I scramble for a question. "Um. What do you do with your free time, besides work receptions at the Arboretum?"

"I play sports and watch documentaries."

That a Harvard grad watches documentaries for fun doesn't surprise me. "Which sports?"

"I enjoy playing most sports, though my favorites are volleyball and basketball. I also golf, mostly to schmooze other lawyers."

"I bet your height makes you an amazing hitter in volleyball. Probably helps your serving as well."

He smiles. "You're correct. Do you play volleyball?"

"I did in high school."

"Were you any good?"

I shrug and keep my face neutral. "We won state my junior

year, and I received the MVP award."

Jayson's face opens in surprise, which makes me chuckle. "How many kills did you get?"

"None. I was the setter."

He sits up straight, eagerness in his expression. "No way! You should be on my team next season. I bet we'd make a great duo."

"I haven't played in forever. I'm probably super rusty."

"Well, let's knock that rust off with some practice. I've got a ball and net at my house."

Whoa, he's a serious athlete if he has equipment at home. I'm not sure I'd even want to play in such a competitive league. Oh, who am I kidding? It'd be fun to get back into it, if I could fit it into my schedule.

"Maybe."

Jayson grins. "I'm going to turn that *maybe* into a *yes*. Speaking of sports, I have a basketball game tonight at eight at the community center. Would you like to come?"

The thought of watching Jayson run up and down a court in shorts and a t-shirt immediately has my mind going haywire. I bet he looks good even when he's sweaty. I open the calendar app on my phone. The store's closed tomorrow and I don't have a wedding reception on Saturday to prepare for. Seems like the stars have aligned. "Okay, sure."

I'm rewarded with a beaming smile and my stomach squeezes in more-than-friendly delight. *Calm down. Ease into this. Feel him out and find out what you're getting into.* I let my relationship with Xavier move too fast. Slow and steady is probably the right move. To distract me from my feelings, I pick up my burger and take a bite, savoring the mouthful of pickle, beef, cheese, and mustard. After swallowing, I dip an onion ring in ketchup and pop it in my mouth. "I would argue that these are the best onion rings in the city," I say, grabbing a second one and shoving it in my mouth. Maybe food will dislodge my budding feelings for Jayson.

"I'd love to disagree with you just to hear your arguments, but I can't. These are heavenly."

Jayson grins and my stomach swoops. I'm in so much trouble.

Emily bumps her hip against mine. My knees bend and I sway to the side, grabbing the counter in front of me to regain my balance. "Earth to Julie."

When I look at her, she's wearing a knowing grin. "What?"

"Your head's been in the clouds all afternoon. What's on your mind?"

I shrug. "Nothing really. I think eating a big lunch made me tired." It certainly didn't dim my attraction to Jayson.

"You don't have the look of a tired person. You look like someone who's got a secret."

Sometimes it's a real pain having a best friend who knows me so well. "It's nothing," I insist, but it's obvious I'm lying.

Emily purses her lips. "Let me know when you're ready to talk about this 'nothing.'" She uses air quotes for emphasis. "I'm already dying of curiosity."

23

Jayson

I GLIDE DOWN the lane, dribble the ball between my legs, then gently lay it up against the glass. It swishes through the net. I retrieve the ball and pass it to a teammate before heading over to the bench for a drink of water.

"Hey, man," Carlos says, joining me at the bench. "Is that your woman friend over there?"

My head whips around. "Where?"

Carlos laughs and tilts his head toward the opposite side of the gym. Julie steps up onto the bleachers and takes a seat. She scans the teams on the court and I wave when she looks my direction. I smile when she waves back, starting across the court toward her. The buzzer sounds, stopping me in my tracks. I sigh and shrug apologetically at Julie. She waves her hand, motioning her understanding. I turn and head to the bench.

"Okay, coach," I say. "Who's starting?"

Carlos looks at me and grins. "Jayson can start today because his girl is here."

I narrow my eyes. "My *friend.*"

"Whatever. Keith, Luis, Andre, and I will be the other

starters. Travis, you come in for me after about four minutes. Jon, I'll put you in after I'm back on the bench. Alright, fellas, we beat this team by four last month. Let's see if we can make it double-digits tonight. Hands in. One. Two. Three."

"Ball-Stars," we yell in unison.

I make my way to center court for tipoff. My skin feels jumpy and I'm already sweating, though I barely warmed up. Am I nervous about a rec game? I'm never nervous. Of course, I've never had a fan in the stands before either. I toss a quick glance at the bleachers. Julie catches my eye and gives me a thumbs up. I sure hope I don't make a fool of myself. I turn away, squaring myself up next to my opponent and try to focus on the court.

As soon as the ball's tipped, my mind snaps into the zone and I play like I belong in the NBA. I almost couldn't miss a shot from any range. The entire team plays better than usual. When the final buzzer sounds, the Ball-Stars have won by fifteen points. We all high-five one another.

Carlos, our team captain and unofficial coach, gathers us in a circle after we shake hands with our opponents. "That was awesome, guys. Props to our MVP, Jayson, who was on fire tonight."

I duck my head to hide my delight at the praise. "Everyone played well tonight. It's the team's energy that helped me up my game."

"Indeed," Carlos says, nodding. "Let's bring our talent with us next week for the tournament. Our first opponent will be the Sky City Ballers, which we've beaten before. But then it looks like we'll be playing The Ball Boyz for a place in the championship."

"They were tough last time," Luis says.

"They beat us last time," Carlos reminds us, frowning.

"We'll get them this time," I say.

"I sure hope so. Let's practice Thursday night and possibly Saturday or Sunday to make sure we're ready. Again, great job tonight, guys."

Everyone grabs their stuff and clears off the court for the next game. I pick up my bag and walk over to Julie, who's standing next to the bleachers.

I wipe my forehead and neck with a sweat towel, not wanting to drip on her. "Thanks for coming."

"Thanks for the invite. Congrats on your win."

Something equally sweaty nudges my shoulder. Carlos must have followed me across the gym. And now he's grinning like a fool. I know why he's here.

"Julie, this is my friend Carlos. Carlos, this is Julie."

"Very nice to meet you, Julie," Carlos says, sticking out his hand.

"Nice to meet you, too," she says. "You look familiar. Have we met before?"

"Maybe you've seen me at an Arboretum reception. Sometimes I help Britt out when she needs extra hands."

Julie tilts her head, studying Carlos. "That's thoughtful of you. But, no, I don't think that's it."

I bristle at Julie's compliment to Carlos. I, too, am thoughtful for helping my sister out. *Chill out, Jay. She's just being nice.* I try to get my emotions under control.

"Jayson and I usually grab food at Mr. Twisty after games. Would you like to join us?" Carlos says.

Julie's gaze flicks over to me. "Are you sure? I don't want to intrude on guy time or anything."

Why didn't I think to invite Julie? I mentally apologize to Carlos for all the unkind thoughts I just had about him. "You should definitely join us," I say. "But we have to shower first, so it'll be fifteen or twenty minutes before we can go."

"If you don't mind, then sure. I'll meet you guys over there."

💼

I'm standing near the entrance to Mr. Twisty, perusing the cars in the parking lot. I don't know what Julie drives, but it doesn't look like she's here. Did she change her mind? I pull out my phone to check for missed texts, but find nothing. I'm just about to send one of my own when a car zooms into the lot, going a little too fast. It brakes suddenly, swerving into a spot. Julie emerges, looking frantic. She dashes toward the entrance before slowing when she sees me. Concern swells in my gut.

"Is everything okay?"

She stops in front of me and releases a long breath. "Everything's fine. Sorry I'm late. I thought I'd have time to run home and let my dog out, but, of course, she took her sweet time."

I put a hand on her arm and give what I hope is a reassuring squeeze. "It's okay. I wasn't worried." *Liar,* my mind counters.

"Well, I'm here now. Let's go in."

Despite having already had one earlier today with Julie, I order my usual burger with onions, fries, and a lemonade. Julie gets a grilled chicken sandwich and a small chocolate shake. When our food is ready, we join Carlos in the booth. I hesitate, trying to decide whether I should sit next to Carlos or make Julie sit next to me. Carlos seems to notice my dilemma and spreads himself out across the bench seat. I'm not sure whether to give him the side-eye or thank him. Instead, I slide into the empty booth, as close to the inside as possible, and Julie sits down next to me.

"So," Carlos says, looking at Julie and munching on a french fry. "Have you figured it out yet?"

"Figured what out?"

"How you think you know me?"

Julie shakes her head. "I don't. Do I look familiar to you?"

"Nope, sorry."

She shrugs. "What do you do?"

"I'm an elementary art teacher by day and artist by night."

"What kind of art do you make?" Julie's interest is palpable, and my gut twists. It makes sense one creative person would be interested in another.

"I paint, mostly."

"Do you have a studio?"

Carlos takes a sip of his drink. "I rent a space over in the River Arts District."

"What's the name of your shop?"

"Double Rainbow Designs."

"Do you have any photos of your art?"

Carlos smiles. "Yeah, I do."

He pulls out his phone and taps on the screen a few times before handing it to Julie. "It's a small album. Swipe right."

I watch Julie while she scrolls through the photos, complimenting Carlos on his work. His stuff really is amazing, but I'm suddenly feeling like a third wheel on a date. They have an easy rapport which must come from their mutual creativity. I want my friend to like someone I'm interested in, but I don't want him to like them *too* much.

Julie pauses at a photo. "I've seen this before."

Carlos furrows his brow. "I doubt it."

"I'm pretty sure I have. It's very familiar." Julie squints her eyes and looks into the distance. She taps her finger to her lips for a moment. "Ah-ha! The Asheville Food Pantry!"

Carlos sits up straight and leans forward onto his elbows. "Do you volunteer there?"

"I do. I mean, I have, but not recently. Usually, I go on Tuesdays because the store's closed, but I've been working seven days a week to keep up with demand."

"That must be where you've seen me. I volunteer there on various days. Perhaps we've crossed paths on a Tuesday."

"I bet that's it." Julie beams at Carlos, and my lips press together. This is not how I expected dinner to go.

Carlos lowers his voice. "So tell me. What do you think of Bryce and his puns?"

The intimacy of their insider knowledge makes me glower across the table at him, but he doesn't seem to notice.

Julie grins. "Now that's something to taco 'bout!"

He groans in response. "Oh no! Are you a pun person, too?"

"Not really, but sometimes they're so terrible they're good. I'm always curious to see if he's come up with something new."

"I must admit, I'm impressed at his volume of puns. He must have hundreds."

"Probably." Julie motions between me and Carlos. "How do you and Jayson know each other?"

"We played basketball together in high school."

"You guys went to the same high school?"

This conversation about me that doesn't include me only enhances the feeling that I'm intruding on someone else's date. I need to reinsert myself into this conversation pronto.

"We didn't," I cut in. "We were both picked for a summer all-star team after our sophomore years and played together for three summers until college."

Julie turns toward me, and I feel a puff of pride at snagging her attention. It doesn't last long because, after a quick smile, her face swings right back to Carlos. "Where did you go to college, Carlos?"

"I went to SCAD."

"What's that?"

"The Savannah College of Art & Design. Where did you go?"

"I went to AB Tech."

I sink down in my seat, having given up on participating in this getting-to-know-you back and forth. The conversation turns to favorite things to do in Asheville. I should jump in and contribute to the conversation, but my brain's too busy trying to determine if this is just a friendly interest between Julie and Carlos or something more. She's paying him an awful lot of attention.

When we finish eating, Julie asks me to walk her to her car. My stomach sinks as I wonder if she's going to ask me if Carlos is single out of his earshot. We pause near the trunk of her car. She turns and smiles up at me. "Thanks for inviting me to the game and dinner. This was a lot of fun."

I return her smile, but it doesn't reach my eyes.

"When's your next game? Maybe if work isn't too busy, I can come?"

"Next Tuesday."

She leans forward and gives me a quick hug before pulling back to place a hand on my forearm, her eyes trained on my face. "Is everything okay?"

"Yeah, I'm fine. Just a little tired." And a little jealous of my friend.

"Okay, well, get some rest."

I step back to give her room to maneuver to the driver's side door. She waves through the window before backing out and driving away. My gaze trails after her until her taillights are no longer visible. I'm conflicted. I thought I was making steady progress with Julie, but she opened up like a flower greeting the morning sun while talking to Carlos. Why isn't she that way with me?

She came to the game tonight because I invited her, which has to mean something. And she initiated our get together earlier today. Maybe she was being friendly toward Carlos for my benefit. Don't people usually try to get to know their significant other's friends? Not that we're significant to each other yet, but I feel like we've got loads of potential. My thoughts are a jumble of worry, envy, and frustration swirling around in my mind on the drive home.

24

JULY

Julie

I SET DOWN my tray of food and take the seat across from Rachel.

"Thanks for inviting me to lunch. This was a great idea."

Rachel smiles, her eyes creasing at the corners. "I thought it'd be fun to have some sister-in-law time. It seems like I only see you when Tom's around or we're at book club."

"How's married life treating you?"

Rachel's face turns dreamy. "It's fantastic! I love having Tom around all the time, though I think he's getting a little restless. I don't think he's used to being in one place for so long yet."

"Well, November will be here before you know it."

"True, but at least I'll be able to join him for part of it."

"You're not going for the whole time?"

She shakes her head. "I don't think work would look too fondly upon me being gone for several months."

"But you're an author now. Can't you quit the bookstore?"

She chuckles. "I've sold one book, and, until it's published and the sales numbers come in, I won't know if they'll offer me a contract for another. So, no, I still have to be a regular working stiff until I reach Stephen King status or something."

"What about Tom's money?" I immediately color. "Sorry, that's rude."

Rachel waves away my faux pas. "I like working. Maybe if we have kids I'll quit the store, but until then I want to keep working in one of my favorite places *and* hang with the Book Babes each month. Speaking of which, did I tell you my sister's moving to Asheville?"

"No, but that sounds like great news." My brow furrows in confusion. "How did your job remind you of your sister?"

Rachel grins. "I'm going to get her to join Book Babes, of course!"

"Does she like to read as much as you?"

"No, but I'm planning to bribe her with your chocolates." Her devilish smile makes me laugh. "Speaking of work, how are things going with your new business manager?"

"She's been a tremendous help. She's smart, detail-oriented, and really whipping our business into shape. I feel like I have some breathing room again."

"That's good to hear. Now, for the juicy gossip. Does your breathing room allow you to go on dates?"

I look away, but can't stop the blush creeping up my neck.

Rachel's face shines with delight. "Oooh, spill it!"

"There's really nothing going on."

"Then why are you blushing?"

I sigh, cursing my traitorous skin, though part of me is glad for the opportunity to talk about Jayson. "There's someone I'm sort of interested in, but I want to take it slow. It's been a long time since I put myself out there."

She nods. "There's nothing wrong with being cautious. I'm glad you're trying again."

I smile, but say nothing. Trying again still feels a little scary, but also worthwhile, when Jayson's nearby.

"New subject," Rachel says, nibbling on a french fry. "Tom told me you're officially doing wedding cakes now. How's that going?"

I can't help but laugh.

"What'd I say?"

"The sister of the guy I like is the event coordinator for the Arboretum."

Rachel smiles widely and claps her hands. "That's fantastic! Built in opportunities to interact and for him to see how awesome you are."

"Or I'll have more opportunities to embarrass myself in front of him."

"Embarrassing myself in front of a guy worked for me!"

I grin, my mind recalling the stories Tom told me about his early encounters with Rachel. "True. I guess I'd just prefer a less mortifying method."

"Don't knock it until you try it," Rachel says, giving me a playful wink.

25

Jayson

I DROP ONTO the bench next to Carlos and take a swig from my water bottle. My eyes wander over to the bleachers for the twentieth time tonight, wondering what kept Julie from coming. When we'd texted yesterday, she said she'd try to come.

"Great game, Jay."

"Thanks, 'Los. You didn't see Julie come in during the game, did you?"

He smacks the side of his head. "Oh, I forgot! Julie said she couldn't make it tonight and asked me to wish you and the team good luck. Which obviously worked, since we flattened the Sky City Ballers."

Julie and Carlos are communicating with one another? I don't like that at all. "When did you talk to Julie?"

"She was at the AFP today."

"I thought you went to the food pantry on Thursdays?"

He shrugs. "I had some free time today. Julie's really cool, man. We talked about owning our own businesses and all the stress that comes with it."

The back of my neck heats, unease prickling my scalp. "What

kind of stress?"

"Oh, you know, feeling like everything is up to you. That if the business fails, then it means you're a failure. Concern that any current success is just a fluke and it'll all come crashing down. You know, light-hearted things." Carlos grimaces comically, but then his expression sobers. "She also told me about how she feels like an impostor, and I definitely know what she means. I've struggled with that a lot myself. Especially with there being so many artists in the area. It's super intimidating."

I can't believe Julie shared so much with Carlos. Why hasn't she confided in me like that? I guess, technically, we've only had three meals together, one of which included my best friend, so we haven't spent enough time together to have conversations about deep subjects. Did he go to the food pantry today just because it's Tuesday and he knew she might be there? The memory of the meal at Mr. Twisty the previous week plays in my mind. Their banter and easy connection floods my brain and envy blooms in my chest. Although I don't like the fact that Carlos knows so much, I'm willing to learn more about Julie any way I can. Like, why she might feel like an impostor when her business is exploding with new opportunities.

"Why does she feel like an impostor?"

Carlos bends over, stuffing his shoes and water bottle into his bag. "Oh, you know, because her uncle willed her the business and she thinks its current success is all because of what he built, not her own savvy. She's just waiting for the day when everyone finds out she's a fraud and the store goes under."

I'm incredulous. "What? The business looks like it's thriving. Especially with her branching out into wedding services. She's done so much, and her hard work and ingenuity are paying off."

Carlos shakes his head. "Yeah, that's what I told her too, but I don't think she believed me."

As much as I hate how cozy my friend is getting with the woman I'm trying to pursue, I can't help but be glad she has someone to talk to about everything. "Well, I'm glad you and Julie both have someone who understands the creative life."

"It's kind of reassuring to be reminded I'm not the only one who deals with these thoughts. She told me about the Asheville Small Business group and said it's really helped her make connections and feel less alone. She offered to take me to the next one. I think I might go."

Another streak of jealousy courses through me, but it's quickly followed by guilt at being upset in the face of my friend's excitement. I should be happy the two of them have hit it off. I just need to find things Julie and I have in common.

"Cool man," is all I say.

"Yeah. It is. Are we still going to Mr. Twisty?"

"Of course. I need to send a quick text first."

Jayson: Are you free for dinner on Friday?
Julie: Yes!
Jayson: Great! I'll pick you up after work.

Julie's apparent enthusiasm gives me hope things are still going well between us. Feeling pacified, I head to the showers.

26

Julie

I LOCK THE front door of the store, and then walk to the passenger side of Jayson's SUV parked at the curb. His smile is as warm as the sunshine slanting in the windows of the vehicle. My lips curve up in response. I'm tempted to lean over and kiss him on the cheek, but instead grab the seatbelt and fasten it across my lap. I've never been one to make the first move in relationships. It's a huge act of vulnerability and I don't know if I'm ready to risk rejection again.

"Thanks for the dinner invitation," I say. "I've been working so much this week I've forgotten to eat a few times."

He nods, his smile dimming. "I'm sure it's stressful running a business. I can't imagine all the plates you have to keep spinning."

I'm touched by his concern. "You have no idea. I felt like a headless chicken for a long time. Nikki has finally allowed me some breathing room. Thanks for encouraging me to hire more help."

He breaks my gaze and puts the car in gear, pulling out onto the road. "It was really all you. You're a smart, savvy businesswoman."

I'm thankful he's distracted and doesn't seem to notice the way my skin heats at his compliment. We're both quiet the rest of the way to the restaurant. I don't know what's on his mind, but I'm thinking about the fact that this is our fourth time eating food together. Even though Carlos was with us last time, it could possibly be considered a date. When was the last time I went on four dates with a man? I've had dates here and there since my divorce, but never felt a connection strong enough to put myself out there and truly try to get to know another man. Is Jayson special? The thought gets my heart beating faster, both from excitement and fear. I sneak glances at Jayson while he drives, but his face gives nothing away.

After we've ordered and sat down with our food, I smile across the table at Jayson. He furrows his brow. "What?"

I wave my hand around the room. "Did you know Blue Goose is my favorite restaurant?"

"No."

"I guess you're just good at picking places to eat, then."

"Actually, I've never been here, but my aunt recommended it and she's never steered me wrong. Why is this your favorite restaurant?"

A happy sigh escapes me. "I enjoy the variety of options. They're always working on new tacos, so there's often something different to try."

"Which one is your favorite?"

"The lamb gyro taco hands down, but the spicy shrimp taco is a close second."

Jayson waves a hand over his basket of food. "And how do you rate my choices of the duck and beef bulgogi?"

"The bulgogi is good. I haven't tried the duck taco. I'm not sure I'd like how it tastes."

"Try a bite of mine and find out, then." He lifts his basket out toward me. "Go ahead."

"Don't you want the first bite?"

"Nah, it's fine."

I pick up the duck taco and take a bite, setting the rest back in the basket. He places it back on the table in front of him without removing his eyes from my face. I chew slowly, closing my eyes to focus on the flavors melding together in my mouth and also to take a break from Jayson's penetrating eyes. It almost feels like he can see into my thoughts, which would be a disaster. I'm not ready for him to know how much I like him already. I swallow, smile, and open my eyes.

"That's actually pretty good. The sauce really enhances the flavor profile of the taco."

Jayson rolls his eyes. "Flavor profile, wow. Didn't know I was eating with a food critic."

My smile falters. Is he just teasing or actually bothered? "Hey, my family loves good food. You should hear Tom's reviews of the places he's eaten at around the world."

We lapse into silence for a few minutes.

"So," Jayson says when his basket's empty, "it must be hard sometimes owning your own business."

I don't know where that question came from, but I'm pleased by his interest. People don't ask me often about what it's like running a business. "It can be. There's a lot of pressure because I'm responsible for everything. If something goes wrong, then I have to figure out how to fix it. There's no one to shift blame to."

He's quiet for a moment, seeming to digest the heaviness of my words. "What's been the most surprising thing about owning a business?"

"It surprised me how lonely it felt."

"Does it not feel that way now?"

I shake my head. "I recently joined an entrepreneur group that meets monthly and realized how common my experience is among small business owners. The connections help me feel like I have resources if I need advice."

"That's good to hear. Anything else you've learned that's different from when you were just an employee?"

What's up with all these questions about my business? It's flattering, but I can't help wondering if there's an ulterior motive. I choose to give him the benefit of the doubt. "How personally I take everything related to the business. When I see a negative review online, I feel attacked. Even if it's something as minimal as the store was out of a particular truffle the day someone came in, it can make me feel like a failure."

I duck my head in embarrassment. It's hard to admit not everyone has a stellar experience with my store. It's hard to predict what every customer will want and seasonal truffles are obviously not available year-round, but it doesn't keep people from posting one-star reviews about not being able to get a pumpkin-flavored truffle in March.

"And also, just how time consuming it is. A business can become your whole life if you let it, as you've probably noticed." I feel really vulnerable sharing that. As a distraction from the discomfort, I dip a tortilla chip in queso and shove it in my mouth.

Jayson nods. "I definitely understand work monopolizing your time, but you seem to do well at delegating and letting others fill their roles."

I shrug off his compliment. "It's not optional if I really want to have any type of work/life balance."

"Since we're having dinner together, I'd say you're having some success."

"I suppose so." I still don't get Jayson's motives for this conversation. Might as well be up front. "What's with all the questions? Are you thinking about starting your own firm?"

Jayson's head shake is resolute. "No. Definitely not."

"Why not?"

"First, I really love working with my aunt. She's a great boss and I learn a lot from her, which is a big plus, being only a few years into practicing. Second, I don't know that I'd want all the pressure and responsibility that you've described. I don't think I have the courage to do what you've done. I admire you."

I wave away his words, refusing to let any of his kind words settle into my heart. "It's not like I started from scratch. Uncle Bill left me with a very healthy business."

"True, but you've been keeping it going for what, four years now? That says something about your own business acumen."

"I'm sure continuing with his business model has been the key." I pick up my lamb taco and take a large bite, hoping Jayson will drop the subject. He doesn't.

"But you haven't really done that. I mean, you're expanding into additional revenue streams like with the wedding cakes, right?"

I want to be upset at his persistence, but truthfully, I feel pride over some of my recent accomplishments. Not that I'd ever say that out loud. "I also convinced Samuel over at Hill of Beans to sell pre-boxed chocolates in his store. I'm thinking about opening an online store and shipping within the U.S. I haven't checked out the costs of that yet, but it'd be another way to gain customers."

Jayson's eyes fill with what looks like admiration mixed with something fiery that makes my stomach flip. "See, you're so creative. You don't give yourself nearly enough credit."

I allow this compliment to sink in and smile my appreciation. Jayson's hand rests on the table and I reach over and squeeze it in thanks. His eyes capture mine. He pulls his hand back a bit, then splays his fingers, interlacing them with mine. His thumb rubs against mine and a shiver travels up my spine at the intimate gesture.

"I heard you saw Carlos at the food pantry the other day," Jayson says.

My head snaps back at the sudden topic change. Our conversation is all over the place tonight. "I'm sure I'll see him in there all the time now that I know who he is."

"He said you two had a discussion about being business

owners."

Carlos talked to him about our conversation? The heated look in Jayson's eyes makes me wonder if he's a little jealous. The thought gives me a zip of pleasure. "We did. I invited him to come to one of my group meetings with me. There are quite a few artists who attend, so I'm sure he could make some useful connections."

Jayson nods. "That's thoughtful of you."

"You two have been friends since high school, right?"

"Yeah. We drifted apart during college, but our friendship picked right back up where we left off after I moved here. He invites me to family events and is always coming up with fun things to do. He knows about all these crazy events that happen in the city, like the Pi(e) Day Run."

"Do people run with pies?" That sounds like a disaster waiting to happen.

Jayson shakes his head, his mouth quirking up into an amused smile. I feel a tiny thrill at this smile just for me. "No. It's a fundraiser where people run 3.14 miles on March 14th and can also take part in a pie baking contest."

"Do you get a piece of pie after you run? Because, if so, I might be interested."

Jayson laughs, and I grin in response. "I don't know. He hasn't been able to talk me into that one yet."

Now I'm intrigued. "What has he talked you into?"

His posture relaxes, and his expression opens. Seeing him like this, and knowing I've had a hand in it, feels like a drug. I want more of this carefree Jayson. "Let's see. We've been axe throwing and broken out of several escape rooms. We've spent the day at Asheville Treetops Adventure Park doing the ropes courses, zip lining, and mountain biking. He's taken me rock climbing, paintballing, hiking, and fishing. If it's something exciting or fun, Carlos has probably already done it and convinced at least one other person to do it with him."

"He sounds like an adrenaline junkie."

Jayson considers my question for a few seconds before nodding. "I suppose he is, but he's awesome. He's always willing to help. He'd do just about anything for anyone. And I'd do just about anything for him."

"Wow. I'm glad you have such a great friend. It's how I feel about Emily."

My phone buzzes and I pull it out, startled to see how late it is. "Oh man, I didn't realize the time. I need to get home and walk Sadie. She's probably dying to go out."

"I can drive you if you'd like."

"That'd be great."

We clear our table before heading out to Jayson's car. When he pulls up to my apartment building a few minutes later, I unbuckle my seatbelt, eager to check on my dog. "Thanks for being my dinner date tonight. It's nice to not eat alone all the time."

"Yeah, I know what you mean."

"Sadie also thanks you for getting me home quickly. If you wait, I can bring her out personally to thank you."

"Nah, that's okay." Jayson's smile vanishes.

"What's wrong?"

The look he gives me kicks up something unpleasant in my gut. "I'm, uh, not a big fan of dogs because I was attacked by one when I was a kid."

My heart twists for him and I reach out for his hand. "Oh, Jayson, I'm so sorry. I'm sure that was terrifying."

"It was."

"Do you dislike all dogs?"

"Small ones don't bother me, but ones taller than my knee make me nervous."

The last bit of joy from my dinner with Jayson evaporates. Our relationship may be doomed before we even start. Sadie and I are a package deal. Still, the more time I spend with Jayson, the fonder I'm becoming of him. I don't want to just give up. "Sadie's very calm and doesn't jump on people, but she's not what you'd call a small dog."

The troubled look on Jayson's face gives me my answer. I pat his arm. "It's okay."

Reaching for the handle, I pop the car door open and get out. "Bye, Jayson. Thanks for dinner."

He nods, his lips pressed together, and I see something like regret in his eyes.

When I open my apartment door, Sadie's standing there with the leash in her mouth.

"I know, girl. Let's get you walked."

I clip the leash onto Sadie's collar, and we head back outside. Jayson's car is gone. We turn toward the park and I replay the evening in my head, troubled by the news that Jayson doesn't like dogs. Is there a way for us to be together and him not have to interact with Sadie? Maybe, but it'll require some effort. Am I willing to try? My heart warms remembering the compliments he paid me tonight, and the memory of our fingers twined together gives it a jolt of pleasure. Yes, I definitely want to try.

27

Jayson

I RUSH INTO the gym, my bag falling down my arm. I grab the strap just before the bag hits the floor and hoist it back up onto my shoulder. My teammates are warming up on the court. I motion to Luis that I'm going to the locker room. Changing in record time, I make it back to the court right as the buzzer sounds. Tossing my bag underneath the bench, I roll through some quick dynamic stretching.

"Cutting it close, aren't you?" Carlos says.

"Work's been crazy. At least I made it."

"Travis, you start for Jayson, so he can warm up some more."

"I'm fine, man. I can start."

"Travis is starting. Get your legs warm."

"Fine." I roll my eyes, but he's right. It would suck to injure myself during playoffs just because I'm stubborn.

The buzzer sounds again, and the starters take the floor. The game is back-and-forth scoring for the first three quarters, but we get a five-point lead late in the fourth and hold it until time runs out. After slapping hands with The Ball Boyz, Carlos gathers us together back at the bench.

"Great game guys. Way to step it up in the fourth. That was our best-played game this season. It looks like we're peaking at the right time. Next week, we play in the championship against either the Alley-Oops or the Monster Squad. They play tomorrow night if anyone wants to come scout our opponent with me. Otherwise, I'll see you at practice."

We all mumble various responses and collect our things. Carlos claps me on the shoulder. "Great playing tonight, Jay. You seemed like a man on a mission. I hope you saved some for next week!"

"Thanks."

I threw everything I had into the game, hoping working out my body would help my mind figure out what to do about Julie and her dog. The more time I spend with her, the deeper my attraction grows. Yet I just can't seem to figure out how my fear of dogs fits in.

"Hey, man. What's up?"

I look up, realizing Carlos and I are the only ones still at the bench. I shrug, not sure how to talk about my dilemma.

"Let's clean up and head to Mr. Twisty. You obviously have something on your mind."

I'm not sure I want to talk about this, but food definitely sounds good. I shower and meet him at the restaurant. When we're seated with our food, Carlos fixes his gaze on me.

"You're a little off tonight. Spill it." He takes a big bite of his burger and chews, his eyes never leaving my face.

Might as well get it over with. "I have a problem with Julie."

"What'd she do?"

I blink, realizing how my words sounded. "Oh, nothing. *She's* great."

He gives me a lopsided grin. "She is, huh?"

I ignore his teasing. "The problem is her dog."

He straightens up, his mouth twisting in concern. "Is it big and mean?"

"I don't know. I've never seen it."

Carlos points a fry in my direction. "So she has a dog, but you don't know exactly what it looks like or what type of temperament it has."

I nod.

"Do you like this woman enough to find out?"

"That's the question of the hour. I *do* like her, but we're still sort of feeling each other out."

He nods. "Well, maybe don't worry about it right now. Give things more time and, if you get to a point where you think you two might have a future, you can revisit the situation then."

"I suppose that's reasonable."

Little flickers of hope that maybe this dog thing isn't a make-or-break issue spark in my chest. My mind roams to memories of Julie. I picture her open and warm expression at the taco shop. A mental image of her laughing, head thrown back and mouth wide with a smile fills my mind.

Carlos clears his throat to get my attention, then gives me a knowing grin. "You're thinking about her right now, aren't you?"

I hang my head. "I'm that obvious, huh?"

"If it makes you feel better, you have the same expression I saw on Julie's face when she was at our game last week."

Excitement thumps behind my sternum. "Really?"

Carlos chuckles. "Wow, man. I've never seen you excited about a woman before. It's pretty entertaining."

I scowl, but it doesn't have any heat. "I could say the same thing about you."

He sobers, and the seriousness of his expression surprises me. Is he a little lonely too? "You're right, but it's because I'm being selective. I need someone who loves adventure. You know me, always on the lookout for the next adrenaline rush."

I nod in agreement. "True. I'm sure you'll find someone when the time is right."

"You're probably right. Maybe by then you'll be happily married to Julie."

I hold up a hand. "Whoa, now. Let's not get ahead of ourselves. I haven't even kissed her yet."

The smirk is back on his face. "Yeah, but you want to. Julie and Jayson, sitting in a tree, K-I-S-S—"

I throw a fry at his face and land it in his open mouth, stopping his teasing for the moment. "Jeez, are you twelve years old?"

My mind turns to thoughts of Julie's mouth and how much I wouldn't mind learning if her lips are as soft as they look.

Carlos snorts, and I look up to see his shoulders shaking, trying to keep a laugh in. I guess my thoughts are written across my face. Well, whatever. He's just jealous and I don't blame him one bit. Who wouldn't want to date a beautiful woman like Julie?

28

Julie

A TAP ON the glass display case next to my arm startles me out of a daydream. I swivel to my right. Nikki's looking at me strangely.

"Sorry, I was kind of zoning out."

Nikki chuckles and shakes her head. "Obviously. I've been trying to get your attention."

"What do you need?"

"Nothing. I just wondered if you're okay. You've seemed off since yesterday. Want to tell me what's on your mind?"

Nikki's been working here for over a month, but despite a couple of lunches, I still feel weird having a heart-to-heart conversation with her. Emily is my go-to person for these kinds of conversations, but she's not here this week. Maybe I need to consider someone else in the meantime.

Nikki's eyes drop from my face to my hands, and I realize I'm fidgeting with the metal trays used to collect truffles for customers. I quickly drop my hands to my sides. Maybe talking about it will dispel some of this restless energy. "Do you remember Jayson?"

"Of course. He's the guy who's sweet on you."

My cheeks heat, the blush spreading down my neck to my

chest. My heart kicks up its pace. Why am I embarrassed that someone else can tell we like each other? If I'm going to date him, it's going to get even more obvious. Which reminds me of Nikki's original question.

"Jayson has a fear of dogs."

"And you have Sadie," she says, completing my thought. A photo of Sadie is my screen saver on the work computer, and Nikki's heard all about her.

"Yeah. I'm not sure how things are going to work long-term."

Her gaze widens. "Are you already thinking Jayson could be the one?"

The statement startles me and my hands shoot out like shields to defend against the idea. "Whoa. No. I'm just getting to know him, but if things continue to go well, we're going to have to deal with this issue eventually."

She nods. "That's true. But you both seem like intelligent people. I'm sure you can figure it out."

"Well, Jayson is, at least. You know, Harvard-educated and all. You and he are the brainiacs."

Nikki tsks. "You're selling yourself short. You run your own business, and I know for a fact you're excelling at it. And you're exploring new avenues to increase your success, which takes brains and guts. Who wouldn't be interested in a creative entrepreneur who makes delicious desserts?"

I smile self-consciously. "When you put it like that, I suppose I've got a decent amount of smarts of my own."

She shakes her head, but she's smiling. "That's the spirit."

"Thanks for letting me share my concern with you, even though it's not really part of your job."

"Hey, the store needs you to focus on being creative. If that requires some unlicensed talk therapy with your business manager on occasion, then so be it."

I give her an appreciative look. "I'm so glad you're here.

You've already done so much for me and this store. You're a treasure."

***

After work, I walk into the back room of Page Turner Books, my copy of *Beach Read* resting on top of a container of chocolates. Rachel's steeping a tea bag in hot water, which seems strange to me because I don't think I've seen her drink anything other than coffee. She's also wearing all black. Was she at a funeral earlier? Her book club attire is usually a book-themed t-shirt. I set the truffles down on the table next to her.

"Hey. Tea tonight, huh?"

A perplexed look crosses her face. "Yes?"

"Is everything okay?"

"Yeah, it's fine."

Rachel isn't normally one to shy away from conversation. Maybe she has something on her mind. "Will you hand me that plate so I can set up the chocolates?"

She wordlessly passes it to me and I arrange the chocolates until I'm satisfied with their presentation. "I'm trying out a new one called the Spicy Sesame. It's dark chocolate with a hint of wasabi topped with sesame seeds. The new sushi place inspired me."

Rachel smiles, her face lighting up. "Ooh, I'm definitely trying that one."

"It's got more heat than the Ancient Treasures truffle."

She rubs her hands together, eying the truffle with sesame seeds dotted on top. "I like spicy things. Excuse me, I need to hit the ladies' room."

My brows scrunch together in confusion. Rachel hates spice. And I've never heard her say she needed to *hit* anything before. I suppose people change, but this all seems out of character. When she comes back, I'll ask if something's bothering her. I put the empty chocolate container under the table and take my book over to the circle of chairs, setting it on an empty one.

"Hey Julie!"

I turn toward the doorway. Rachel's holding a stack of books and wearing a blue shirt that reads *It's a good day to read.* I could have sworn Rachel was just in a black shirt. I hurry to her, taking some books from her to lighten her load. "Did you just change your shirt?"

Rachel glances down, then shakes her head. "No. Why?"

"I could have sworn—"

The woman in black steps up next to Rachel and grins. I release an amused breath and shake my head. "Oh man, Abbie. You got me."

Abbie's smile grows wider. "Sorry about that. It never gets old tricking people with our identical faces."

"I thought something about you was off when I greeted you earlier. Guess I should have trusted my gut."

Abbie points to her left eyebrow. "Was it the scar?"

"I didn't even notice that. No, you were less conversational and making tea." Now that she's pointed it out, I'm curious. "Where'd the scar come from?"

"I got hit with a softball in high school. Nothing exciting."

I nod, slightly disappointed. I was hoping for something crazy, like an archery accident or a knife stab. Not that I *want* other people to get hurt. When I was a kid, I used to make up crazy stories whenever I needed a bandage. The scrape on my knee? Saving a baby from tumbling down a set of stairs. A scratch on my arm? A tussle with a raccoon. I doubt anyone ever believed my tales, but it entertained me.

"I heard you were moving here. Does that mean it's already happened?"

Abbie nods. "I've been here about a week."

"And I see Rachel's already convinced you to join the Book

Babes."

Her nose wrinkles like she smelled something bad. "You call yourselves the Book Babes? Ugh. That's gotta change if I'm going to be part of it."

Rachel laughs. "Good luck convincing Lori and the others."

Abbie wiggles her eyebrows. "I'm quite persuasive, as you know. I'll make it happen."

"I'm sure you will." Rachel looks around the room. "Julie, since the others aren't here yet, what's going on with Jayson?"

"Oooh, who's Jayson?" Abbie says, a gleam in her eye.

"He's a guy Julie likes."

Twin faces, both with the same curious expression, swivel to me. Guess I'm in the hot seat. "He seems nice, but I'm a little apprehensive about dating again. His friend, Carlos, has said good things about him, so maybe I should go for it."

"I knew a Carlos in high school," Abbie says. "Couldn't stand him. He's ruined that name for me forever."

I perk up. This sounds like a juicy story. Even if it's not the same guy, I'm intrigued. "What happened?"

"I don't really want to get into it. All I'll say is that you don't mess with my family." Abbie slings an arm around Rachel's shoulder. "I'm still mad about it, actually. I don't know what I'd do if I saw Carlos Vega again."

Rachel shakes her head. "I think you should let it go. It's in the past and besides, I'm married to an awesome man now, so it doesn't really matter."

Abbie huffs in response.

I'm still stuck on Abbie's last sentence. "Did you say Vega?"

"Yeah."

My eyes widen. "I think that's Jayson's best friend."

"*What?!*" Abbie practically yells the word and I take a step back in surprise. "You should stay away from both of them. Anyone who's Carlos's friend is probably just like him."

"Carlos seems nice enough to me. What do you have against

him?"

"He broke my sister's heart."

I turn to Rachel. "You dated Carlos?"

"No," she says, rolling her eyes like she and Abbie have had this conversation too many times.

I swing my gaze back and forth between the two sisters who are having their own silent conversation. "I don't get it."

Rachel finally shrugs, giving Abbie a look I can't decipher. "It's not really a big deal."

"It *is*," Abbie insists. She turns to me. "Rachel really liked our high school quarterback, and he'd asked her to senior prom. About two weeks before the event, the guy changed his mind and took the head cheerleader instead. Carlos was the one who convinced the guy to dump my sister."

"Why did he do it?" I say, engrossed in the story. My heart pangs with sympathy for Rachel. She's so nice. I can't imagine her being ditched like that.

"Apparently, *Carlos* wanted to take Rachel himself. He asked her to be his prom date, but I told her what I'd heard and she refused him."

I touch Rachel's shoulder. "Oh Rachel, I'm sorry."

Rachel presses her lips together and shakes her head. "Eh, it's not like I was going to marry him or anything. It's just dumb teenage drama. I still went to prom with some friends who also didn't have dates and we had a good time."

"Anyway," Abbie says darkly, "I wouldn't trust anyone who hangs out with Carlos Vega."

"People can change," Rachel says, giving her sister a pointed look.

"I suppose that's true." She turns to me, her face set in a serious frown. "But don't say I didn't warn you. I wouldn't want you to get hurt if you can help it."

Abbie's words slam against my insecurity. I definitely don't want to be hurt again by someone I choose to let into my heart. Maybe I should seriously consider things with Jayson. One big heartbreak in life seems like more than enough.

Voices carry into the room, and soon it's filled with the remaining group members.

"Ladies," Rachel says. "Please welcome my sister, Abbie, to our group. She just moved here from Charleston and is the new athletic trainer for UNC Asheville's men's basketball team."

"Congratulations!" I say, and the other women join in with their felicitations.

"You'll have more time to talk at the end of our meeting," Rachel says. "Grab a drink and some truffles and let's discuss *Beach Read*!"

29

Jayson

THE WHIR OF the garage door opening catches my attention. About thirty seconds later, it starts back up again, making a loud clank when the door meets the floor. Keys rattle as they're dropped into the bowl. The refrigerator door whooshes open, and there's a low clinking of glass bottles on the door shelf as it thumps closed again. The couch dips slightly near my right thigh. "Are you really that interested in some nonstick pans that can withstand nine hundred degree temperatures?"

"What?" I say, blinking out of a trance.

Britt motions toward the TV. "You're watching an infomercial."

I raise my arm, the remote clasped in my hand, and press the "off" button. "Oh. Not really. I turned the TV on when I got home, but I've just been spacing out."

She shifts on the couch to face me. "What's on your mind?"

"I like Julie."

She rolls her eyes. "Duh, Jay. Are you just now realizing this?"

"No, but I recently found out she owns a dog."

My sister slouches deeper into the cushions. "Ah. I could see that being a problem. Does she know the details?"

I shake my head. "I'm wondering if this is a sign we should just go our separate ways."

"No way! I've never seen you this interested in someone. You can't just give up at the first hint of trouble."

Nice to know my attraction to Julie is loud and clear to everyone I know. I thought I was doing a better job of keeping things buttoned up. Though Britt's had a front-row seat to our interactions at the Arboretum so it's likely my eyes following Julie like a magnet around the room was impossible to miss. Still, a dog is more than a tiny possibility of trouble. To me, it's boulder-sized.

"I know you struggle with intimacy, so I'm sure searching for an excuse to end something with real potential is an appealing option."

My head whips to the side, surprised by her words. My little sister thinks I struggle with intimacy? "What?"

She sighs like it should be obvious. "You haven't had a serious girlfriend ever, as far as I know. Why not?"

I can't deny the truth of her statement, though I haven't really thought about why that might be. "Just haven't found the right person, I guess."

"Or maybe you aren't willing to open yourself up and be vulnerable."

I bristle at her words. "No one likes to get hurt."

"Well, no, but you take it to an extreme level. It's like you've encased your emotions in armor, not allowing anyone to really know you."

I open my mouth to respond but close it again, seriously considering Britt's words. I dated one woman throughout college, but it wasn't serious. Neither of us was emotionally invested. We went together to each other's events, but didn't have a single one-on-one date or open up emotionally to one another. When was the last time I truly felt vulnerable with a woman?

The answer slams into me and I suck in a breath, suddenly

winded. I've kept the truth locked inside for a long time. Maybe it's time to share it with someone. "You know why I don't like dogs."

Britt nods. "A dog knocked you down and broke your arm. I wouldn't be a fan of dogs either."

"Right, but that's also when I shut down emotionally."

Britt's eyes widen, as if she can sense the gravity of my words. "Why's that?"

I swallow, but my throat feels like the Sahara desert. I get up from the couch and walk to the kitchen, filling a glass with water and downing it in one gulp. Returning to the living room, I'm feeling too geared up to sit still, so I pace in front of the coffee table, considering how to say something I haven't told anyone.

"That day, I was playing with Nessa, a girl from my class. I had a crush on her and had just gotten up the courage to ask her to be my girlfriend."

My sister's head tilts, and she gives me a funny look. "Weren't you in, like, fourth grade? How can you have a girlfriend when your bedtime is seven o'clock and you have no money?"

My feet still. I snort-laugh, thankful for a sister who gives me grief just to break the tension. "Yeah, it seems pretty silly now, but back then, all the cool kids were pairing up. I was just a scrawny, nerdy kid. Nessa was the popular girl. If I got her approval, I was in."

Britt nods, motioning for me to continue.

"Anyway, before she can answer, there's a loud bark and we turn simultaneously. This huge German Shepherd comes charging at us. We ran as fast as we could away from the dog, but, as you might surmise, two little kids were no match for its speed."

I pull my shirt away from my torso, fanning my body with it. How did it suddenly get so hot? My armpits are damp. I hold up a finger, indicating I'll be right back, then return to the kitchen for more water. After draining another glass, I refill it and bring it back to the living room with me. I take a few deep breaths to get my pulse back under control. My body knows what's coming, even though I'm perfectly safe right now. Feelings of terror and helplessness engulf me just as strongly as they did all those years ago.

"The dog jumped, sinking its teeth into my shoulder and knocking me to the ground. My arm got pinned under me, breaking when I hit the ground. I cried out in pain, tears immediately blurring my eyesight. I laid there for a long time, praying for someone to come rescue me. At some point, the dog got off me and left, but all I remember is my throbbing forearm."

Britt gets up from the couch and wraps an arm around my waist and squeezing herself against me. "Oh, Jay. I'm so sorry. I see how hard this is for you, and I'm honored that you're sharing it with me. You felt all alone and so now you don't feel you can count on people."

I shake my head. "Uh, not exactly."

She pulls away so she can look up into my face. Her forehead creases. "There's more?"

"The next day at school, kids were looking at me and giggling. At first, I thought maybe it was nervous laughter because of how banged up I was. I know I looked rough. Our parents even have a picture to prove it."

"Oh yeah. And they have a picture of when I tried to style my hair by myself and looked like I'd stuck my finger in a light switch."

Her words spark another memory. "Remember Quinton's superhero phase?"

Britt's eyes shine with amusement. "Yeah. He wore dad's boxers with suspenders as his costume and tied a towel around his neck for a cape. Face it, our parents have a lot of embarrassing stuff on us, which I'm sure they'll use at an inopportune moment. Like when we introduce them to our significant others."

It suddenly makes sense. "Is that why they haven't met Neil yet?"

"One of them. We've gotten distracted. You're still telling

your story."

"Oh, right." The smile drops from my face as I remember where I was in my saga. "I found out Nessa spread the story at school, but changed some facts. She said I ran from a chihuahua and called me Cry Baby. The name stuck until middle school."

"That's terrible." She places a hand on my arm. The warmth helps calm my heightened nervous system. "Why didn't you tell our parents or a teacher?"

"What could they do? I'd have been teased worse for being a tattletale. Eventually, someone else did something that knocked me out of the spotlight. From then on, I've kept my head down and vowed not to put myself in a position to be teased like that again."

"Man. That's some seriously messed up stuff. Kids can be ruthless. I'm really sorry that happened to you."

"Thanks, Britt."

She puffs out her lips and gives me her tough-love face. I brace for whatever she's going to say, knowing I won't like it, but it's probably something I need to hear.

"Here's the thing, though. Are you going to let what some immature girl did to you almost twenty years ago keep you from pursuing a potentially great relationship now?"

I drop my head to my chest. When she says it like that, it sounds pretty dumb. "You're right. I shouldn't."

She sits down on the couch, patting the cushion beside her until I sit down. "Tell me more about Julie."

"I really don't know that much about her."

She gives me a look that says her patience is wearing thin.

"I know she likes Orange Dream smoothies from Hill of Beans. She's part of a book club at Page Turner Books. Blue Goose is her favorite restaurant, and her dog's name is Sadie. She has two brothers and owns her own business. She doesn't care for raw onions. I think that's about it."

"You're right, that's not a lot to go on."

I turn to glare at her, but her smile tells me she's just teasing me, so I relax.

"How'd you learn the onion thing? You try to kiss her?"

"What? No. She said it when we got burgers together. There have been no kissing attempts."

Britt rolls her eyes. "You know onions are code, right? Man, you really are clueless about women, huh?"

I do a double take. "Hold up. Are you saying she *wants* to kiss me?"

She looks at me like I'm a lost cause. "Duh."

"Huh."

A slow smile spreads across my face at the idea of kissing Julie. If I end things now just because of something that happened to me as a kid, I'd regret that missed opportunity for a long time. Can't have that. I should just take things one day at a time and find some way to hurdle the obstacle that is my fear of dogs when the time comes. In the meantime, I'd better double down on my efforts to spend time with the woman I like.

30

Julie

I'M LOOKING OVER some paperwork, excited about the challenge of creating a hexagon-shaped wedding cake for two high school teachers. One teaches geometry and the other chemistry. The bride showed me some of the cute ideas they want to use for their math-and-science-themed wedding. I've already sketched a few ideas out and am trying to figure out which the bride might like best when there's a knock on my office door. Emily opens it and sticks her head in.

"Hey Julie, there's a customer out front who asked specifically for you."

"Another prospective wedding client?"

Emily's eyes brighten and her lips quirk up into an amused smile. "I'm not sure. Maybe."

"Send them back so we can have some privacy."

"Sure thing, boss."

I grab my work notebook out of a drawer and snag a pen off the desk so I can jot down the customer's information and what they're looking for. A knock at the door brings my head up and I freeze when I see Jayson enter the room holding a stunning vase of pink and white lilies. My gaze swings between the flowers and his face. Does he look nervous? His Adam's apple bobs when he swallows. I shoot up from the chair. It bumps loudly into the wall behind me.

"Jayson, hi. What are you doing here?"

Definitely not a wedding client, unless Emily was insinuating we should get married. Um, no. I barely know him. He steps closer, holding the vase out.

"I wanted to see you."

I take the vase, lifting it so that I can smell the flowers' sweet scent. "Thank you."

Jayson nods, his face serious and focused. I bet he looks exactly the same when he's in front of a judge.

"I came here to tell you I like you. I'd like to spend more time together to see where this might go. Would you be interested in dating me?"

Wow, okay. He's just putting himself right out there. My mind flits to Sadie, but I push the thought down for now. There's nothing wrong with going to dinner with a guy who's kind and smart and very easy on the eyes. "I'd like that."

I'm rewarded with a beaming smile from Jayson. "I'm so glad. Can I take you to lunch today?"

I look down at my computer. "It's only ten-thirty."

"I know. I'll pick you up at noon if that works."

"It does if we go somewhere within walking distance. I like to stay accessible during operating hours."

He nods. "No problem. I'll see you later, yeah?"

"Yes, you will."

I hesitate for a moment, but then set the vase on the desk, walk around it to where Jayson's standing, and wrap my arms around his waist. When his hands settle on my back, pressing me closer to him, I can't help but squeeze my arms a little tighter. A quick breath in sends the heady smell of his cologne into my nose and I sigh out my exhale. He smells even better than the lilies.

Reluctantly, I release my arms and step back. When I look up, he's grinning broadly.

"Have I turned you into a hugger, too?"

I shrug. "Not yet, but I think I could be converted. Thanks again for the beautiful flowers."

When he leaves, I turn back and stare at the gorgeous arrangement. The lilies are so bright and open. My smile widens as I think about the last few minutes, especially the sensation of Jayson's arms around me. I felt safe nestled into his body like that, which is something I haven't felt in a long time.

"Those are gorgeous flowers. What'd Jayson want?"

Emily leans in the doorway, making me wonder how long she's been there. I wouldn't put it past her to have been lingering in the hallway while Jayson was here.

"He wants to date me. We're going to lunch later."

"Ooooh, exciting! Take your time. I can keep things handled here."

I shake my head. "You really want something to happen between us, don't you?"

"As your best friend, it's my duty to cheer you on, especially toward happiness. I've noticed the way your eyes light up when you see him and how your body instinctively leans toward him."

"What? I do that?"

Emily laughs. "You sure do. I'm proud of you for stepping out of your comfort zone with Jayson. I know the idea of opening your heart to someone is scary, but he seems like a great guy. And if he does anything stupid, I'm here to put him in his place."

Emily's too sweet to issue any real threat, but I appreciate the sentiment. "Thanks, Em. You're the best."

"I am, aren't I? Anyway, I better get back out front. Congrats on your lunch date." She wiggles her fingers and leaves.

My eyes scroll back and forth over the sidewalk outside the shop windows. My hands fidget with the clasp of my purse. I check my phone for a missed text. Nothing. He's late. Did he change his mind? No, surely not. He's probably dealing with a work thing. *How much time should I give him? I don't want to look desperate. Maybe five more minutes and then I'll just go find something to eat myself.*

My shoulders drop and my fingers relax when Jayson and his dapper navy suit flash by the window. He stops just outside the door and brushes the front of his suit before pulling the door open. When he steps inside, his eyes catch mine and I know my grin makes it obvious I saw him running down the street. He turns to assess the glass windows that run the entire length of the storefront before turning back with a sheepish grin.

I step out from behind the counter and walk over to him. I consider kissing his cheek, but I'm too much of a chicken. "Hey. I'm guessing you lost track of time?"

He ducks his head. "Yeah, sorry. I have an adoption hearing this afternoon and I wanted to make sure I had everything in order. When I realized I was late, I ran to make up a little time." He motions toward the windows. "Which, I guess you saw."

My smile widens. "I did. You could have just texted me."

"Oh yeah! Duh, Jayson." He rolls his eyes.

We walk to the door and he holds it open for me. I walk through, pausing on the sidewalk. "Where are we going?"

"It's a surprise."

He offers his hand, and I hesitate for just a moment. I slide my hand into Jayson's, feeling warmth shoot up my arm as our fingers intertwine. It's been a long time since I've held a man's hand in public. It feels a little odd, but also comforting. I smile at how small my hand looks in his. When I look up, Jayson smiles, then gently tugs me by the hand, and starts us up the hill.

He leads me past the Haywood Street Market, turns right, and walks another few blocks until we're standing in front of a tall building. He motions me through the front doors, greeting the security guard by name, and over to the elevators. We ride to the top floor. When the doors open, Jayson presses his hand to the small of my back, guiding me over to a door. He scans a card and opens the door to a stairwell. Walking ahead of me up the stairs, he scans his card again, gesturing for me to proceed him through the door.

I don't know what's happening, but the intrigue's exciting. When I walk through the door, I realize I'm on the roof of the building. Over by the wall, there's a table for two set up with an umbrella overhead and two coolers nearby. I peer over the side of the building, admiring the view. It's a gorgeous view of this part of the city. Below us is a grassy area with a pavilion. It's really cool to see Asheville from above. I feel Jayson's presence next to me and turn.

"Jayson, this is incredible! I have so many questions about how you found this spot. Where are we, by the way?"

He smiles, but instead of responding, pulls out a chair at the table. "Have a seat, and I'll tell you everything while we eat. I don't want you to be late getting back and get in trouble with the boss."

I smile at his teasing reference to our previous conversations about my tough boss. Jayson takes off his suit jacket and places it on the back of his chair before sitting down on the opposite side of the table.

"I don't think she'd mind me taking a more leisurely lunch just this one time."

"Oh, good."

Jayson opens one cooler and removes two plates, setting them on the table. He places bottles of water next to them before opening the second cooler. Delicious aromas waft out from inside, making my stomach growl. Jayson pulls out a large cardboard to-go container, places it on the table between us, and pops the lid. Inside are a dozen different tacos. I look up into Jayson's face, impressed by what he's pulled off.

"Blue Goose!"

"I got your favorites, but they had two new ones on the board I hadn't seen before, so I got one of each and a few others that sounded tasty. I wasn't sure what you might be in the mood for."

The earnestness on his face squeezes my heart. What a sweet gesture. "We won't be able to eat all this."

"That's okay. You can try whatever you like and take the rest home with you."

"Jayson, this is so wonderful! Thank you." I reach across the table, grab his hand, and give it an appreciative squeeze.

"You're welcome. Dig in."

I select a taco I don't recognize from the container and take a bite.

"This tastes like bacon."

"I think that's the pork cheek taco."

I scrunch up my nose at the name, but can't deny the wonderful flavors in my mouth. "It's delicious."

"Good. You wanted to know where we are?"

I nod.

"This is the Jackson Building. It was the first skyscraper in western North Carolina, completed in 1924. Built on the lot formerly occupied by a tombstone business operated by William Wolfe, father of novelist Thomas Wolfe, it currently holds the record for the tallest building built on the smallest lot, which is twenty-seven feet by sixty feet."

"Wow, you know a lot about this building."

"I should. The offices of Thompson and Associates are on the eleventh and twelfth floors."

That bit of information surprises me. "This is where you work?! Do you come up here all the time to take in the view?"

"Not as much as I'd like, but I think of it as my private rooftop of solitude."

A rooftop of solitude. I could use one of those now and

again. Makes me think of Superman and his fortress. *Jayson's definitely built like a superhero.* I imagine him with a pair of glasses that he rips off his face before tearing open his shirt to reveal a spandex super suit. I flush at the thought. *Get your thoughts back on track, Julie.*

"I feel honored," I say.

"It seemed like an appropriately romantic gesture."

Nice to know he's trying to be romantic with me. It lets me know I'm not the only one becoming more invested in whatever this is between us. I motion to the wall beside us, which has heart-shaped cutouts in the stone. "It definitely has a naturally romantic quality to it. I bet it's gorgeous up here at night with lights below and stars above."

He looks off into the distance before returning his gaze to me. "Never been up here at night, but I bet you're right. I usually try to be out of the office by seven."

"That sounds like a wonderful goal. How's it working out for you?"

"Okay. Sometimes I end up taking work home with me instead."

Not surprising, based on how focused and serious he is. "Mmm."

"I know, I know. But it's not that often. Besides, are you really one to talk about work/life balance?"

I purse my lips, bristling at his accusation. Or is he teasing me? I can't tell. "I'll have you know I've hired another part-time employee and given a key to a third person to spread out closing responsibilities."

He gives me a wide smile. "Oooh, Julie, that's big for you. Way to go. I'm proud of you." He raises one hand over the table toward me.

Is he seriously offering me a high five? Eh, it comes with praise, which I can't help but feel pleased about. I'll go with it. I slap his hand. "Thanks."

"Tell me about some of your favorite things."

"Like what?"

"Favorite color, favorite movie concessions, and favorite place in Asheville."

This feels like one of those online "five facts about me" posts. I love those. I sit up straighter. "My favorite color is emerald green."

"Because of your eyes?"

"Well, yes, *and* because I look great in it."

Jayson nods. "You really do. But you looked great in that blue dress at your brother's wedding, too."

I blush at his compliment. I'd forgotten how wonderful dates can be for one's self-esteem. At least, dates with someone who seems to like you. "Thanks. You look fantastic in your suits."

"I should hope so for what the tailoring costs. Okay, movie treats."

"I'm kind of boring—soda and buttered popcorn."

Jayson shakes his head. "Not boring. Perfect. That's my choice, too. What type of soda?"

"Sprite. You?"

"Same."

We smile at each other for a beat. "What's your favorite color?" I wonder if it's green as well.

"Red, but I'm warming up to emerald green."

He looks me right in the eye when he answers, and my blush deepens.

"See, something red I like," Jayson teases, his finger reaching out and tracing a line down my flaming cheek.

My breath catches at his touch. I roll my eyes to play off how much he's affecting me.

"Let's move on to favorite places in Asheville," I say, getting back to the questions. "Before today, I would have said the Blue Ridge Parkway. I love being able to see for miles, but I can see both downtown and the mountains from here, so maybe it's a tie."

"The mountain views are magnificent, but they're not my favorite place."

"What is?"

"I know it's kind of cliché for Asheville, but I like the Biltmore Estate."

"Really?"

"Yeah. It's fun to hike around the grounds and see the different ponds and streams. Once Carlos and I took a paddle board tour down the French Broad, passing through the Biltmore property, and it was so neat to see it from a different angle. It feels like no matter how many times I go, I discover something new or interesting there. And it's really cool when the place is decorated for Christmas."

"You know, I've lived here fifteen years and only seen the Biltmore at Christmas one time."

The shock on Jayson's face is almost comical. "What? That's a tragedy. We'll have to fix that in about four months."

"Sure, why not?"

"Great. It's a date. Speaking of which, tomorrow my basketball team's playing in the championship game. Can you come?"

My face scrunches, disappointment thudding in my chest. "I'd really like to, but I'm providing dessert for an event at the convention center. It'll be all hands on deck staffing our station. If it goes well, it could lead to more business."

"Julie, that's great! What about dinner on Wednesday?"

"I should be able to swing that."

We lock eyes across the table, and I wonder if he's flooded with nervous excitement like I am. It's been a long time since I've allowed myself to care for a man. The mix of exhilaration and fear is giving me an adrenaline rush.

The conversation flows while we eat, and I'm surprised at how much Jayson makes me laugh. When I can't possibly eat another bite, I lean back in my chair, staring at the mountain of tacos still on the tray between us. When was the last time I had this much fun with another person? It's been too long. It makes me want to be a little reckless and prolong the enjoyment.

"I suppose I should return you to work," Jayson says, catching my gaze. "Emily's probably wondering where you are."

"It probably wouldn't hurt her to wait a *little* longer."

A surge of boldness bubbles up and, before I can second-guess myself, I lean halfway across the table, hoping Jayson will understand my message. His forehead furrows with an unspoken question. My tongue darts out to wet my lips, and I tilt my head to the side, raising my eyebrows. His gaze turns from questioning to heated. He leans forward until our faces are just a few inches apart. Blood whooshes in my ears and I will myself not to faint, my skin tingling with anticipation. I pause, debating whether to close the remaining distance and kiss him or enjoy the prolonged anticipation. It's been so long since my last first kiss and I've never been good at these games.

Before I can ponder the dilemma more, Jayson presses his hands into the table, lifting himself out of his seat until our lips meet. My eyes drift shut at the slight pressure, my body indecisive about whether to melt into the sensation or explode like fireworks. My mind tries to memorize every detail of the moment—how his soft, warm lips feel against mine, the electricity coursing through my body, the slight breeze tickling my skin and ruffling my hair. The pressure against my lips eases when he pulls back. My arm flies up from the table, cupping the back of his head with my hand, and I bring his lips back to mine, reinstating the delicious pressure my lips now crave. I'm so focused on the feel of his mouth on mine that all other thoughts disappear.

A buzzing sound pulls me out of the moment. My brain catches up with my body, and I realize I'm still clutching Jayson's neck. My eyes open and I break the kiss, sitting back in my chair. Part of me feels embarrassed for getting carried away, but a bigger part yearns for more.

"Wow, that was—" I don't know how to finish that sentence. Why am I so breathless?

"Yeah, that certainly was."

The teasing in his voice breaks the tension and I relax, realizing we're both grinning from ear to ear. My cheeks and neck are on fire, but I decide to ignore the embarrassment that wants to surface and enjoy the present. Unfortunately, the sensible part of my brain breaks in reminding me it's the middle of the workday. I sigh, returning more and more to real life. We can't stay up on this roof forever, as appealing as that idea sounds.

"I suppose we should both probably get back to work."

"I'll walk you back." Jayson stands, pushing his chair back.

"You don't have to."

"I know. It's an excuse to spend a little more time with you."

Thoughts of our sizzling kiss fill my head. Spending more time together sounds like an excellent idea.

31

AUGUST

Jayson

I'M A FEW minutes early for my date with Julie. Maybe I can help with whatever still needs to be done inside the store. The pleasing chocolate aroma wafts into my nostrils when I open the door. I take a deep breath, then look around. Emily's the only employee out front. Her hair's lavender today.

"Hey Jayson. I assume you're here for Julie." She motions toward the doorway that leads to the office. "She's in the back. I doubt she'd mind you coming to find her."

The door to the office is closed, so I knock and wait. When I hear a muffled "come in," I open the door. Julie's sitting at her desk, papers scattered all over the surface and some on the floor near her chair. "Hey. I'm a few minutes early, so finish whatever you're doing."

Julie's wide grin makes my heart flip.

"I'm not working on anything that can't wait until tomorrow. Let me run to the restroom and then I'll be ready."

"Take your time."

Julie pulls her purse from a desk drawer, walks over to me, and, after a moment of hesitation, kisses me on the cheek. Then she moves around me before darting out the door.

I touch my fingers to my cheek. The sensation of her lips against my skin is fading quickly, but I console myself with the thought that I'll probably get to feel them again later. It feels weird being alone in her office space, so I walk to the main area of the store. I use my camera app to double check my appearance while I wait. I smile at the camera to see if there are any remnants from the Everything bagel I had at lunch still in my teeth. My stomach growls as if to remind me a bagel is not a substantial lunch. *Duly noted, stomach.* A door opens behind me, and Julie emerges from behind it.

"Okay, I'm ready. Where are we going?"

"We've eaten at your favorite spot, so tonight we're going to mine."

Julie's eyes widen at the plate of lobster nachos set between us. "These look amazing!" she says.

"Wait till you try one."

She smiles slyly. "How long do I have to wait?"

I motion with my fork. "Dig in."

Julie moves a pile of chips to her plate with her fork before picking up a loaded chip and taking a bite. Her eyes close, and she sighs.

My body relaxes with relief at her reaction.

"It sounds like I made the right call."

She opens her eyes and smiles. "You certainly did. I have to admit, while I adore the lobster mac and cheese here, the idea of seafood together with nachos has always sounded a little dicey to me, but the flavor combo is superb."

"Does everything meld together just right?" I tease.

"It does."

"You know, it's kind of funny. Both of our favorite restaurants are in the same food family—tacos and nachos."

"That *is* funny. I bet your brilliant lawyer brain figured that connection out quickly. By the way, this coconut margarita is the best drink ever. It's like a beach party in my mouth."

I laugh. "Glad you like it. I've never had a margarita here. I'm more of a Dos Equis man myself."

Julie raises her glass toward me, which I take without hesitation. I take a small sip, then hand it back with a nod. "That definitely tastes like a tropical vacation. What else do you like to do with your free time besides eat good food, walk your dog, and go to book club?"

"That pretty much sums up my life right now."

"What did you used to do before you owned the store?"

She nibbles on a nacho while she thinks. My eyes can't stop roaming down to her mouth tonight. I keep flashing to our kiss up on the roof and hope for an encore today. Not here in the middle of a crowded restaurant, but maybe at the end of the date.

"I used to love going to concerts."

"What kind of music?"

"All kinds. I like rock, pop, classical, alternative, just about anything on the radio. I don't care for heavy metal or country, though. I really just enjoy the experience of watching people do what they love and getting swept up in the music with the crowd."

"If you could see any band in concert right now, who would it be?"

"Two Left Feet."

That sounds like a fake name, though there was no hesitation in her answer. "Never heard of them."

"They're a local band, but their shows are so much fun. They mainly play covers, but occasionally play songs they've written. It's two hours of dancing and singing along and it's a blast."

"Do you know when their next show is?"

"Next weekend."

"Do you want to go? I'd be interested in experiencing it with you."

"No."

The speed at which she issues her response surprises me. For someone who seems really into the band, I'd think she'd see them every chance she could. "Why not?"

"They're playing at The Xcape."

"And that's a problem?"

A deep sigh escapes through Julie's lips. "It is."

"How so?"

"The Xcape is owned by my ex."

"You'd miss seeing your favorite band perform because of a guy you used to date?"

She shakes her head. "I wish it were that simple."

"I'm obviously missing something."

Julie sighs again, and leans back in her seat, rubbing her temple. She looks uncomfortable and an urge to do whatever I can to ease her troubles wells up inside.

"Xavier is my ex-husband. He cheated on me with one of his bartenders. Probably with other women, too."

My neck snaps back and I feel like I've been struck. "What?"

Julie looks embarrassed. "Which part shocks you? That I've been married, or that my husband cheated on me?"

I blink a few times, still trying to wrap my head around the fact that someone as beautiful and kind as Julie received such treatment is despicable. "Both. How could anyone do that to you? He obviously couldn't see how wonderful you are. You didn't deserve that."

She waves her hand like she just wants to move on from this topic, and I can't blame her. "I know. I shouldn't have married him in the first place, but I was young and dumb and thought I was in love."

I'd like to let this be for her sake, but I just have so many questions. If I don't get them out, they'll keep running through my mind for the rest of our date. Still, I don't want to force her to talk about something so obviously painful. "Do you feel comfortable talking about it with me? If not, no problem. We can talk about something else."

Julie lifts a shoulder and then drops it. "Might as well. You should know what you're getting into with me. Where should I start?"

I don't like her resigned tone, but I don't know what to do about it. "How about at the beginning? When did you two meet?"

"We met at The Xcape, actually. I had just turned twenty-one and came to see Jack Wylie perform. Xavier was working the bar when I sidled up, pronounced I was of legal age, and asked what he recommended. We flirted as he made my drink, a Fuzzy Navel, and he gave me a business card with his cell phone number scrawled on the back."

The back of my neck heats with jealousy. I don't enjoy hearing about Julie with another man, but it's not like I expected her to have never dated. I work to keep the emotion from showing on my face. She doesn't need to deal with my insecurity while she shares her story with me. I concentrate on the raw emotions flashing over her face while she talks.

"I didn't call him, but I returned to The Xcape a few weeks later for another show. I was asking for a drink recommendation from the bartender when someone stepped up next to me. Xavier told the bartender that whatever I wanted was on the house and then asked me why I hadn't called. I told him I didn't think he'd been serious. He then asked if I was free for dinner later in the week."

Her tone is monotone as she speaks, making my heart twinge with sympathy. I reach across the table for her hand, giving her what I hope is a reassuring squeeze. She catches my eye before looking back down at the table.

"At dinner, I found out he owned the venue and was in his early thirties. The age gap concerned me initially, but he didn't seem bothered by it. He showered me with compliments, telling me I was the most beautiful woman he'd ever seen and how he felt so lucky to be with me.

"He bought me lots of gifts and gave me free entrance to any concert I wanted to see. I was at The Xcape any night I wasn't working, enjoying the concerts but also soaking up all the attention Xavier gave me. After six months of constant affection and attention, he proposed, and I said yes. We had a quick wedding with just my uncle, the officiant, and one of his friends in a park on a random Monday."

The way she says the last sentence gives me the feeling that wasn't the wedding of her dreams. That she jumped into marriage so quickly surprises me, though it makes sense why she's been skittish about admitting her feelings for me. I've been hesitant to get serious with women and I've never truly given my heart away and had it crushed like she has. I'm not sure what to say to all this information, so I settle on the most recent information. "Is that the wedding you wanted?"

"I honestly didn't think much about it. But I was so infatuated with Xavier that I did anything he wanted."

"That doesn't sound good."

"It wasn't healthy, but I didn't know any better. I hadn't dated a lot, and I'd certainly never been swept off my feet before. I felt like a princess in a fairytale romance."

"Obviously, things changed at some point."

Julie nods. "I moved out of my apartment and into Xavier's place after the wedding. I was busy working during the days and Xavier's work took up most evenings, so I'd usually go to the club after I finished work for the day. All those late nights followed by early mornings at the store left me completely exhausted. I asked

Xavier if he'd mind if I stopped coming in after work, and he was completely supportive of my desire to get more rest. I thought it meant he was a considerate husband."

She pauses and screws up her face in discomfort, letting me know this story is about to take an unpleasant turn.

"Everything seemed fine between us until I surprised him for our one-year anniversary. I hadn't been to his work regularly for at least six months, so it didn't seem odd that we wouldn't see each other that night. I even told him we'd celebrate our anniversary on his next evening off to keep him in the dark about my intentions."

Even knowing where this is going, my stomach still twists with sympathy for Julie. She's so brave for sharing this with me. Her hand fidgets with her fork on the table. I reach over and gently take her hand, squeezing it for reassurance.

"I'd snuck a cake into the back office and was coming out to the lobby when I saw Xavier behind the bar with his arms wrapped around one of the bartenders. I watched in horror as he leaned down and gave her a long, passionate kiss, his hands roaming down to her rear."

"On your anniversary?"

"Yes. After I unfroze myself from the shock, I marched over to the bar and slammed my hand on the counter, startling them apart. Xavier didn't even sound convincing when he said, 'It's not what you think, Honey Bear.' I held up a hand to stop his flimsy excuse, saying, 'Worst anniversary ever, Baby Cakes, and—'"

"Wait." I hold up a hand. "I'm sorry. Baby Cakes?"

"Yeah, that was my nickname for him."

My nose scrunches. "Yeesh. I demand veto power on any future nicknames."

Julie raises an eyebrow. Despite the depressing subject, the corner of her mouth twitches like it wants to curve up.

"Getting ahead of ourselves, aren't we? I don't give nicknames to just anyone, you know. Only the important people in my life."

"Oh, *excuse* me," I say, thankful for the bit of levity in this heavy conversation. "Well, *if* I reach Important Person status, may I humbly request a say in what you call me?"

Julie taps her chin. "I suppose. But I request you show me the same courtesy."

"Of course. Didn't you like Honey Bear?"

Julie purses her lips. "It wasn't my favorite. I called him Baby Cakes because it sounded as sickeningly sappy as Honey Bear."

"Yeah, it definitely sounds like you had a healthy relationship."

Julie sticks out her tongue, which makes me chuckle. "Do you want to hear what happened next or not?"

"Oh, I definitely do. Please continue. You just called him Baby Cakes."

Julie narrows her eyes at me, but then relaxes her face and continues. "I told him it was over and left, but I heard the other woman lay into him. I guess she was new enough that she didn't know he was married. I called a few friends, and they came over with a truck and some boxes and helped me pack up my things and move out while he was still at work. He called me but I didn't answer. He came to my work the next day to apologize and said the other woman meant nothing to him, that it was a mistake. But you don't kiss another person when you're married to someone else. Besides, I couldn't trust him anymore and I told him that. He was at least gracious enough not to contest the divorce. Not that we really had much to divide. I obviously wanted nothing to do with The Xcape. And that was that."

"Oh Julie, I'm so sorry you went through that."

"Like I said, it was a long time ago."

"How long?"

"About eleven years."

That knocks me back in my seat. It really shouldn't shock me, as I've been feeling the effects of trauma that happened almost twice as long ago.

"Long story short, that's why I won't see my favorite band play at The Xcape next week."

I can hardly blame her. The venue holds some terrible memories for her. "Have you been back there at all since your anniversary?"

Julie shakes her head. "Nope."

I know firsthand how stuck you can get in your past. Maybe we could help each other move forward into a future where our hurts don't define us or dictate our decisions. "Do you think maybe it wouldn't be so bad now that so much time has passed?"

"I don't know. It'd just be weird seeing Xavier in that environment again after so much of our story together was there."

I try a new tactic, feeling out whether our fledgling relationship might help her open up to the idea of reckoning with the past. "Would it help if someone went with you?"

"Like you?"

"Yes. I don't want you to miss doing something you enjoy if I can help it. Maybe going with me could help you overwrite those terrible memories with some good ones."

Julie twists her lips to the side, considering my proposition. "I just don't know."

"Please think about it. I won't put any more pressure on you, but if you'd like to go, I'll gladly be your date."

"Thanks, that's very sweet of you."

"Speaking of sweet, do you have room for dessert?"

Julie shakes her head and pats her belly. "Could we walk instead?"

"Sure." I motion for the check, then turn back to Julie. "Thank you for sharing your story with me. I'm sure it wasn't easy."

"Thanks for being a compassionate listener, Jalapeño."

I frown. "Jalapeño?"

Julie grins. "Just trying out a nickname. You're definitely not a Jalapeño."

I smirk. If she's trying out nicknames, does that mean she

thinks this has long-term potential? I sure hope so. "What is it with you and food names?"

"I make chocolate for a living. Must be a hazard of the job."

"Whatever you say, Butter Cup."

Julie groans and rolls her eyes. "Okay, I get it. No food names."

32

Julie

"SO," I SAY, once we're out front of the restaurant. "Where to?"

"You take the lead," Jayson says. "We can walk until you're ready for dessert and then see what's around us."

"Sounds fun." I turn left and Jayson falls into step beside me. "I've told you about my dating history. What's yours?"

I'm acutely aware of how the backs of our hands brush together every few steps. I stay quiet, waiting for Jayson to speak. Finally, he does.

"I know this sounds like a cop out, but I don't really have much to tell."

"You're right, it does. Especially after what I just shared."

There's no way someone as attractive as Jayson didn't have girls falling all over him. Though, I suppose there's the possibility that he grew into his looks. Maybe he was awkward in high school. Hard to imagine looking at him now, but I suppose it's possible.

"I took a girl to senior prom in high school, but we were just friends."

"I didn't really date in high school either, so I get that. Surely you dated in college, though."

He shakes his head. "I went to some parties and made out with girls I met there, but it never turned into anything. There was one girl who was my date for events and vice versa, but we were more like good friends than a couple. In law school, I spent all my time studying or networking, trying to figure out how to get quality internships for the summer."

"That doesn't sound like a lot of fun." I'm finding this hard to believe. Well, not the making out at parties part. That sounds right, though the idea of him kissing random girls raises the little green monster inside me, but I remind it this story is from years ago and he's here with me now. Maybe he was more focused on school than on relationships. It's just kind of unbelievable to me that someone as great as Jayson is still single.

One of Jayson's shoulders raises, then drops. "I mean, no, but I was there to get my degree and then pass the bar. I figured I'd have time for dating once I was working."

"And is that what happened?"

"Not exactly. I moved here after I graduated and dove into learning the ropes at my aunt's firm. I've just recently felt like I'm at a place where I can handle adding a relationship."

"Oh." I'm not sure whether to be pleased or worry about his lack of dating experience. Does it mean he's not looking for anything serious? I don't want to put my heart out there if there isn't a chance he's interested in doing the same. "What are you looking for in your dating life?"

"That's a good question. I guess someone I can have fun with and talk about work and life. A person I can connect with on a deeper level, something potentially long-term."

That's a surprise. Not the fact that he's thought about it, because obviously he's someone who considers all his options before making a decision, but that he seems to see us as having long-term potential. "Wow," is all I can say at the implication of his words.

"Am I scaring you with my straight talk?"

Scared? No. A little overwhelmed at the thought of potentially trying another serious relationship? Yes.

"Not really. I just didn't think you'd be ready for something serious since you haven't dated much yet."

"To me, the purpose of dating is to find someone you can intertwine your life with, someone you can support who will support you, possibly someone to become family."

I'm quiet, considering everything he's said. He bumps my shoulder, drawing my attention to his face. There's uncertainty in his eyes when he turns the question back to me. "What are you looking for in someone you date?"

"I guess someone who supports me, like you said. Someone faithful and honest, someone I can trust completely."

Jayson nods. "I can understand that. Have you dated anyone seriously since your ex?"

"No."

"It sounds like we both have limited experience, but we're looking for the same things, right?"

He's got me on both points. "Yes, it does."

I sense Jayson tense next to me and look over. His eyes are glued to a couple coming up the sidewalk toward us, walking two dogs. One is a fluffy little Pomeranian, and the other is a Great Dane who looks like it's smiling widely. The disparity of their sizes makes me chuckle.

Jayson drifts over into my space, his shoulder pressing against mine. His eyes are wide with concern. I grab his arm and slide him over toward the buildings so I'm closest to the couple. I link his hand with mine and squeeze firmly. His fingers tighten around mine and my knuckles pop from the pressure.

They pass us and Jayson swings his head around, following them up the street with his eyes. He pulls me around a corner, then leans back against the building, running a hand down his face. He lets go of my hand and bends at the waist, hands on his thighs, his breath short and fast.

Unsure what to do, I place one hand on his shoulder and use the other to rub slow, firm circles on his back. "Everything's okay. Breathe in and out. With me."

I bend down to catch his eye, then exaggerate my inhale and exhale until our breaths align. After a minute or so, Jayson straightens.

"You okay?"

The weird look on his face makes me wonder if he's embarrassed by what just happened. He shakes his head, as if he's trying to get rid of whatever's in his head.

"Yeah, I think so."

He told me he didn't like dogs, but I didn't realize it's actually fear rather than dislike. The dogs looked harmless to me, but Jayson didn't see them that way. I don't know how he's going to react to Sadie. My throat tightens at the thought.

"Can you explain what just happened?"

He sighs. "I was attacked as a kid. Ever since, large dogs have made me nervous. However, that gray dog was *enormous*. The thought of him wrapping his jaws around my face psyched me out. Thanks for helping me recover. You're a very calming presence."

I want to tell him the dog looked more likely to lick his face than bite it, but I doubt it'd help. Words fail me, so I wrap my arms around his waist and squeeze. He hugs me back for a few seconds before letting go. I step back from the embrace, wanting to give him whatever he needs. I search his face for guidance.

He grasps my hand, intertwining our fingers. I look between our clasped hands and Jayson's face. A tentative smile crosses his lips, which I take to mean he's ready to move on. I smile back before a question pops into my head. "I can't believe I almost forgot to ask. How did the championship game go last night?"

"We won. It was close, but Carlos made a last-second shot to give us a two point victory."

I squeeze his hand, trying to convey my excitement for him. "Congratulations, Jayson! I'm so happy for you and your team. Did you get a trophy or something?"

"The team got a trophy. We'll take turns keeping it and then it'll stay at Carlos's place since he's the coach."

Pride rushes into my chest, and I need to express it. I rock up onto my tiptoes and kiss his cheek. My heels barely touch the ground before he tugs me closer. I keep our torsos from colliding by putting my free hand on his chest to stop my momentum. The feel of his muscles under my fingers momentarily distracts me. My fingers trace the outline of his pectorals. My eyes roam from my fingers up to his face. His eyes sparkle, crinkling at the corners with laugh lines. He leans toward me, his eyes closing. My lips twitch in anticipation of what's coming. I tip my chin up, stretching onto my toes once again. When our lips meet, it feels electric.

Jayson pulls back after only a few seconds. Disappointment shoots through me. I want to reach up and drag his mouth back to mine for more, but he drops my hand and takes a step back, leaving a foot of space between us. I immediately miss his warmth.

He clears his throat and glances around. "I really like kissing you, but we probably shouldn't do it in full view of a bunch of strangers."

I blink and look around. *Oh right. We're standing in the middle of the sidewalk.* My cheeks heat at the realization. "You're right. This isn't the time or place."

"I definitely want to make time, though." He says, his gaze heavy with meaning.

"How about you drive me back to my place?" The words are out before I even have time to consider them.

Jayson's face opens in surprise at my words, but then he gives me a devilish grin. "Let's find the car."

33

Jayson

WE PULL INTO a parking space in front of Julie's building, and I cut the engine. I unbuckle my seatbelt and grab the door handle, before freezing when I remember a crucial fact. Julie seems to sense the change in my demeanor because she places a hand on my arm.

"Is everything okay?"

I slump back in my seat and cover my face with my hands. "No."

She pries my hands away from my face, turning my chin toward her. Her concerned look only twists my gut more. "What is it?"

"Your dog. I don't know how I could forget." *Especially after what just happened.* I release a breath and rub a hand over my hair. "I can't come in with you."

Julie squeezes my arm, and the heat radiates up to my chest. I can't believe I'm turning down a chance to hold her in my arms.

"That's okay," she says. "We can end the date here. Thanks for a lovely evening."

I'm relieved that she's being so considerate, but this is not how I wanted the night to end. The disappointment in her eyes tells me she feels the same. "I appreciate your understanding, but I feel bad that you didn't get any dessert."

"How about we have a little something sweet right here before I go inside?"

My eyes brighten at her meaning. I lean toward her, and our lips connect over the center console. My hand cups Julie's cheek. Light pressure on my neck draws me closer to Julie. When she deepens the kiss, desire swells deep within me. Kissing has never felt as good and right as it does with Julie. I'm overwhelmed by the sensation of our mouths pressed together, the hum of pleasure coming from Julie, and the warmth of her hand on the back of my head. A groan erupts from me when Julie pulls back.

"This has been nice, but it's a little uncomfortable here in the car and I need to let Sadie out."

The mention of her dog is a wet blanket over my desire. I can't disagree with her assessment that a car is no place for a prolonged make-out session. I could take her to my place, but Britt will be there. The thought of being in an enclosed space with any dog makes me nervous. My skin prickles with goosebumps just thinking about it. I should be able to move on, but my ragged heartbeat confirms that I'm still scarred by the past. If only there was something I could do.

"Hey, uh, is it okay if I sit out here in my car and see Sadie when you bring her out for a walk?"

"Yes, that's fine. Why?"

"I should at least see the animal that's preventing me from visiting your apartment, right? Size up my obstacle and see if it's something I can overcome."

Julie smiles. "Of course. She really is a sweet dog. Do you want me to bring her to the car?"

"No, that's okay. Just pretend I'm not here and do what you usually do."

"Alright. Before I go, I wanted to see if you're free on Friday night."

Julie's asking me out? Even after seeing a glimpse of my fear? That's got to be a good sign. "I am. What'd you have in mind?"

"It's a surprise. We can meet here. I'll let you know what time when I get the details worked out, okay?"

"Works for me."

She gives me a quick kiss before heading into her apartment building. My leg bounces up and down while I wait for her to return. This is hardly a step at all, but I really like Julie and know she loves her dog. Maybe Sadie isn't as intimidating as I'm imagining in my head. I certainly can't ask her to get rid of a pet she's had much longer than she's known me. It's up to me to make our relationship work.

The door to the building opens and a black dog emerges, its tail wagging and its tongue hanging out. My eyes round into giant saucers. It's not nearly as big as the dog we saw earlier, but it's no tea cup poodle. Those don't bother me at all. Julie appears holding the leash and waves in my direction before they head down the block in the other direction. I watch them go, my heart beating faster than normal.

I don't want to give up on the new relationship just because of my fear. Surely we can figure out a way to make it work. Perhaps I should talk to a professional about my issue. The idea of therapy makes me a little uncomfortable, but if it could help me make peace with dogs, then it'd be worth it. Julie's worth it.

Back home, I walk into the house, tossing my keys and wallet in the direction of the bowl on the kitchen counter, and hear a satisfying clang when they land inside. I slip my shoes off on the mat next to the fridge. Grabbing a glass from the cabinet, I fill it with water and drain it in one gulp. I refill it and carry it into the living room, where Britt is watching a competitive baking show.

"What's the challenge today?"

"To make a dessert that perfectly captures the story of *Sleeping Beauty*."

"How are the competitors doing?" I sit down next to her on the couch.

"One seems quite focused on the dragon protecting the castle. It's quite intricate, but I'm afraid they're forgetting about the main character. Another is channeling the movie with Angelina Jolie rather than the original telling of the story. I'm rooting for the person trying to recreate the wobbly cake from the cartoon movie. She's got a sleeping girl on top and a prince riding a horse up the side. It's pretty cool."

I watch the screen for a few minutes. "I see what you mean. That dragon looks pretty fierce, though."

"Indeed."

Britt glances at me before doing a double take.

"Hey, bro, you look troubled? I thought you had dinner with Julie."

"I did, but we went for a walk after and ran into a ginormous dog."

She squeezes my arm, her mouth puckered in sympathy. "I'm sorry, Jay. Did it jump on you?"

"No, but it reminded me that Julie's dog might ruin our relationship if I can't interact with it without hyperventilating."

"What're you gonna do?"

I shrug and take another drink of water. "That's the big question. I really like Julie. I think it's time I get some help and overcome my fear."

"That's really brave of you. Can I help?"

"Thanks, but I can do it."

34

Julie

ZIPPING UP THE cooler, I glance at the microwave to check the time. Jayson should be here shortly. When I texted Tom yesterday to see if he could let Sadie out for me tonight, he offered to have her spend the night at their place. I gladly took him up on the offer. I'm grateful to have someone dependable looking after Sadie for me most of the time. And Sadie loves Tom so much. They make a great pair. Perhaps I should see if Tom has any interest in adopting Sadie.

My heart twists painfully at the thought, but if things continue to progress with Jayson, I'll eventually have to choose between him and my dog. I definitely don't want him having to relive his trauma every time he visits my apartment. Of course there are complications with my love life. It can't ever be easy for me, can it?

My phone pings with a message.

Jayson: I'm downstairs whenever you're ready.
Julie: Be right down.

I grab the cooler, a tote bag of blankets, and my purse, and head downstairs after a quick pat and kiss for Sadie, letting her know Tom will be by for her in about an hour. Not that I believe she knows what I'm saying.

I'm greeted with a brilliant smile from Jayson when I step outside. I smile back, my cheeks stretching wide, and lift my chin up toward him for a quick kiss. "Hey, there. Ready for some fun?"

"Sure. What are we doing?" Jayson takes the cooler and tote from my hands.

"Still a surprise. We have to go around the corner to get my car."

"I can drive." He nods toward his SUV parked down the street.

"Nope. This is my date. I'm driving."

"Yes, ma'am."

We load everything into the trunk of my car and get in. Jayson slides the seat back as far as it will go, but still looks cramped in my Honda Accord.

"Maybe we should have taken your car for the leg room. Sorry about that."

Jayson waves off my apology. "No worries. I'll be fine. It's better than being on an airplane."

"I suppose that's one way to look at it. We don't have far to go."

Leaving the garage, I navigate the streets until we're headed west on the interstate. After ten minutes, I take an exit and drive along winding roads, then turn down a long gravel driveway.

"Where are we?" Jayson says.

"You'll see."

We pass through a copse of trees into a large, open field with brown posts spaced in even rows and a large white screen in the distance.

"A drive-in theater?"

I grin. "Yep."

"I didn't think these things still existed."

"There aren't as many as there used to be, that's for sure. This one only shows classic movies. I hope that's okay with you. Tonight's feature is *Charade*."

"What's that about?"

"A woman's husband is murdered and she and a stranger try to figure out what happened while also searching for the money her husband was killed for. Audrey Hepburn and Cary Grant are the stars."

"That sounds interesting."

"I think so."

I pull up to the gatehouse and purchase our tickets. After parking, I pop the trunk and get out of the car. Jayson follows me to the back of the car, and I hand him two bag chairs. "Set these up in front of the car, please. I'll bring the rest of the stuff."

I carry a tote bag of blankets and the cooler to the front of the car, setting them on the hood.

"I didn't even know you could get lounging bag chairs," Jayson says. "These look nice."

"They're pretty comfortable. I brought blankets in case it gets cold after the sun sets. Oh! I almost forgot."

I dash around to the back of the car, remove a small folding table, and then shut the trunk. I set the table between the two chairs. "There. Now we can eat."

I unzip the cooler and hand Jayson two bottles of water. Next, I retrieve plates, napkins, chopsticks, and a few packets of soy sauce, arranging them on the table before adding several plastic to-go containers. "I thought sushi sounded good tonight. I hope that's okay."

"That sounds wonderful. Where's it from?"

Jayson's eyes light up. Looks like he's a sushi fan. Good.

"Dragon Sushi. I've heard it's good, but haven't made it there yet."

"It's fantastic. Excellent choice. Did you get the Tipsy Tiger?"

"As a matter of fact, I did. I also got a Rainbow, a Shrimp Tempura, and a King Crab."

"A woman after my own heart."

His wide smile combined with the intense way he's staring at me makes my face heat.

"Sit down and let's dig in."

We discuss our workdays and some of our favorite movies while we eat. Jayson is very skilled with the chopsticks while I fumble with mine until he reaches over and helps me situate them properly in my fingers. After that, I do much better holding onto my food.

When we're finished, the sky is nearly pitch black and we can barely see our plates. Jayson uses his phone as a flashlight while we clean up. The large screen in front of us lights up and a countdown begins.

"It's almost showtime," I say. "Can you put everything in the cooler? I'll be right back."

"Where are you going?"

"To the concessions stand. We're at a movie, after all."

Jayson grins. "Cool."

I return with a giant tub of popcorn and two cans of Sprite. "I hope you're not too full for popcorn."

"Never." As if to confirm his words, he grabs a handful and pops it in his mouth. His brow furrows, and he glances down at the palm of his hand before holding it out to me. "That's a lot of butter."

I forgot we're still learning about each other. I've felt so comfortable eating and talking with him tonight that this feels like we've been hanging out forever. In reality, we've only been on a handful of dates together. "I love buttered popcorn."

"Me too. I could use a napkin, though."

"Luckily for you, I came prepared." I hand him a stack of napkins. "Those are all for you."

I set the tub on the table and grab the tote bag of blankets, placing it down on the ground, scooting the table back behind the chairs. "Would you like a blanket?"

He takes one from the bag and I grab another, sitting down and settling it across my lap. When I reach over to the popcorn, my hand brushes Jayson's. We grin at each other. He takes my hand and brings it to his lips for a soft kiss, his eyes never leaving mine. The hunger in his eyes makes me shiver with pleasure. I take my hand back so that I can scoot my chair next to Jayson's until the arms overlap slightly. The corner of his mouth hitches higher, and then he leans toward me.

When our lips meet, a soft sigh escapes my lips and I feel Jayson smile against my mouth before pressing more firmly against my lips with his. My hand reaches up to the back of his neck and his hand drapes over my hip. It's a good thing I've seen this movie before because it looks like I might be missing most of it tonight.

35

Jayson

SITTING DOWN IN a chair near a window, I look around the waiting room. It contains half a dozen chairs, a coffee table with some old magazines, a half-completed puzzle, and a small fountain with water bubbling out of the top and trickling down the sides of the rock-like structure into a small bowl below. There are two doors on the wall opposite the one I entered, each with several name plates affixed to them, letting me know this office houses multiple therapists. The door on the right lists three names, one of which is the person I'm here to see, Gabrielle Martin, LCSW.

Unsure whether I'm supposed to knock on the door or do something else to signal my arrival, I open my email to double-check the instructions. I'm just supposed to wait and the therapist will come get me when it's time. I pick a seat in front of the coffee table.

My knee bobs up and down rapidly, and I place a hand on it to calm my nerves. I shove my phone into my pocket and pick up a magazine from the table. It's a Sports Illustrated from two years ago with a picture of LeBron James on the cover. I thumb through the pages until I reach the featured article.

I try to read it, but my eyes kept returning to the door. Anxiety wells up inside. Can she really help me overcome my fear of dogs? Will she make me interact with dogs? Are there methods that don't require contact with actual dogs? I'll just have to wait and see.

I force my eyes back to the article, but I'm just reading the same sentence over and over without comprehending. My heel begins tapping again. I give up on trying to keep myself preoccupied and toss the magazine back onto the table. I turn my attention to the fountain, concentrating on the water bubbling out of the top. It helps, but only a little. I close my eyes, hoping to get my mind to focus on the sound. My breathing deepens and my foot stills as I imagine sitting next to a small stream in the middle of a quiet forest.

Door hinges squeak, breaking my concentration. My eyes fly open and all feelings of calm dissipate. Out steps a woman in a smart business suit. Her brown skin glows and her short, curly hair is perfectly styled. She offers me a smile I can tell is meant to put me at ease. Unfortunately, it doesn't work. "Jayson Thompson?"

I stand up. "That's me."

The woman holds out her hand. "I'm Gabrielle Martin, but you can call me Gabi if you'd like."

I wipe my sweaty palm on my suit pants before shaking her hand. "Hello, Gabi."

Gabi leads me down a hallway to three doors. Gabi pushes open the door with her name stenciled across it and motions for me to enter and take a seat. This room is fairly simple, with a desk pushed against the wall in front of a window and a small seating area with a sofa, two chairs, and a small side table, a tissue box the only thing on its surface.

On the desk is a laptop, several legal pads of paper, a cup of pens, and a small plant in a bright green pot that reminds me of Julie's eyes. I take a deep breath and catch a whiff of something.

It's a clean scent. Not sterile, more like linen or cotton. It reminds me of spring and renewal. Maybe it's a sign I'm in the right place.

I choose the couch and sit on the side closest to the corner of the room. Gabi picks up a pad of paper and a pen from the desk and sits down in the chair across from me. I stare out the window, wondering if I'm supposed to be saying something.

"Okay, Jayson. Why don't you tell me why you're here today?"

I drag my eyes back to Ms. Martin. Or is it Mrs? My eyes flick down, but the yellow legal pad hides her hands from me. The pad looks just like the ones I use. My gaze returns to her face and she flashes me an encouraging smile. I've only got an hour, so might as well jump right in.

"I have a fear of dogs and I'd like to get over it."

She nods, scribbling something with her pen. "Are you aware of the reason for this fear?"

"When I was a kid, a dog chased me and knocked me down."

"Did it bite you or hurt you in any way?"

"It bit my shoulder, and I broke my arm in the fall."

"Before that incident, did dogs bother you?"

I shrug. "I didn't love them, but they didn't scare me."

"Has a dog attacked you again since that incident?"

"No."

"When you see a dog now, what happens?"

My skin prickles at the memory of the big dog I saw when I was with Julie. "I usually try to steer clear. If one gets too close, I sweat and my breathing gets shallow."

"Does this happen around all dogs?"

I shake my head. "Little dogs don't bother me. Their loud yipping is annoying, but that's it. It's bigger dogs that are the problem."

"Do you know what kind of dog attacked you?"

"It was a German Shepherd."

She makes another note, then meets my eye. "Tell me why you've decided that now is the time to overcome your fear of dogs."

My body heats immediately at the thought of Julie. I rub the back of my neck and stare up at the ceiling. "I'm dating a woman who owns a big dog."

"Mmhmm."

I look at Gabi, but she's quietly waiting for me to say more.

"I like her. A lot. And I know if there's any chance of it going somewhere, I have to be able to interact comfortably with her dog."

Gabi writes some more, then brings her attention back to me. "I prefer to use EMDR therapy for situations like these. It stands for Eye Movement Desensitization and Reprocessing. This involves following my finger movements to distract your brain as we talk through your trauma experience. It may seem a little weird or silly at first, but it can be quite effective. Would you like to try it?"

"Sure." Following fingers and talking I can do. It sounds so much better than being thrust into a room full of dogs.

"Excellent. What I'd like to do for the rest of today's session is have you give me as detailed an account of the attack and then try to identify the emotions you felt and the beliefs that were created from the incident. Are you able to do that?"

Okay, maybe this won't be easy peasy, but I told Britt the story without too much trouble. I can definitely do it again if it means getting rid of the obstacle in my relationship with Julie. "Yes."

I slump down in the driver's seat of my car and lean my head back against the headrest. I'm exhausted. Who knew digging through memories, thoughts, and emotions could be so tiring? I'm glad I scheduled my next appointment for the end of a workday. I don't know how I'll focus on anything for the rest of today.

The therapist gave me some homework to complete before my next session. She wants me to take the list of limiting beliefs we discovered during our hour together and come up with statements I can speak to myself to counteract them. I'm not sure how much help they'll be, but I want to give therapy a fair shot so I'm doing everything Gabi says.

Now back to the real world. Taking a deep, steadying breath, I pull my phone out of my pocket, preparing for the bombardment of messages I expect to have after an hour of not being available. I switch it off airplane mode and see my email, text, and voice mail numbers appear. It's not as bad as I'd feared. I start with voice mails.

The first one's from someone interested in local adoption and was referred by one of my other clients. I'll call them back after lunch. I hit play on the second one and my mouth curves into a wide smile when I recognize the voice.

"Hey, Jayson, it's Julie. I was calling to see if you might be free for lunch. I was thinking maybe Blue Goose? If I don't hear from you by noon, I'll assume you're busy. Hope your day's going well."

I pull the phone away from my ear. Two minutes to twelve. I click on her number and put the phone up to my ear.

"Hey, Jayson!"

My smile grows even wider at her enthusiastic greeting. "Hey, Julie. I just got your message. I'd love to go to Blue Goose with you."

"Great. Do you want to swing by here or just meet there?"

"I'm not at the office right now, so how about we meet out front of the restaurant?"

"Sounds good. How long will it take you?"

I go through the route in my head. "Probably about seven minutes, depending on traffic."

"Okay, see you soon!"

I hang up, click my seatbelt into place, and head back toward downtown, listening to my remaining messages over the car's audio. When I reach the restaurant after parking the car, I don't see Julie, so I pull out my phone and start working through my texts. Nothing too major, thankfully. I reply to a few and receive more in return. I'm working on yet another reply when something makes me look up. Julie's standing right in front of me, an amused look on her face. I wonder how long she's been standing in front of me. I drop my phone into a pocket and pull her in for a quick kiss and a prolonged hug. It feels so good having her in my arms. *This is why I'm going to therapy. Worth it.* I'd be content to stay like this indefinitely, but Julie's stomach growls loudly, killing the moment.

Julie's smile is now a concerned frown. "Is everything okay?"

"Yeah, why?"

"You were pretty focused on your phone. Are you having a really busy day?"

"No. I had my phone off for a while this morning and was just trying to catch up before you arrived."

"I suppose you turned it off so you could concentrate on important matters."

I analyze the statement. It's definitely true. Overcoming my fear of dogs is important to me. I don't want to tell Julie where I was in case it doesn't work out the way I hope. I'm also not ready for her to know just how much I like her. I just nod.

"Wish I could do that sometimes, but I worry about missing potential business, you know?"

"Should we really be accessible *all* the time, though?"

"Good point." She takes her phone from her purse and sets it to silent. "There. Now, let's eat." She grabs my hand and leads me into the restaurant.

Back at the office, I settle in at the conference room table to look over client files. Late in the day, there's a knock at the door. My aunt pokes her head in.

"I'm heading out for the day. You should, too."

I roll my neck around, feeling the stiffness of minimal movement for several hours. "You're probably right. I'll head out soon. Thanks for checking on me."

My phone vibrates on the desk with a text message. Julie sent me a kissy face emoji. I smile, pondering a response.

"What'd Julie say?"

My head snaps up from my phone to my aunt. I'd momentarily forgotten she was still here. How'd she know it was Julie? Does she have eagle eyes that can see my phone screen from that far away? The question must be obvious on my face, because she smirks and shakes her head.

"I know a smitten look when I see one. It's obvious you like her."

She walks over, pulls out the chair next to me, and sits, pinning me with a serious look that has me straightening in my seat. "You know I think of you like a son, right?"

I'm completely alert now. Whenever she says something like that, I know we're in for a serious, possibly unpleasant, discussion. I stay silent, my chest constricting, but I nod.

"I love you very much, so I would be remiss if I didn't ask you if you understand what you're getting yourself into by dating this woman. You're very intelligent and I trust you to make good decisions, but the world isn't as open-minded as your family. Are you prepared for everything this choice may bring you?"

"Yes, Aunt Alicia, I understand. I've considered the potential ramifications, but, as you can obviously tell, my feelings for Julie are strong. I'm prepared to see where things will go, but appreciate your concern."

She nods and pats my hand. "Okay. Just had to check."

I stand, pulling her into a hug. "Thanks. I love you."

"Love you, too." Her hold on me relaxes, and she steps back.

"Don't keep your girlfriend waiting for a response. Better yet, get out of here and go see her."

I'd love to, but seeing her means coming face-to-face with her dog. One therapy session was not enough to give me the courage to tackle that challenge. Still, I have hope I'll get there one day. But I'm too tired to have that conversation with my aunt right now. "Great idea, but I'm beat."

She shrugs. "Your life. I'll see you tomorrow."

After she's gone, I ponder a response to Julie's text, but am too worn out to be clever or flirty, so I respond with the same emoji. Maybe tomorrow I can be more creative. I organize my folders and take them to my desk before leaving the office.

36

Julie

"I STILL CAN'T believe you talked me into this," I say, staring up at the sign over the building. Memories flood my mind of the dozens of shows I've seen inside. They all feel tarnished from the last time I stepped foot inside The Xcape.

"I'm proud of you for facing your fear. I know it's difficult, but you shouldn't let your past keep you from enjoying the present." Jayson's hand, clutched tightly in my own, gives mine a reassuring squeeze.

"I suppose. Maybe he won't see me or remember me."

Jayson chuckles. "You don't give yourself enough credit. You're impossible to forget. Believe me."

That's meant to be a compliment, but it just makes dread pool in my gut in anticipation of seeing Xavier again after so long. "What if he's still with that bartender?"

"I doubt it. From what you've told me, he doesn't sound like someone who wants to settle down."

My head tilts in acknowledgment of Jayson's words. "That's true."

"The show starts in fifteen minutes. Should we go in and get something to drink?"

It's the moment of truth. I swallow down the bile rising in my throat. "I suppose."

"If you want to avoid the bar, I'd be happy to get us both drinks while you figure out where you want to stand for the show."

I give Jayson a grateful smile. "Thanks. That'd be great."

"Tell me now what you'd like in case it's hard to hear inside."

"It'll be fine until the band starts, but I'd like an Xcape, please."

"That's a drink?"

"It's their signature cocktail, an alcoholic pink lemonade. I'll look for a spot to the left of the stage. If you can't find me, send a text."

"I'm sure I can spot you in a crowd just by your hair."

I run a hand over the top of my head. My hair's in a sleek top knot in anticipation of how hot it'll be with everyone crammed together, but it's still a date, so I'm trying to look good for Jayson. I've dressed in skinny jeans tucked into black lace-up boots with a heel and a black tank top with Two Left Feet's logo on it that highlights my curves. He showed up in a pair of jeans that hugs his thighs and rear quite nicely and a fitted t-shirt that shows off his muscular chest, shoulders, and biceps. I'd like to run my hands all over his torso, but nervousness at possibly seeing Xavier keeps my desire in check. "Right."

I square my body with the entrance and will my legs to move, but they aren't complying.

"We really don't have to go in if you aren't ready," Jayson says, noticing my hesitancy.

"No, I want to. I'm just struggling to take the first step."

Jayson grins down at me. "Well, I can help you with that."

He releases my hand, then bends down in front of me. "Hop on, I'll carry you inside."

I laugh at the image of being piggy backed into the concert.

His concern's sweet, but I couldn't take the embarrassment if Xavier saw me on his back. It shouldn't matter what Xavier thinks, but if I'm going to see him, I want to appear put together.

"I appreciate the offer, but I'll walk."

He straightens and gestures for me to lead the way. My feet disengage from the piece of sidewalk I'm occupying, and move to the doorman. He scans the bar codes on my phone and ushers us inside.

Jayson looks around, then turns to me. "I'm heading to the bar now."

"I'm going in that door," I say, pointing, "and will be over to the left."

"Great. See you soon."

Jayson kisses my cheek, then turns away. I make a beeline for the door into the stage area, avoiding looking at the bar. I don't know what my body might do if I recognize anyone. Possibly have a nervous breakdown. I want to avoid all the drama tonight if possible.

When I pass through the doors, I pause and look around at the large, open room I used to spend so much time in. At the far end is the stage, a drum kit in the center and several guitars on stands resting near microphones. My excitement grows as my mind recalls all the fun I've had at the previous Two Left Feet shows. I hope Jayson enjoys it. He seems to enjoy novel experiences, so perhaps it'll entertain him even if he doesn't like the music.

The room is about half full but becoming more crowded by the minute. I make my way to the left side of the stage and smile at the girl next to me. She looks college age. I'm impressed the band has a younger following. Would it be weird to talk to her? Before I've decided, Jayson appears at my side and hands me a cup.

"An Xcape for my lady."

"Thanks."

"FYI, the bartenders are all men tonight."

My relief is palpable. One hurdle managed. "Next round is on me, then. Cheers."

I clink my plastic cup with Jayson's, which is filled with an amber liquid. "What'd you get?"

"Nothing fancy. Just the Sierra Nevada Pale Ale."

I scrunch up my nose. "I'm not much of a beer drinker, which is a shame with all the breweries here."

Jayson shrugs. "To each their own."

The lights flicker and dim. The crowd cheers in anticipation, and I grin at Jayson. "I hope this is as fun as I remember." I'm almost yelling to be heard over the buzzing crowd.

"We're about to find out."

The opening band enters from the right side of the stage and takes their places, picking up guitars and checking the sound one more time. The lead singer approaches his microphone. "Hello, Asheville!"

The crowd erupts. The man grins at the warm welcome and waits for it to die down a bit.

"We're Blueberry Jones and we're happy to be here with Two Left Feet tonight."

More cheers. "We're going to have a rocking good time, aren't we?"

The audience claps and whistles their agreement. "Let's get to it, then."

He nods to the drummer, who counts off with his sticks before starting the intro. The guitars join in and I feel the vibration of the instruments under my feet. I close my eyes, savoring the moment. I've missed this. It's so crazy to think I stopped doing one of my favorite things because of someone who's no longer a part of my life. I should evaluate other things I love but haven't done in a while.

Life's supposed to be enjoyed, but I shut down after Xavier. Maybe I'd have gotten back to things I love if the responsibility of owning a business hadn't piled onto my shoulders after Uncle Bill's death. Not that I blame him for my closed up life. I can see now I've used everything as an excuse to keep from getting hurt again, but now that I'm reengaging with life, I don't want to go back to how life was before.

My body moves to the music. I lift my face, my soul full of joy. When the song ends, I clap my free hand against my thigh. Jayson smiles at me. Maybe I should feel embarrassed about getting swallowed up by the experience, but I'm too happy to worry about what others think of me right now. I reach up, grab Jayson's shoulder, and pull him down for a kiss. When we separate, I lock eyes with him. "Thank you," I mouth, knowing there's no way he can hear me with the band playing right in front of us.

Jayson grins and gives me a quick peck in response. The volume in the room increases as the band moves into the chorus of the song and many in the crowd sing along. It occurs to me I've heard this song before and join in. The band plays a few more songs before announcing that Two Left Feet will be out in a few minutes.

"Do you want another drink?" Jayson says.

I down the last few drops from my cup. "Sure. I'll go get them this time."

He takes my empty cup. "No, stay. I'll go. I want to try a different beer, but I'm not sure which one. What would you like?"

"Another Xcape, please. I try to stick to one liquor per night."

"That's probably a smart plan. I'll be back. "He kisses me before heading toward the door at the back of the room.

I pull my phone from my pocket. I want to take a few pictures to document the enormity of this night. Angling myself so that The Xcape's logo is visible on the wall behind me, I snap a few shots. I'll get one with Jayson when he returns so I can give him proper credit for this big step.

"Julie?"

My head snaps up and unease trickles down my spine when I find myself face to face with Xavier Quinn.

37

Jayson

MY FOCUS IS trained on making sure I don't spill our drinks on my way back into the main hall. I look up to see how far I am from Julie and frown when I spot her. Something about her body language is off. Her shoulders are back and she's glaring at someone I can't see, her lips moving. I pick up my pace, no longer concerned about spilling. When I reach her, she looks over at me and something flickers in her face. She steps closer to me. I hand her a cup, then wipe my damp hand on the leg of my jeans.

"Thanks," she says, draining half of it in one gulp.

I turn my attention to the man staring at Julie. He's about her height, but built like a competitive weightlifter. His black t-shirt tugs against his muscular torso and arms. Tattoos cascade down his arms to his wrists. This must be her ex. While he's more muscled, I have him in height. Not that I expect an altercation. It is the man's place of business, after all.

"Hi, I'm Jayson," I say, extending the hand not holding my beer.

The man glances briefly at it, then returns his gaze to Julie. "I'd better get back to work. Let me know if you want to catch up sometime."

He winks at Julie and blood pulses in my veins. Maybe something *will* happen if the man keeps hitting on my girlfriend. Xavier turns and disappears into the crowd before I can say anything.

I follow him with my eyes until I'm sure he's not coming back before shifting my attention to Julie. She's shaking, though I can't decipher the emotions behind it. I wrap my arms around her, careful not to spill my drink on her. "Are you okay?"

She nods against my chest.

I kiss the top of her head, compassion welling up in my chest. "Do you want to leave?"

"No," she says, stepping away from me, her jaw set. "I came to see Two Left Feet, and that's what we'll do. I'm fine. Everything's fine."

"Whatever you want. If you change your mind, let me know."

"Thanks."

My heart lurches at her tight expression. Her anger is clear from the lines creasing her forehead to her narrowed eyes and puckered mouth. I want to draw her back to me, but she seems to want space, so I keep my arms to myself. "I assume that was Xavier."

"Yes."

"Do you want to talk about it?"

The lights flicker, drawing our eyes toward the stage.

"Let's talk after," she says.

Unable to maintain our awkward distance, I reach for her hand and squeeze it, an attempt to remind her I'm here for her. Her face relaxes from its tense expression and she tightens her fingers around mine. The crowd cheers and she turns back toward the stage, a smile finally gracing her face when the band comes out from the wing.

Guilt creeps up my spine knowing I put Julie in the position where she ran into her ex without me by her side. At least she agreed to talk about it after the show. Maybe it wasn't as terrible as I'm imagining. A guy can hope.

I hold Julie's hand the whole way to the car. I'm dripping with sweat and feel disgusting, but don't care because I had a fun time and Julie is just as sweaty. She grins up at me when I open her car door.

"Thanks for convincing me to come tonight. I haven't had this much fun in a long time. I'd nearly forgotten how much I love concerts."

"You're welcome. I had a lot of fun too. We should do it again."

Julie beams. "Sure. I'll check out who else is coming to town."

I close her door first and then get in on the other side. Taking her hand again, I breathe deep before broaching the subject that's been on my mind most of the night. "Do you want to talk about whatever happened while I was getting drinks?"

Julie wrinkles her nose, grimacing. "He just kind of appeared out of nowhere. He said he saw me come in and that he missed me."

"He missed you?" A strong, protective feeling wells up in my gut.

She rolls her eyes. "That's what he said. He acted like we were just old friends who'd been too busy to get together. He even flirted a little." She sticks out her tongue, her disgust clear. "It really wasn't long before you returned, but the whole thing just felt gross. When he bragged about dating a college student, all the anger I pushed down over the years came rushing up. If you hadn't returned when you did, I might have done something I'd regret."

She shakes her head. "He hasn't changed a bit. I don't know what I saw in him all those years ago. I wasted so much time wondering how things might have been different, but after tonight, I'm glad we're not together. I deserve so much better than him."

She shudders. I'm glad she's unimpressed by her ex, but keep this thought to myself. "Is it going to keep you from returning to The Xcape in the future?"

"No. I'd built everything up so much in my mind and seeing him again punctured it like a balloon. I was dumb and made a mistake. I'm older and wiser. I think I really can put the past behind me now."

I squeeze her hand. "I'm glad. Though I'm still sorry I put you in a position to be alone with him."

"Don't worry about it."

My lingering doubt must be noticeable on my face because Julie chuckles and tries to smooth out my forehead with her fingers.

"Really, Jayson, it's fine. I'm fine. Though, now that my adrenaline is waning, I'm feeling a little tired. Can we go home?"

I drive to Julie's apartment and put the car in park. Julie releases her seatbelt and leans toward me. I meet her in the middle of the car. After a few minutes, Julie pulls back and grins flirtatiously at me. "Do you want to come up for a bit?"

A part of me is already out of the car and pulling Julie into the building. The other part, the more powerful part, is trembling in fear of what's waiting behind her front door. I've made some progress in therapy, but am still not ready for an up close and personal experience with a dog. I don't want to reminder her of my dog phobia, so I play off my hesitation. "It's pretty late. We probably both need sleep before work tomorrow."

Julie's expression sobers. "Oh yeah, work. You're probably right. Thanks again for a great evening."

She gives me one more lingering kiss before exiting the car. I watch longingly after her as she walks up to her building door. She waves and smiles before disappearing inside. I sigh, put the car in gear, and head home.

38

SEPTEMBER

Julie

I PULL INTO the driveway and park, smiling at the cute two-story house. The front flower beds are neatly landscaped, with small bushes and a colorful smattering of perennials. On my way to the front door, I smell one of the knockout roses, inhaling its pleasant scent. The door swings open before I can press the doorbell, revealing a grinning Rachel. She pulls me into a hug.

"Your landscaping is gorgeous."

She releases me and smiles widely. "Thanks! Put down your stuff and I'll give you a tour before dinner."

I hand over the gift bag. "For you and Tom."

She looks inside and pulls out a bottle of wine. "Thanks!"

"There's more."

Placing the bottle on a nearby table, she removes the tissue paper. She gasps when she pulls out a gold-lidded box. "Ooooh, double thanks! Are there Blackouts in here?"

"And a couple Ancient Treasures for Tom."

"Great. We'll open the wine for dinner."

I wave my hand. "It's for you two to share whenever. I'm fine with water."

"Nonsense. It's our first dinner party at our new house. We should celebrate."

My forehead creases. I thought it was just the three of us for dinner. "Are more people coming?"

"Just Abbie. She's out back with Tom."

I relax. Only a family thing, then. "Okay."

Rachel takes my purse and hangs it on a hook above the table. "Let me show you the house."

She leads me upstairs, where there are two bedrooms and an office. The first floor comprises a foyer, a kitchen that opens into the dining area, a laundry room near the garage, a living room, and a third bedroom. We return to the kitchen to grab drinks and then head out back to join Tom and Abbie.

I hug Tom, realizing how much I miss having him as a roommate. It's kind of lonely having only a dog for company. Sadie's not great at surprising me with dinner or washing dishes while I'm at work like Tom was. "It smells good, bro. What are you grilling?"

"We're having chicken kabobs," Tom says.

"Yum. Hey, Abbie."

She waves her cup at me in greeting. "Hey, Julie. Have you started reading *The Great Alone* for group yet?"

"Not yet. I'm hoping to start it this weekend."

"It's pretty engaging. I finished it in a couple of days."

"That's what I like to hear. Rach, I'm sure you're already finished with it."

Rachel nods. "I am. I really enjoyed it."

I turn to survey the backyard. We're standing on a raised deck with steps down to a fenced-in yard. A couple of fallow raised garden beds line one side of the fence. "I really like your yard. It's got plenty of room for kids or a dog."

"Or both," Tom says, winking at Rachel.

I quirk an eyebrow. "Do you have big news to share? Is that what tonight's about?"

Rachel laughs and shakes her head. "No news. We just wanted our favorite siblings to see our new house!"

Abbie grins and elbows her playfully in the ribs. "I can't wait to tell Paul I'm your favorite sibling."

Rachel rolls her eyes and turns her focus on me. "Julie, how are things going with Jayson?"

"It's going well, I suppose."

"What does that mean?" Abbie asks.

I sigh, but am grateful for the opportunity to share my frustration with people I trust. "Jayson's afraid of dogs."

She grimaces. "Uh-oh."

"Uh-oh is right."

Rachel reaches over and covers my hand with hers. "Did you tell him Sadie's really sweet and doesn't bite or jump up?"

I nod, frowning. "It didn't seem to help. I really like Jayson, but I've had Sadie since she was a puppy. She's my family."

"What are you going to do?"

I shrug. It's the same question I've been asking myself lately, and I've only come up with one palatable solution. I don't love it, but I can't think of any other recourse. I know what I want to ask, but courage fails me. Maybe if I dance around my request, they'll get the hint.

"I've been feeling guilty lately for leaving Sadie in the apartment all day while I work. I didn't feel so bad when Tom was staying with me because she'd get company for a week or two a month. Hiring a dog sitter would help, but that just doesn't feel right to me."

"I could come by and walk her for you," Tom says.

"I couldn't impose on you like that. Especially now that you live here. It's out of your way."

"You know I wouldn't mind. I love Sadie."

My heart kicks up. We're getting somewhere now. Just a few more nudges. "I know you do."

"Maybe I could come by, pick her up, and keep her here for a few days at a time." Tom looks at Rachel, who shrugs and gives a slight nod.

Or maybe just one big nudge. "That's a possibility." I pause, gathering all the courage I can muster. "Is there any chance you two might consider taking Sadie permanently?"

My head swivels between Tom and Rachel, who converse silently through facial and body movements. I add quickly. "I know it's a big ask, so don't feel bad if the answer's no. It was just a thought."

Rachel turns, looking me straight in the eye. "Wow, Julie. This is a big deal. For all of us. I know how much you adore Sadie. If I'm reading between the lines, this is your way of telling us you want to make your relationship with Jayson work?"

I nod, grateful for her understanding. Inexplicably, my eyes fill with tears. I swallow the lump in my throat, but my voice still trembles slightly when I speak.

"I hate that I have to make a decision like this, but I really like Jayson. I don't think I've ever felt this way about anyone, not even Xavier."

Tom whistles. "Wow, that's saying a lot. Julie, I'm happy for you. Obviously, Rachel and I will need to discuss this more on our own, but we'd really like to help you out."

A tentative smile creases my lips. "I understand. A dog is an enormous responsibility and one that I took on, not you. I'd hate to lose her completely by giving her away to strangers, but ultimately, it's my problem."

Rachel puts an arm around my shoulders. "You're right, though. This yard would be great for a dog."

"The kebabs are ready," Tom says, moving the skewers to a plate and shutting the grill lid. "Let's eat."

My stomach churns with all the uncertainty I'm facing. Am I really willing to give up Sadie for a potential happily ever after with Jayson? I think so, but how can one really ever know where a relationship is heading? That it'll go the distance?

A glance at Rachel lets me know she's concerned for me. Guilt covers me like a blanket. This was supposed to be my brother's housewarming party and I've made it all about me. I can deal with my issues later. It's not like they're going anywhere. I take a deep breath and plaster on a smile.

"It smells delicious," I say, linking my arm through Rachel's and steering her inside.

39

Jayson

MY EYES FOLLOW Gabi's fingers as they move back and forth at a rapid pace. It's hard to keep up, but I'm familiar enough with the process now to know that's normal.

"Alright, Jayson. What came up for you right there?"

I open and close my hands. "I remember the way the gravel bit into my hands."

"Go with that."

Gabi resumes the finger movement.

"What popped up then?" she says.

"Feeling powerless to stop the pain."

"Okay. Your ten-year-old self felt powerless. What can your older self say to your younger self?"

I take a deep breath. "It wasn't your fault."

"Go with that."

My eyes track Gabi's fingers again.

"What came up?"

"I'm not powerless anymore." The words release something inside me and I straighten, feeling lighter.

I drop into the driver's seat of my SUV and lean back against the headrest. A faint smile forms on my lips. That was a good session. I definitely feel like I made more progress. While the dog attack was a scary experience for a small boy, I now have the physical ability and skills to fight off a dog if needed. Not that I expect to be attacked again. I almost feel silly for still being afraid of dogs, but Gabi reminded me that my brain is still trying to protect my 10-year-old self.

I'm still not quite ready to play fetch with Sadie or anything, but I can picture myself doing so eventually. A few months ago, that would have never seemed possible.

Pleased by the noticeable progress in my thoughts and feelings, I turn my mind to the next thing on today's schedule—lunch with Julie. I have just enough time to get to the parking garage and walk to Haywood Street Market, where we're meeting. A wide smile lights up her face when she spots me approaching. I pull her into a hug and give her a long kiss. Moments like this are a big part of why I'm doing the hard work of therapy.

"Hey there," Julie says. "Everything okay?"

"I'm fine. Why?"

"That was quite a greeting, considering I just saw you yesterday."

I relax my posture, hoping to look more casual than I feel. My feelings for Julie are growing stronger by the day. "What can I say? Seeing you makes me happy and, when I'm happy, I go a little overboard."

"Well, I'm certainly not complaining." Julie grabs my hand and pulls me through the doors.

"What do you want to get?" she says.

"I'm in the mood for a Cuban sandwich. How about you?"

"I think I want some dumplings and lo mein. Meet you at a

table?"

"Sure."

I let go of her hand and watch her until she turns the corner, then make my way to Papi's Pan Sandwich Shop. When my food is ready, I find a vacant table for two and take a seat. Julie joins me a minute later with her tray and we chat while we eat.

"You seem a little tired," Julie says. "Did you not sleep well?"

She reads me well these days, which I take as a sign things are going well between us. "I slept fine. I probably just need some food to perk me up."

"How was your morning?"

Is she on to me? Has she figured out what I've been doing? Can she tell that I'm hiding something from her? *Calm down. It's just an innocent question.* I want to tell her about therapy, but only once I'm finished and can consider it successful. It would be fun to surprise her on a walk with Sadie sometime. I think that's what I'm waiting for—the opportunity for a big reveal to show her what I've done for her.

There's no way she knows, I remind myself. I've only told my aunt, and that was to explain why I'm unreachable for an hour each week. Aunt Alicia was supportive when I told her. It feels good to have her in my corner. And it provides a little accountability to help me push through any discomfort I experience through the process. I realize Julie's still waiting for a response. I shake my head and give an embarrassed grin.

"Sorry about that. What did you say?"

"I asked about your morning, but something's occupying your mind. Do you want to talk about it?"

"No, it's nothing." She looks skeptical. "Really, I'm fine. How was your morning?"

"I'm glad you asked!" She nudges me playfully, breaking the slight tension between us. "I booked another wedding event."

"That's great! At the Arboretum?"

"No, this one's at the Homewood."

"What's that?"

"It's a castle."

I set down my sandwich and focus on Julie, disbelief creasing my forehead. "There's a second castle in Asheville besides the Biltmore?"

"I'd never heard of it either until the bride told me about it."

"That's pretty cool. Will this be your first wedding event not at the Arboretum?"

Julie nods. "I'm branching out!"

"Good for you. You're an amazing business woman."

"Thanks, Jayson." Her face flushes at my compliment and I don't think she's ever looked more beautiful. I could stare into her emerald eyes all day. She leans over and gives me a long, tender kiss. "I really appreciate your support and encouragement."

"You're welcome, Juicy Fruit."

Her nose wrinkles. "No. No food names, remember?"

I grin. "I know. It's just fun to tease you, Julie Bean."

"Ugh. Sometimes I wish I'd never told you about Xavier."

That sobers me right up. I put my hand on top of Julie's. "I'm glad you told me. It's important to know about one another's pasts. I never want to hurt you. If you really don't like me teasing you in that way, I'll stop."

"Thanks, Jambalaya. That's sweet of you to say."

It's my turn to scrunch up my face. "Yuck. That's definitely a no. Maybe I'll try a different route. Like Crown Jules. Or Freckles. Oooh, yes, Freckles!"

She reaches up to her face, running her fingers along the freckles on her cheeks. "Mmmm. I may actually like Julie Bean better."

"Too late."

"Guess that means I need to work harder on a nickname for you." Julie's lips pursed as she thinks. When her eyes sparkle and a slow grin spreads across her lips, I know I'm in trouble. The mischievous look in her eye tells me I may have made a mistake goading her about nicknames. "I've got it."

"I'm a little nervous."

"Then, I won't tell you now. I'll wait and use it at a more opportune time." She leans back and crosses her arms over her chest, a smug look on her face.

I shake my head. "Nope. Don't like that either. Just tell me now and put me out of my misery."

When she leans forward, her forearms on the table, her eager expression tells me I've fallen into her trap. "You sure?"

"Yes, I'm sure."

"Sweet Lips."

I rear back, appalled. "What?!"

"I mean, I do love your kisses."

"I'm cool with *that*, believe me, but Sweet Lips? It isn't very manly."

Julie shrugs. "Too bad it's ultimately up to me."

She plays hard ball. I like it. I bet she'd make a brilliant lawyer herself. "Okay, I'll drop Freckles if you drop Sweet Lips."

"Deal."

She holds out her hand. "Let's make it official."

I shake my head in amusement but take her hand.

"You think you're pretty clever, don't you?"

"If I'm going to be dating a lawyer, I should probably work on my negotiating skills, right?"

My heart squeezes with joy. I love being with Julie. She's fun and smart and beautiful and keeps me on my toes. I reach across the table, place my hand behind her head, and pull her face to mine. Our lips press together before I shift my head slightly and deepen the kiss, trying to express everything I'm feeling through my actions.

After a few moments, I pull back, remembering we're surrounded by people. A look at Julie's flushed face gives me the impression she enjoyed it as much as I did.

I probably have a stupid, smitten look on my face, but I really don't care. Julie is amazing and exciting and surprising and like no other woman I've met. My heart slams against my ribcage at the realization I'm falling in love with her. The thought is both exhilarating and scary. Now I have no choice but to overcome my fear of dogs. I want nothing to stand in the way of this relationship.

40

Julie

PLACING THE LAST chair on the stack, I turn and survey the room. Abbie rolls the round fold-up table over to the wall and leans it against the chairs. Rachel's at the sink, rinsing out the coffee carafe. I enjoy the new ritual of cleaning up after book club. It's an opportunity to spend more time with my sister-in-law and Abbie. "What else needs to be done, Rachel?"

Rachel makes a quick sweep with her eyes. "I think we've done it all. Thanks for your help."

"No problem. I've been meaning to ask, how's your new manuscript going?"

Rachel turns off the water, grabs a towel, and dries the carafe. "It started out a little slow," she says, returning the carafe to the beverage table. "But the action's picking up and I have an idea of where things are leading. I may have to go back and cut the first chapter so the book starts with a bang, but that can wait for the first round of edits."

"What's the overall premise?"

She straightens, eyes shining, clearly excited about this new book. "Macy Graves discovers a plot to overthrow the Costa Rican government and enlists the help of fellow CIA operative Rhys Carlson to stop it."

"That sounds action-packed."

"It should be. Tom's about got me convinced to take a trip for research purposes, but I know he really just wants us to go on vacation."

"Well, that sounds wonderful to me," I say. "I can't remember the last time I've gone on a real vacation. Just home to see the family and a quick trip to NYC for Charlie's wedding."

"It sounds like you could use one," Abbie says. "Why don't you make it happen?"

"Probably because the idea of a solo vacation sounds a little depressing. Besides, I don't even know where I'd go."

"I'd be happy to go with you. I know how awkward things can be for us single women. We have to support one another."

"Julie's not exactly single," Rachel says, looking my way. "Am I right?"

I can't stop the smile from spreading across my face. "That's true."

"Oh, yeah?" Abbie says.

"She and Jayson are dating," Rachel says.

Abbie narrows her eyes. "Is this the guy that's friends with Carlos?"

"Yes," I say, "but they're both great guys. Perhaps it was just the immaturity of high school. Carlos seems very grounded and trustworthy now."

Abbie shrugs. "Maybe. I just hope I never run into him again."

"Then stay away from the River Arts District. He has a studio over there."

"Carlos is an artist?" Rachel says.

"Yes, and a pretty good one, too. He showed me pictures of his stuff."

Rachel nods thoughtfully. "That makes sense. I remember

him designing theater sets in high school. Anyway, somehow we've gotten off topic. Do you think you could convince Jayson to take a vacation with you?"

"I don't know. Our careers are pretty demanding, but we'd probably both benefit from some time away."

"And some serious one-on-one time, I'm sure."

"I can't say I don't like the sound of that." I imagine us walking hand-in-hand along a beach and my cheeks warm.

"It seems like you two fit well together," Rachel says. "He's gotten you to spend more time away from the store, which is good. And you really seem to like him."

My heart pounds as I turn over Rachel's words in my head. Jayson's definitely helped curb my workaholic tendencies. He's fun to be around and is extremely supportive. I can definitely see us together long term. My eyes widen at this revelation.

"What is it?" Rachel says, noticing the change in my expression.

I swallow, wondering if she can hear my heart slamming into my ribs. "I think I'm falling in love with Jayson."

Rachel squeals and pulls me into a hug. "Oh yay! I'm happy for you."

"I'm glad *you're* happy. My stomach is churning with nerves."

"I know it's a little scary, but really it's a good thing, right Abs?"

"Sure." Abbie nods, but there's no enthusiasm in her voice.

I release my hold on Rachel, my throat tight and tears pricking my eyes. "Thanks. I honestly didn't think I'd ever be ready for a new relationship, but Jayson just kind of burrowed himself into my life and heart. Speaking of my heart, how's Sadie doing over at your place?"

Rachel's smile dims with the change of subject. "Sadie's adjusting well. She likes the yard. Tom's lavishing her with love."

Sorrow pangs in my chest. It's good to hear, but it still hurts.

"I'm glad she has such a good place to live."

"Why's your dog at Rachel's house?" Abbie says.

"Jayson has a fear of dogs. If I really want to make an honest go of our relationship, I couldn't ignore the obvious problem between us."

Abbie frowns, sympathy washing over her face. "Oh. I'm sorry. What did Jayson say about it?"

"I haven't told him. I didn't want him to feel bad about something he can't control."

"Wow. You must really like him to give Sadie away."

I nod, a fresh wave of sadness cascading over me. "It's been hard, but knowing she's with people I trust and still close enough to visit has made things easier."

"Speaking of visiting, I had something made for you," Rachel says, digging into her purse and setting a shiny new key in my outstretched palm. "Please come over whenever you want."

"Thanks." Fresh tears well up in my eyes at the gesture. "You're the best. Thank you for taking care of my Sadie."

"Not a problem. And, hey, maybe Jayson will eventually warm up to Sadie and you can have her back."

If only it were that simple. "Not likely, but I appreciate your positivity."

41

Jayson

THE SHARP CRACK of the can opening is a welcome sound. I lift it to my mouth and take a long swig. The ice-cold beer lowers my temperature from the inside out. Kicking the cooler closed, I scan the backyard from my spot on the porch. It's an unseasonably hot day, but perfect for a Vega Family Cookout. Near the back corner of the yard, Carlos is laughing with a couple of guys, probably cousins. Two of Carlos's sisters, Sara and Monica, fix hot dogs at the food table. I'm struck by how similar the women look even though they're two years apart. Carlos's third sister, Angelica, is cuddled up on a two-seater swing with her husband, James.

All the Vega women are knockouts, though I'll never say that out loud to Carlos. He'd be horrified to know I think they're attractive. Though, to be fair, I'd be weirded out if Carlos said something similar about Britt. I smile and wave when Angelica catches me looking at her. She waves back. There are a few other familiar faces, probably aunts and uncles. Sometimes I'm a little jealous Carlos has so much family living in the area. At least I have my sister, aunt, and uncle. It's better than nothing.

I step off the porch and head in Carlos's direction. He waves me over when he spots me.

"Jayson, you made it. You remember my cousins, Tomás and Matteo?"

"Of course I do," I shake their hands. "Hot day."

"Yeah. Thanks for bringing me a beer," Carlos says, gesturing at the one in my hand.

I take another swig, finishing it. "I need another. I'll grab you one."

"I'll go with you." Carlos nods at his cousins. "Hasta luego, hermanos."

We walk back across the yard to the porch and the drink coolers. "Did you just call your cousins, brothers?"

"I did. I've known them so long, that's what they feel like to me. Especially since I have three sisters. Have you eaten yet?"

I open the cooler closest to me and grab two cans, tossing one to Carlos. "Nah. Just arrived."

Carlos opens the can and drinks deeply, releasing a satisfied "ahhhh" when he's finished. "Let's make plates and find some shade."

I bypass the hotdogs in favor of the empanadillas, rellenos de papa, and arroz con gandules. Carlos's family can cook. I'm always thrilled to be invited to their parties.

We fill plates and carry them over to a couple of empty chairs shaded under a giant maple tree. The savory empanadilla delights my tastebuds. "Oh man, I've got to visit Puerto Rico. This food is amazing."

Carlos grins. "I know you only come to these things for the food, but it's still good to see you. Now that basketball's over, we'll have to find more reasons to get together."

I gesture around the yard. "I'm good with coming to more family cookouts."

"The issue with that is I see my family enough as it is. I was thinking more like going to the movies or something."

"Sure, that'd be cool."

"I thought you were bringing Julie today."

I swallow my food. "She has a wedding event. She sends her regrets."

He says nothing, but I turn toward him when I feel his eyes on me. He's studying me like he's trying to figure something out. I grow uncomfortable when he continues to stare at me. "What?"

"You really like her, don't you?"

A smile breaks across my face. "I do. I think she could be *the one*."

"Whoa. That's pretty serious."

"I know."

"I don't want to rain on your parade, but you haven't really dated many people. Are you sure it's not just infatuation?"

I shake my head. He isn't saying anything I haven't already considered myself.

"No. I mean, sure, I want to be with her all the time, but I also admire her business acumen. We're both serious about our careers and respect one another. Our goals seem to line up. And I think I love her."

He nods. "I suppose I can't argue with that. I'm happy for you, Jay."

Glancing around the yard, I notice Angelica looking our direction. She's tilting her head and raising her eyebrows, contorting her face into crazy expressions. I nudge Carlos with my elbow. "Hey, is your sister okay?"

He jerks his head up from his plate and looks around. "Which one?"

"Angelica."

"Oh, right. There's something I wanted to talk to you about."

His words make me immediately wary. I never know whether that means he has an idea for some insane adventure like hiking up the side of a volcano, needs me to help him move one of his outrageously heavy sculptures, or wants my opinion about the latest season of the shows we both watch. Hopefully, it's the last one, but I doubt it. "What's up?"

"Angelica and James have been talking about adopting, and she wanted me to ask if you'd be willing to meet with them and talk through the process. You know so much about what's involved, and they want to know everything before they commit to it."

My muscles relax, grateful they're not being asked to move some art this time around. "That's great! I love that they're considering adopting. I'd be more than happy to talk with them."

Carlos gives a thumbs up sign, and I turn in time to see Angelica clasp her hands together and smile. She blows me a bunch of air kisses. I wave back. "Tell her to call me and we'll set something up."

"I will, thanks."

"Are you ready to be an uncle?"

Carlos's smile drops and his eyes widen. "Oh man, I hadn't even thought about that part of it."

I smile. "Well, I'm sure you'll be an awesome tío."

He nods slowly, his smile returning. "Tío Carlos. I like the sound of that."

42

Julie

THE DELICIOUS AROMA of my lamb gyro wafts out of the bag in my hand, making my mouth water. My steps quicken when my stomach rumbles. I'm in the middle of completing a wedding cake order, but need to eat so I can stay focused. Hence the quick stop at Haywood Street Market. When I pass by Apollo's Tavern, the place with a huge Greek chicken salad and to-die-for homemade dressing, I glance in the window. Something catches my eye and speeds up my heartbeat, so I pause for a closer look.

Over at a table near the back is a beautiful woman with long, straight black hair wearing a dress that flatters her curvy body. She doesn't look familiar, so what made me pause? My gaze flickers to the woman's companion, whose back is to me. He's a tall man in a crisp, white dress shirt and short, black hair. I eye the navy suit jacket on the back of the chair and goosebumps rise on my arms. I definitely recognize that jacket.

My heart is in my throat as I watch the woman pat the man's arm before resting her hand leisurely on top of his. The woman turns her head, laughs, and then points at something inside the restaurant. The man turns to look and his profile leaves no doubt it's Jayson sitting in a restaurant with a beautiful woman. He hasn't removed his hand from underneath hers. My heart squeezes uncomfortably.

There could be a reasonable explanation for what I'm seeing. Maybe she's a client, and he doesn't want to offend her. It's not like he's actually holding her hand or anything. I'm on the verge of going into the restaurant and clearing things up when the woman clasps her hands to her chest in what looks like adoration. Her eyes brighten and her smile beams like the sun. There's no ignoring her beauty, but clients are allowed to be gorgeous.

The woman grabs Jayson's hand with both of hers and then leans over the table toward Jayson, her lips pursing. I want to turn away, afraid of what's happening, but a stronger part of me keeps my eyes open, determined to witness whatever this is. A server passes in front of my view and when it's clear again, the woman is pulling back toward her side of the table, her cheeks pink. This only adds to her beauty. My heart deflates like a punctured balloon. This isn't a client meeting at all. Jayson's seeing another woman.

I pace around the living room at Rachel's house, trying to get my thoughts in order. My stomach feels like there's a swarm of bees inside. My back is damp with perspiration, and I have to pause and grab the couch when a bout of dizziness hits me. Sadie's lying on the floor, tracking me with her eyes, but when I stop, she hops up and leans against my leg for support. I reach down and bury my hand in her fur, looking for something to anchor me.

I'm not sure how I ended up here. I should be at the store finishing up the order, but some part of me needed to be near a friendly face, even if it's furry. Rachel's probably at work, but I'm not sure why Tom isn't home. No matter. It's probably better I have some time alone to process what I just witnessed.

Facts first. Jayson was in a restaurant with another woman. He'd told me he couldn't have lunch because he was meeting with clients. Plural. I only saw one person at his table, and it certainly didn't look like they were working. That looked like a personal matter. A very *intimate* personal matter. I shake my head to get rid of the images in my mind. I can see why he's attracted to her. She's undeniably beautiful.

We haven't explicitly said we're exclusive, but Jayson's been calling me his girlfriend. He has to know how I'd feel about him dating someone else while we're together. *Which is obviously why he didn't tell me.*

If he'd said he wanted to see other people simultaneously, I would have refused, and that would have been the end of that. I wouldn't have gotten so emotionally involved and my heart wouldn't be breaking now. Tears well up in my eyes at the thought that something that started off so well has gone up in flames, scorching my heart to ash. *Keep it together, Julie. You're stronger than this. A man shouldn't be able to break you.*

I pick up a pillow from the couch and scream into it. Weight presses against my leg and I look down to where Sadie's staring up at me. I reach down and scratch her head, embarrassed at how I'm behaving, and fall onto the couch. Sadie jumps up and curls herself against me. I wrap an arm around her, absently rubbing her side. I can't believe I gave her up for a man. What a terrible pet parent I am.

Should I tell him what I saw? No, that would be too humiliating. He obviously doesn't care about me as much as I care about him. No need to give away my deep feelings for him. I can just tell him we aren't working out. I don't have to justify my reasoning and it lets me keep my dignity. He probably won't care anyway since he's got the bombshell who's obviously smitten with him. It's best to make a clean break.

Of course, I'll have to avoid Hill of Beans now. I can always send Emily to pick up smoothies. Problem solved. But what about my events at the Arboretum? It requires working with his sister, after all. What if Brittina knows Jayson's dating multiple women at the same time? Was he even telling the truth about not dating much in college? He could have just said what he thought I wanted to hear. The thought sparks an ember of anger inside. I can't believe he played me.

A tear slips from my eye and I can't tell if I'm sad crying or angry crying. Probably a little of both. I give myself a few minutes to release the emotions swirling inside through my tear ducts before trying to pull myself together again.

I can't let my personal life ruin my professional one. I'll just have to ignore Jayson if we run into each other at the Arboretum. Besides, I usually only have to deal with the dessert setup. I can always send someone from my staff to stay if needed. See? I'll be fine.

Now, if only the ache in my chest could be managed as easily. I rub circles over my sternum, hoping the gesture will encourage my heart to unclench. It doesn't. Maybe if I tell someone, it'll start the healing. But first, I have to figure out how I'm going to break it off with Jayson. A text is definitely too impersonal, but I don't think I can stand to see him face-to-face right now. I'll call him this evening.

The sound of the garage door startles me and I sit up quickly, wiping my hands across my cheeks. That must be Tom back from wherever he was. I don't want him to see me like this. I hear some shuffling in the kitchen and fan my face, hoping it's not red and blotchy.

A feminine giggle makes me freeze. I shoot up off the couch when I hear a soft moan. I turn toward the kitchen, but then cover my eyes when I see a flash of skin. It's probably just an arm, but I don't want to be proven wrong. I clear my throat, then shout to make sure I'm heard.

"Hey, guys. Julie's here."

It's eerily silent for a few seconds, and then I hear Tom's voice, overly chipper.

"Julie! What are you doing here?"

My hands are still over my face when something gently circles my wrists and pulls them down. Tom's humored grin confirms what I suspected.

"I just came to see Sadie, but I think I'll go. Give you two some privacy."

Rachel enters the living room from the kitchen, smoothing down her hair. "Hey, Julie. We didn't know you were here."

"My car's parked out front."

"Is it? I guess we missed it."

Rachel looks over at Tom, eyebrows raised. He shakes his head and shrugs.

"No worries. I'll get out of your way. Just stopped by to see Sadie for a bit."

"Are you sure? You don't have to leave on our account."

I don't miss the exasperated look Tom sends Rachel's way. That's exactly what he wants.

"No, no. It's fine."

I head for the door without turning around. "Have fun."

As soon as the words leave my mouth, I wince. I can't believe I just told my *brother* to have fun with his wife. No time to correct myself. Instead, I continue through the front door, shutting it firmly behind me. When I drop into the driver's seat of my car, I pause for a moment to get my bearings. That was an unexpected turn of events. It took my mind off of my own issues for a few minutes, but now they're back. I lean against the headrest while I think for a second. Deciding, I grab my phone and dial a number. It rings twice, then connects. "Hey, it's Julie. Are you busy right now? I could really use someone to talk to."

"I'm free," Abbie says. "Where are you?"

"I'm at Rachel's house."

"I'll be there in ten minutes."

"No, don't!" I don't want to explain why we can't meet at their house, no need for both of us to be traumatized, so I quickly think of an alternate location. "Can we meet at Wolfe Ridge Park?"

"Sure. See you soon."

Abbie's eyes are wide and she shakes her head, her mouth pursed with righteous indignation. "Wow, Julie. That sucks."

I slouch down on the bench next to her. "I know."

"I'm honored you called, but why me?"

I heave a deep sigh. I could really use Sadie's comforting presence right now. Instead, I wrap my arms around my torso. "You're the only other single person I know. My brothers and best friend are married, and they'd probably talk about how there are other fish in the sea, but they haven't been in the sea in years. I just need someone else who's still in the dating world and understands the water has a lot of undesirable creatures in it as well."

"Gotcha. Do you know what you'll say to Jayson?"

"Not quite, but I'll figure it out."

"I don't envy you."

I grimace. "Me neither."

We sit in silence until a question pops into my head. I blurt it out before I can think too hard about it. "Have you ever been in love?"

"Once." If the question surprises her, she doesn't show it.

"I gather it didn't work out."

"Obviously."

"What happened?"

She's quiet, staring out across the park. I wonder if I've crossed a line, but then she sighs and turns to face me.

"We met in college and dated about a year. He was fun and

enjoyed adventures like I do. We were always doing something new. But then, as graduation approached, he seemed to flip a switch. He decided it was time to get married and fulfill his responsibilities. He told me all about our future that he'd planned out."

She scowls. "We'd get married the following summer at the same place where his parents and brothers had, move to Maryland where his family lived, and I'd stay home to raise our four kids. Three boys and a girl, by the way."

My face screws up in distaste. "Yikes. That doesn't really sound like you, from what I know."

Abbie nods, her mouth in a straight line. "You're right. It's not. I told him he was welcome to that life, but he'd have to find someone else to be his wife. And that was it."

"He sounds like a bit of a control freak."

Abbie twists her lips to the side. "That's the strange thing. He really wasn't. Apparently, his father told him he could do whatever he wanted during college, but once he graduated, they expected him to join the family business and settle down. He'd failed to mention that when we started dating."

I wrinkle my nose, my heart lurching on Abbie's behalf. "Ouch, I'm sorry. It sounds like he misled you."

"I agree. But I feel like I dodged a bullet, so for that I'm grateful."

"That's a good attitude to have."

"Well, it didn't come overnight, that's for sure. It took me a while to see the blessing in the pain."

Abbie glances at her phone and stands up. "I hate to go, but I have students to get ready for basketball workouts this afternoon. There are ankles to tape and injuries to assess."

I nod. "I understand. Thanks for giving me some of your time. I feel a little better now that I've told someone."

"You're welcome. Call or text if you need to talk some more.

I'm free tomorrow morning if you need another face-to-face."

"Thanks, Abbie. That's very generous of you."

Abbie heads for the parking lot, but I stay seated, pondering our conversation. It probably is better that I found out about Jayson's double life before it was too late. Aww, who am I kidding? It's already too late.

I know I deserve to be the only woman in a man's life and shouldn't settle for less, but a small part of me wishes I could ignore what I saw earlier today. At least I found out before I married him, but I can't believe I picked another cheater. I guess Abbie was right about staying away from Carlos and his friends. Maybe I'm just that gullible, wanting to believe the best about others. Well, I've been fooled twice. It won't happen again.

43

Jayson

I'M SURROUNDED BY piles of files in preparation of an upcoming adoption court hearing. It's really exciting being part of making a child an official member of a family who loves them. A knock startles me. My aunt's face peeks around the conference room door.

"Don't work too late, Jayson. It's good to have a life, too, you know."

I'm shocked to see it's nearly nine p.m. Where did the day go? "You're one to talk since you're here, too."

"I'm leaving right now. Do you need anything before I go?"

"No, I'll be fine. Thanks."

She opens the door wider and steps into the room. "You don't have a date with Julie?"

"Not tonight."

My phone vibrates on the table in front of me. I smile when Julie's name pops up. "Speaking of which," I say, holding up the phone, "she's calling."

She blows me a kiss and leaves, shutting the door behind her. I slide the answer button to the right and put the phone to my ear.

"Well, hello there, beautiful. I was just talking about you. Guess you could feel it."

"Oh yeah? What were you saying?"

The flat tone in Julie's voice turns the fluttery feeling in my belly to lead. Is something wrong? Maybe I'm just tired and misreading the situation. "Nothing really. My aunt asked if we had a date scheduled for tonight."

"Ah."

Silence drags for a minute, which is weird since she called me. Shouldn't she be guiding this conversation? Something's definitely not right. "Is everything okay? You sound odd."

"No, things aren't okay."

My heart lodges in my throat. I jump to my feet, grab my suit coat off the back of my chair, ready to find her and fix the problem, whatever it may be. "What happened? Where are you?"

Julie sighs loudly through the phone and my heart pounds painfully inside my chest. I check my pockets for my keys, but her next words make me freeze.

"Jayson, this isn't working out."

I'm stunned. Surely I'm not understanding correctly. "What do you mean?"

"I don't think we should date anymore." Her voice wobbles on the last word, telling me she's upset.

"What? Why? I thought we were having fun together."

Another deep sigh. "We *were* having fun, but I just don't think we're in sync with what we want. I'm sorry to do this over the phone, but I didn't want to drag things out."

My brain scrambles to make sense of her words. "I don't understand. This seems so sudden. Tell me what happened. We can fix whatever the issue may be."

"No. We're just not compatible. Goodbye, Jayson."

"Julie, wait—"

The call disconnects, and I pull the phone away from my ear. What in the world just happened? Everything was going so well between us. Did I miss signs that something was wrong? I fall back into my chair, letting my coat drop to the floor. My elbows perch on the end of the conference table, and I cradle my head in my hands. Racking my brain to come up with a plausible explanation for Julie's phone call yields nothing. She'd sounded certain about her proclamation, though her voice wavered toward the end. She obviously has feelings for me if she's emotional.

I consider driving over to her apartment, but don't know what I'd say. I'd also have to face Sadie, which I'm not quite ready for. I stare into space, trying to process our brief conversation. It makes no sense to me. Did Julie find someone else? Was my inability to hang out with her and her dog too frustrating?

I curse myself for my fear of dogs. Why did I have to fall in love with someone who makes me face my greatest fear? I suppose it's actually a good thing. My feelings for Julie led me to therapy. At my last appointment, Gabi had praised my progress. Which apparently doesn't matter now. It's too little, too late.

Numbness invades my chest. At least the shock will stave off the pain for a little while. I straighten up and look down at the table before me. There's no way I'm getting any more work done tonight. I shove papers into my briefcase, turn off the lights, and make my way to the parking garage with a head full of questions and a heart that's shattered.

44

Julie

MY BRAIN SWIRLS with melancholy thoughts, making it a struggle to concentrate on work. I haven't seen or heard from Jayson in over a week. It's been radio silent since that tense phone call. *This is what I wanted, right?* I should be grateful he respects my wishes, but my stubborn heart still longs for him. It baffles me I gave my heart away so easily again. I should know better. Didn't my relationship with Xavier teach me anything? I sigh, frustrated with my stupidity. How could I make the same mistake twice? I'm done with love. I don't need it, and it obviously doesn't agree with me.

"Julie," Emily says, knocking on the door frame to the office, "there's someone—" She stops mid-sentence, scrutinizing me. "Are you okay?"

I meet my best friend's eyes and tears well up immediately at the concerned look on her face. I shake my head, unable to speak for fear the tears will spill over. I look at the ceiling and blink, trying to keep them from falling. Emily walks quickly to where I'm seated at the desk and wraps her arms around my shoulders.

"What's wrong?"

My hands reach up and squeeze Emily's arms, grateful for her presence. I swallow hard, trying to force my emotions back down, but then a sob escapes from my mouth. Before I know it, I'm crying into Emily's shoulder. She rubs my back and makes soothing sounds until I'm able to calm down. I release my hold on Emily, lean back and take a deep breath, fanning my flushed and tear-stained face. Emily passes me a tissue, which I use to wipe my eyes, cheeks, and nose. I take a few stuttering breaths to get myself back together.

"Whew. Sorry about that."

"Hey, I'm your best friend. It's what I'm here for."

"But still. It's not exactly professional." I wave a hand around the office.

Emily puts her hands on her hips and tsks. "We can't just turn our feelings on and off with a switch. Is this about Jayson?" I nod. "What happened?"

I drop my head, embarrassed. "Nothing. I just miss him and I feel so stupid for letting myself get involved so quickly. I should have listened to my gut when we met. It said he seemed too cocky and self-assured. I shouldn't have trusted him."

Emily puts a comforting hand on my shoulder. "Hey, don't be so hard on yourself. He seemed like a nice guy to me, too. It's always a risk to open yourself up to someone, but when you find someone who truly values you and guards your heart, it makes all the past heartaches worth it."

I roll my eyes. "I'm glad it worked out for you."

"And it can work out for you, too."

"There's obviously something wrong with me. I can't keep a guy's attention. Somehow, I'm not enough for them."

"They're the ones with issues, not you. You're a wonderful person."

I grab another tissue and swipe at my eyes to get rid of any errant tears, then toss it in the trash. "Whatever. I don't want to talk about this anymore."

"Okay, but I'm here if you change your mind."

I can feel the beginning of a headache and rub my temples. "I know, thanks. Was there something you needed before I assaulted you with my emotions?"

"There's a woman who wants to talk to you about designing a cake for a party. Do you want her to make an appointment for a later date?"

"No, I'll be fine. Give me a minute and then send her back."

Emily gives me one last pat on the shoulder before turning and exiting the office, shutting the door behind her.

I take a few deep, steadying breaths, sip some water, pat down my hair and clothing, and pull an event form from my top desk drawer. When there's a knock on the door, I get up to answer it. After one more fortifying breath, I pull open the door and freeze mid-smile. Standing in front of me is a short, curvy woman with long, dark, straight hair, and a beautiful face I recognize immediately as belonging to the woman I saw having lunch with Jayson.

My breath quickens as thoughts race through my head. Did she notice me staring in the window the other day? Did Jayson tell her about me? What in the world is she doing here? As quickly as I can, I push the thoughts down, forcing myself into professional mode. I stick out my hand. "Hi, I'm Julie."

The woman smiles and accepts my hand. "I know who you are. I'm Angelica."

Her words put me on guard. Is she here to tell me to stay away from Jayson? If so, she doesn't have to worry. "What can I do for you?"

"I heard you make amazing cakes and I'm in the market for one."

What? Why does she want me to make her a cake? "What's the occasion?"

"My husband and I are adopting a baby."

Jayson's married? He doesn't wear a ring, so how was I to know? I can't believe I bought his "too busy to date" act. He probably just said it so I'd feel like we were on the same page. The truth is, he's busy because he already has a wife. My heart pulses with pain. I wrestle to keep my face neutral to resist giving away my tumultuous thoughts and emotions. *Be professional, Julie.* "How exciting."

Angelica's brilliant smile feels like a sucker punch. "It is. We can't wait to be parents."

Jealousy flares inside me. I bet Jayson will be a great dad. It makes no sense why he'd date me, knowing it couldn't go anywhere. If he's going to be a father, how does he expect to have time for a mistress? The thought makes my stomach clench. Because that's what I was—his *mistress*. Do I tell Angelica? I know how devastating it is to find out something like this, but she should know before bringing a child into this mess.

"The baby isn't due until January, but my parents offered to host a baby shower. I love planning parties, so I'm in charge of everything. I was hoping you have an opening for the second Saturday in November."

She seems nice. The thought of being mean to her feels like injuring a baby deer. At a loss for how to graciously bring up the subject of infidelity, I hear myself speak almost on autopilot. "Let me look at my calendar."

I lead Angelica over to the desk and wave my hand at the chairs. When she sits, I take my seat behind the desk and flip my calendar over to November. My heart sinks at the blank square staring up at me. Part of me hoped I had already booked the date for an event, but it's wide open. I hadn't even thought about doing desserts for baby announcements, but I'm sure expanding to those types of events would be lucrative. "I'm available that day. Where are you having the shower?"

"The Arboretum. They have a gorgeous indoor space that will

hold everyone, and Britt's giving us a discount, which is even better."

Of course, Jayson would use his sister for this event. *Maybe I can send Nikki or Emily to do the setup and teardown at the event to avoid all the awkwardness that's bound to ensue at my ex-boyfriend's baby shower.* Though maybe in two months I'll be completely over him. *Yeah, right.* He obviously isn't broken up about our breakup. "You're right. The main hall is beautiful."

"Jayson and Britt both speak highly of you, so I can't wait to work with you. He said your truffles are to-die-for, so I definitely want some of those to go along with the cake."

At the mention of his name, my stomach heaves and my eyes dart to the trash can at my feet. *Please don't let me vomit in front of Jayson's wife.* Is she rubbing their relationship in my face? She doesn't seem like the type. Maybe she has no clue we were together. I should tell her. It's not her fault her husband's a cheater. If someone as beautiful as her can't keep a guy's full attention, there's no hope for the rest of us. Angelica's talking about the type of cake she wants, most of which I've missed because of my troubled thoughts. I quickly refocus my attention.

"We love hiking, so I thought the truffles could look like small boulders around a cake shaped like a mountain? I know it's not a traditional baby cake, but we're not exactly traditional people."

I'll say you're not traditional people. Maybe she knows about me and doesn't care. I obviously wasn't a threat to her. Well, if this is who Jayson really is, I'm glad to be rid of him. I didn't know he enjoys hiking. He didn't once mention it as an activity we should do together. Guess that was information reserved for people he really cares about.

"I can definitely make your vision happen. May I ask how you two met?" Yes, I'm a glutton for punishment.

"We met while hiking. The sole of my hiking boot came off when I crossed a stream. I slipped on a rock and fell into the cold water. Jay scooped me up out of the water and carried me to a log to assess my injuries. I ended up with a twisted ankle and he carried me back down the mountain and drove me to a doctor." Angelica's face glows with fond remembrance. She obviously loves telling this story.

"You call him Jay?"

"It's my nickname for him."

My ears heat with indignation. They have nicknames for each other. Of course, they do.

"What's Jay's nickname for you?"

"He calls me his Angel."

"Ah." I just stop myself from rolling my eyes. Maybe if I pretend this is a generic client, I can survive the rest of this meeting. I'm too far in to back out now.

"Anyway, I think on the mountain peak, I'd like there to be a cake topper of our initials, A and J, and a plus one."

"Of course. Would you want them rustic looking, maybe made from wood?"

Angelica claps her hands together. "Oooh, that sounds great."

"I'll sketch up some designs for you and we can schedule a flavor tasting whenever you'd like. I have a few more logistical questions as well."

As our meeting wraps up, my conscience twists my stomach. Angelica is a genuinely sweet person. I'd feel terrible if it turns out she really doesn't know that Jayson has been cheating on her. *Be the bigger person, Jules. You wish someone had told you.* I suck in a breath for courage. "I'm sorry, but I just have to ask. Do you know Jayson and I dated?"

Angelica's smile fades. "I did. I was sorry to hear that you two broke up. He really liked you."

I frown. What a weird thing to say. At least I have my answer. Maybe I truly avoided a bigger disaster by breaking up with Jayson. I smile, hoping Angelica can't tell how upset I am right now. So much for a generic client. "I'll try to have some designs emailed to you within the week."

"That's wonderful, thank you."

"You're welcome."

When she's gone, I fall into my chair, drained. I can't believe Jayson suggested they use me for their cake. Is he being spiteful? Well, I can be professional about it at least. I'll make the most amazing cake and show him he can't hurt me, that he didn't mean that much to me. Only he meant the world to me, and I'll have to be the best actress ever to truly pull it off. What other options do I have?

Something hits my calendar, blurring the note I made for Angelica's party. Another drop of water hits the paper. I'm crying. Of course. I reach for a tissue and do my best to dry off the page, then rewrite the entry. I grab another tissue and press it against my eyes, hoping to stave off the waterworks. *Pull it together, woman. You can do this. You have to do this.*

45

OCTOBER

Jayson

HUMMING AS I approach the house, I leap up the two steps to the porch and knock on the door. The bright red door swings open and I'm enveloped in a hug by Carlos's mother.

"Hola, Jayson."

"Hola, Señora Vega."

She lets me go and ushers me inside. "You know you're welcome to call me Veronica. Everyone is out back."

Never gonna happen. My parents instilled in me the value of respect by calling friends' parents by their last names and, even though I'm an adult now, I just can't break the habit. "Where should I put this?" I hold up a gift wrapped in light blue paper.

"There's a table out back. It should be easy to find."

I follow her through the house to the kitchen, where she stops to stir something in a pot on the stove.

"Mmmm, that smells delicious. Arroz?"

"Sí, gracias. I'll bring it out soon." She shoos me toward the sliding glass door.

I step through it onto the back patio. Streamers and crepe paper bells are everywhere, strung between trees, along the fence line, and hanging from all the porch railings. The gift table is a mountain range of packages of all sizes in various shades of blue. I perch mine on top of a peak and then step down into the yard. Angelica and James sit under a tree in two wicker chairs covered with more streamers and bows. Carlos stands next to James, appearing to be in a very animated discussion with his brother-in-law.

When I get closer to them, Angelica jumps up and throws her arms around me. "Jayson! So glad you could make it."

I kiss her on the cheek. "Of course, I'm here. Britt sends her congratulations. She had an event today she couldn't get out of, but said she'll see you at the big one."

"Oh, that's okay. I know how busy she is."

"Speaking of which, your parents are throwing you *two* baby showers?"

Angelica rolls her eyes. "It's ridiculous, right? Mom is over the moon about her first grandchild and wanted to cook in celebration. Since the Arboretum party will be catered, she threw a small one here."

"This is small?" I look around the yard, taking in the decorations anew. There are at least fifty people here. "I'd hate to see what she considers big."

She laughs. "You'll find out next month."

"How are preparations going for that?"

"Everything's falling into place. Thank you so much for recommending Little Shop of Sugar for the cake. Julie did a great job of capturing my vision. I can't wait to see it and eat it."

"That's great to hear. She really is amazing." My smile falters. I still don't know what happened between us. I've been tempted to visit her store for more of an explanation, but it wouldn't be right to ambush her at work. Visiting her at home would show her how much I care for her, but I can't quite bring myself to drive over there. She hasn't contacted me, which means she was serious about ending things. I should respect her wishes even if I don't agree with them.

Angelica puts a hand on my arm. "I'm sorry again about the breakup."

"Me too. I just don't get it. What could've happened for her to end things so suddenly?"

"If it's any consolation, she didn't seem too happy about it either. She actually mentioned it to me at our meeting."

Julie talked to Angelica about our relationship? "What did she say?"

"Just that you two dated. She seemed a little cool toward me. Is that her personality?"

I frown. Maybe the breakup is hitting her as hard as it is me. But then why did she do it? "No, she's usually somewhat bubbly, especially about desserts. She loves her work. Maybe she was having an off day." Or she could be feeling overwhelmed with this new part of her business. I wonder if Carlos knows anything. He might have seen her at the food pantry recently. I'll ask him if I get the chance.

Angelica twists her mouth to the side, not fully convinced. "Maybe. She gave me a discount, though."

"Why?"

Angelica shrugs. "Who knows? Maybe it's because I mentioned your name."

My heart lifts with hope. Maybe I still have a chance with her. What can I do to fix whatever went wrong? Now isn't the time to think about this. "Anyway, enough of this talk. Congratulations to you and James! I'm excited you were matched so quickly."

"Me too. We were planning to visit Puerto Rico over Christmas so I could introduce James to relatives he's never met, but that'll have to wait."

I nod. "They say a baby changes things. Guess this is your

first taste of it."

Angelica laughs. "Yeah, but it's worth it. We're just pushing back our trip until next year. Then the family can meet my husband and my child."

"What are you two talking about?" Carlos looks between the two of us.

"How babies affect plans."

"Exciting stuff." He turns toward the house and rubs his hands together. "Hey, the food's out. Angelica and James, can we bring you plates? The tías are heading over here to see you, probably to give you lots of advice about parenting. I doubt you'll be able to go anywhere for a while."

Angelica gives Carlos a side hug. "Yes, please. Get me plenty of arroz!"

"Me, too," says James. "And a few empanadillas."

"Coming right up," says Carlos.

We make plates for the couple before returning for our own, then sit down with our overflowing plates. "Man, two parties in two months," I say. "If your family has any more parties, I'm going to have to get a gym membership."

I pat my flat stomach, and Carlos rolls his eyes. "Whatever, man. What's been going on?"

"Nothing. Work is about it." I take a bite of rice and close my eyes, enjoying the flavors.

"Have you figured out what happened with Julie?"

I open my eyes and sigh. "No. I've tried to be respectful and give her space, but it's really been bugging me. Angelica said Julie seemed sad about the breakup too, but I still don't know what her reasons were."

"I think you should talk to her. You both seemed pretty serious. You deserve to know the truth."

If Carlos thinks I should talk to her, maybe it isn't such a bad idea. "She doesn't owe me anything, but it's really bugging me. If I do it, it'll need to be in person so she can't hang up on me like last time."

He waves his fork at me. "Yeah, but probably not at her work. That wouldn't be cool."

"I doubt she'd agree to meet me. I'll probably have to go to her apartment."

"Doesn't she have a dog?"

"She does."

"How's that going to work?"

I haven't told Carlos what I've been doing. What's he going to think? "I've been going to therapy."

His eyebrows shoot up in surprise. "What? When?"

"For a couple months."

"Has it helped?"

I tilt my head back and forth, considering. "I think so. She helped me work through my fears and I actually think I'd be okay now. I mean, I know I have more power and control now than I did as a kid."

Carlos gives me a skeptical look. "And you're planning to test it out on Julie's dog?"

"Well, I pretty much did it *for* Julie, so yeah."

"Wow. You really like her." His voice is tender, like he's finally realizing how much I care about Julie. The lump forming in my throat keeps me from speaking, so I just nod. "Then go talk to her, man."

I clear my throat. It's time. No more excuses. "I'll go after the party."

Carlos pumps a fist in the air. "Yes! I'm proud of you, Jay."

I smile at my best friend, but my stomach churns in nervous anticipation now that I've decided to visit Julie and her dog. I'm not sure which makes me more anxious. At least I should know exactly where I stand by the end of the night.

My car is a comfortable cocoon of safety. Am I really ready to do this? I take deep, calming breaths, then practice the countdown exercise to align my senses. It's time to really face my fears.

After a few more seconds of courage gathering, I get out and walk up the steps to the intercom next to the front door. I look over the list of names until I find J. Quinn in apartment 4D. I take another few breaths. Will she agree to see me or leave me standing on the front stoop? When the front door opens, I decide not to announce my arrival so she can't shut me out. We need to have this conversation face-to-face. I grab the handle just before it shuts and step into the lobby.

There's an elevator at the other end of the lobby, but I take the stairs to give myself more time to compose my thoughts. I reach the fourth floor much too quickly. The stairway door clicks closed behind me. The welcome mat in front of Julie's door gives me pause and I feel some courage drain out of me. *All guests must be approved by the dog*, it reads. Is her dog *really* friendly to everyone? There's only one way to find out.

I take two more deep breaths before knocking. Something shuffles toward the door. Is it the dog? There's no barking. Maybe she's well trained. For courage, I recite my power statements in my head. *I can handle whatever's behind that door because I have all the skills I need. I'm not powerless anymore.* The loud clunk of a bolt being turned startles me and I take a step back from the door. It swings open and my gaze latches on to Julie's surprised face.

46

Julie

MY HEART SLAMS against my ribs so hard I swear I hear a cracking sound. What is Jayson doing here? Emotions war inside my head. First, delight at seeing his gorgeous face and then heartache from the reminder of his duplicity. Being forced to face yet another man who cheated on me squashes all positive feelings. I scowl up at him.

"What are you doing here?"

Jayson shifts his weight from one foot to the other, his gaze flicking between my face and the apartment interior behind me.

"I think we need to talk." He swallows hard. "Uh, can I come in?"

The thought of being alone in my apartment with Jayson makes my stomach flutter in anticipation of sizzling kisses. *He's a cheater, remember?* I grit my teeth, both grateful and frustrated by my brain's reminder. Why do all the hot guys have to be such scoundrels? Will I ever learn? I can start right now. I take a step back, using the front door as a shield.

"I don't think so. There's nothing to talk about."

I pull my head in and close the door, but Jayson stops its

progress with his hand.

"I think there is. Julie, what happened? Things were going so well between us."

My shoulders slump, but I keep my weight pressed against the door for protection and support. "I thought so, too."

"I don't get it. Did I upset you somehow?"

"Jayson, I saw you with another woman."

"What? When?"

"At the Greek place. With *Angel.*"

Jayson's brow furrows. "Do you mean Angelica?"

This innocent act is too much. Anger explodes out of me, and I wrench the door open so he can experience its full brunt. "Yes! I can't believe you had the nerve to use me for your baby shower cake!"

"What are you talking about? I thought you'd appreciate more business."

Feeling an obligation to accept his supposed charity chafes me. I'm definitely sending someone else to set up the event. It's too hard seeing his face and being reminded how foolish I've been. "You know I can't say no because I need positive reviews and word-of-mouth advertising, but that's just low. If you weren't sure I'd gotten the message before, I did. Loud and clear. You are some weird people."

"Julie, I don't know what you're talking about. What message?"

I can't believe he's going to make me spell it out. "That you were just playing with me. You had a wife this whole time and continued the charade, even after I told you about Xavier. I'd thought better of you."

His eyebrows shoot up his forehead, his mouth hanging open for a second before he gathers himself enough to speak. "I don't have a wife. Do you think I'm with Angelica?"

"I saw you two kiss at the restaurant. Angelica told me how you met and that she calls you Jay. She even knew about us and didn't seem to care!"

He shakes his head profusely. "It's not at all what you think. Angelica is Carlos's sister. We're just friends, so of course she didn't care you and I were dating. She's married to someone else, not me."

I scoff and cross my arms over my chest. He sounds truthful, but I've been down this road before. I won't play the fool this time. "Nice try, but it won't work. I should have trusted my gut about you from the beginning."

Jayson takes a step toward the door and I take a quick step back. Surely, he wouldn't touch me, but better safe than sorry. He must notice the concern in my face because he quickly retreats, his body deflating. "Julie, I'm telling you the truth. I like you. Only you." He takes a deep breath. "But if you really think I'm this sleazy guy who would date someone behind your back, maybe it should be over."

The hurt look on his face makes my heart lurch, but then I remember how my heart dropped that day on the sidewalk when I saw Jayson and Angelica looking so cozy in the store and my resolve hardens. "I guess so."

Jayson pulls out a small box from the pocket of his jacket and holds it out to me. "Here."

I hesitate. "What is it?"

"Something for Sadie. I wanted to make friends, but I guess it doesn't matter anymore."

When my fingers touch the box, something clicks inside my mind. His eyes darting over my shoulder were in search of Sadie. Because he's terrified of dogs. And yet he came to my apartment, thinking he'd have to see her. Warmth floods my chest at the bravery he's shown. For me.

If only I hadn't seen Jayson and Angelica in the restaurant. No, it's better to know the truth than to live blissfully in a lie. I may not be a super genius Harvard grad, but I'm just as worthy of love and respect. Still, Jayson's show of courage moves me. It's probably the last time I'll see him, so what harm is there in mentioning it?

"I'm sure this wasn't easy for you to come here because of your aversion to dogs. I'm touched by your courage."

Jayson purses his lips, but doesn't look at me. "I've been going to therapy, so I could surprise you one day. I guess it worked, but too little too late. You've obviously made up your mind about me."

My traitorous heart softens. I can't believe he did that for me. He must have really cared for me once. "Wow," is all I can say.

He shrugs. "I'll see you around." He pauses and frowns. "Or not."

He lifts his hand in a half-hearted wave before turning and heading down the hall, disappearing into the stairwell.

Shutting the door, I lean against it for support. I feel guilty for standing firm, but I have to protect myself. I deserve someone who's faithful and trustworthy. Just because Jayson says things I want to hear doesn't mean he's being sincere. Carrying the small package to the kitchen, I set it on the counter before opening the lid. Dog biscuits are inside. Tears spring up in my eyes and I don't stop them from spilling over. Am I crying for the lost relationship or the reminder that I no longer have my dog? Does it matter? I give myself over to sorrow, sliding down the wall into a ball and burying my face in my knees. The knowledge that there isn't a furry face to nudge my knee or lick my face makes me cry harder.

47

NOVEMBER

Jayson

THE COUCH GROANS when I flop down onto my back. My finger presses buttons on the remote, absently flipping channels on the television. There's nothing on, but I need the noise. The doorbell rings. It's probably a solicitor, so I ignore it. It rings again and I turn up the volume on the TV. After a few more rings, someone bangs on the door. No solicitor is *that* persistent. I heave myself off the couch and pad to the door on socked feet. A look through the peephole elicits a resigned sigh. This is worse than someone trying to sell me solar panels for my roof.

I unlock the door and open it, turning away without a greeting and walking back to the living room. I plop back down on the couch and pick up the remote again, changing channels every few seconds. Carlos pushes my legs off one side of the couch to make room and sits down.

"Hey, Jayson, nice to see you, too."

I swing an annoyed gaze his way. Carlos is grinning. He's too happy for my taste. I roll my eyes and return to mindlessly flipping channels.

"Hey, Carlos. What's going on? I haven't seen you in forever," he says, pitching his voice high.

"Thanks for asking, Jayson," he says in his regular voice. "I've sold a few of my pieces lately."

"Wow, that's great," he falsettos.

"Thanks, man, I think so, too."

I continue to stare straight ahead, stone-faced, but I'm no longer aware of what's on the screen. Carlos snatches the remote from my hand and turns it off.

"Come on, man," he says. "I haven't seen you in *weeks*. You missed the family picnic on Saturday. Talk to me."

My head falls back against the couch cushion and I stare at the ceiling, my throat tight. "What's there to talk about? The woman I have feelings for thinks I'd cheat on her—that I *did* cheat on her—and I don't know how to prove it isn't true."

"Couldn't you get Angelica to straighten it out with her?"

"She thinks Angelica's the other woman."

"Huh. Well, that sucks."

I roll my head to the side so I can see Carlos's face. His smile has disappeared. That's better. "Yeah, it does."

"Are you helping Britt with the reception this weekend?"

"No. I told her I couldn't risk running into Julie again."

He winces. "Oh. Yeah. I didn't think about that. You're still coming to Angelica's baby shower, right?"

"I don't know."

"You have to, Jay. You're like an older brother to her. She'll be very disappointed if you don't come."

Way to pile on the guilt, Carlos. Does he think I haven't already thought of that? "It's just too hard right now."

He opens his mouth to argue some more, but the glare I shoot his way seems to halt the assault. "Fine. Do you want to eat?"

"Nah. I'm not hungry."

He gets up and heads toward the front door. Is he leaving without saying goodbye? I guess I can't blame him. I haven't been the best company this evening. He returns to the living room with a cooler, unzips it, and pulls out several glass food containers. He lines them up in a row on the coffee table.

"I hope you don't mind if I eat in front of you."

He doesn't wait for a response, but removes one of the container lids. The aroma drifts over to me and my mouth waters.

"Is that your mom's rice?"

Carlos grins. "Yep. Change your mind about eating?"

"Oh yeah. I'll get some plates and silverware."

"No need. I packed it all."

He sets paper plates and two packets of plastic silverware on the table. He then opens the remaining containers and my eyes widen at the spread of delicious food. My stomach growls, making Carlos laugh.

"Well, dig in," he says.

"With pleasure."

I slump back against the couch, my body satiated and my heart not hurting as much.

"Oh man, I needed that. Thanks for coming over."

"No problem."

Remorse about my earlier behavior bubbles up. "Sorry I was such a jerk to you before."

"I get it. It sucks to be in love. Especially when you can't fix the situation."

"You sound like you speak from experience."

Carlos shrugs. "I've been serious about someone a time or two."

This is news to me. Has he been keeping a secret from me?

"Is there someone right now?"

"No. I've been too busy trying to get my business going."

"You said you've sold a few things?"

"Yeah." He shrugs. "Enough to cover next month's rent, at least. Maybe eventually I can quit my day job and make art my career."

"What would it take to make that happen?"

"I'm not sure. Maybe if I could get a grant or endowment or a steady stream of commissioned work. It's definitely going to be awhile."

"Let me know how I can help." I'm proud he's pursuing his dream. Of course, my mind wanders back to Julie, dampening my mood again.

"Thanks. And if you want to talk any more about Julie, I'm available to listen."

I nod, but reminders of her make it feel like there's a dark cloud over my head, sucking up all my positive feelings and replacing them with despair and gloom. *I can't believe she thinks I cheated on her.* That's mostly my pride speaking, but I thought she knew me better than that. Sure, her ex burned her badly, but why does she have to take out her insecurity on me? She obviously still has some baggage she hasn't dealt with. Not that I can blame her. It took me twenty years to face my fear of dogs. The whole situation just sucks because I really do care for her. Unfortunately, there's nothing more I can do.

48

Julie

THE GIANT WOODEN initials on top of the cake are a glaring reminder I might have to see the happy couple snuggled up together as they celebrate their growing family. My stomach lurches at the thought. Even though he was dishonest, my heart still carries a bit of a torch for Jayson, especially after hearing what he did so our relationship could work. Unfortunately, overcoming a fear of dogs does not make up for infidelity.

I take a step back and admire my handiwork. The table looks perfect. The mountain cake turned out even better than I'd imagined and the collection of truffles around the bottom look just like fallen boulders. Angelica didn't care about the truffle flavors, so I made a mix of Jitterbugs and Sinfuls, hoping my memory of his favorites will please Jayson. Why I still care is beyond me.

Actually, I'm hoping these minor details will make it into the couple's review of my products. More positive reviews can only be good for business. The opportunity for more clients to see my work is the only thing helping me get through this awkward day. Nikki was supposed to handle this event, but her grandmother passed away, so she's in Atlanta with her family. At least now that

I'm finished, I can leave and return when the party's over.

I carry my containers into the kitchen and am surprised to see Britt supervising the food preparation. I thought she'd have put an assistant in charge so she can attend the party as a guest.

"Hey, Britt. Where can I set these containers?"

She smiles at me. "Put them in the supply closet over there. I've cleared a shelf for you."

"Thanks."

I set them down and turn to go. Britt lays a hand on my arm, stopping me. "I'm really sorry to hear you and Jayson broke up."

My hand flops in the air like a limp fish and I swallow the lump in my throat created by the gentleness in her tone. I look up and blink quickly to keep my eyes from producing tears.

It occurs to me that she had to know what Jayson was doing. She apparently wasn't bothered by it. I'd love to be able to cut off all ties with the Thompson family, but the Arboretum is where most of my wedding event income comes from at the moment. I'll have to continue to be professional for the time being. I suck in a deep breath and paste on a smile. "It's fine. We just weren't in sync with what we wanted. Are you excited about the baby?"

She shrugs. "Meh."

This surprises me. I thought she and Jayson were super close. They're sharing a house together, after all. Which, now that I know Jayson's married, maybe that was a lie too. Maybe Britt's reaction is because she's not really a kid person. Nothing wrong with that.

"Well, the cake's all set up, so I'm going to head out. Will you call me when the party's winding down and I'll come back and clean up?"

"Actually, Angelica asked if you'd stay until she could see the cake. She wanted to be sure to thank you in person."

Just kill me now. My stomach curdles at the reality that I'll have to see the happy couple after all. I suppose there isn't a more effective way of receiving closure on my former relationship. I smile, hoping it doesn't look as forced as it feels. "Sure. No problem."

"Great." Britt checks her phone. "She should be here in a few minutes."

I return to the main room, my feet moving like they're wading through molasses. The doors burst open and Angelica rushes in, looking truly amazing in a gorgeous baby blue dress. The doors close behind her and she practically floats over to the cake. She turns to face me, her eyes wide, and her hands clasped together.

"Oh, Julie, it's stunning! It's even more amazing than I imagined it could be. You captured my vision beautifully! Thank you so much."

The praise makes me uncomfortable, especially with all the less-than-kind thoughts I've had about her today. It's not her fault her husband's a jerk. "Don't thank me until you try it."

Angelica smiles. "I'm not worried about that. The samples I tried were divine. What truffles did you end up choosing for the rocks?"

"I used a combination of dark chocolate truffles and espresso-infused ones."

"Oooh, those sound wonderful. I love espresso! How did you know?"

Another way the couple is compatible, I guess. "A stroke of luck."

The doors open again, revealing a man in a pair of khakis and a light blue button-down shirt. He has light brown skin, black hair, and a toned but not overly muscular frame. He looks around until he spots Angelica, smiles, and dashes over, wrapping his arms around her from behind and kissing her cheek. "My Angel."

Angelica giggles. "Julie, let me introduce you to my husband, James."

My mouth falls open and the only proof I'm not a statue is my blinking eyes. *This* is her husband? Where's Jayson? I finally get my brain working again. "Your husband? This is your Jay?"

"He is. Honey, what do you think of the cake Julie made for us?"

James appraises the cake. "Very cool. Those rocks look real. Are they edible?"

"They're chocolate truffles," I say, still not believing my eyes. As the news settles, my stomach clenches uncomfortably. "I hope you like dark chocolate and espresso."

"We're both coffee nuts," Angelica says.

"Well, good." I'm still trying to wrap my mind around the fact it isn't Jayson with his arms wrapped around Angelica. Did I imagine that day in the restaurant? When James releases his wife's side to greet some guests, I decide there's no better time to find out. I clear my throat, suddenly feeling very warm. "Um, Angelica?"

"Yes?"

"This may sound weird, but did you and Jayson have lunch at the Greek place on Haywood Street a couple months ago?"

Angelica purses her lips while she considers the question. Her eyes light with recognition. "Yes. James and I met with him to learn about the adoption process."

That sounds plausible. Jayson handles a lot of adoption cases. But I don't recall seeing a third person at their table. I suppose he could have been in the restroom or something. "Forgive me for saying this, but it's going to drive me nuts if I don't. I was outside the restaurant and it looked like you two kissed."

Angelica tilts her head from side to side. "I probably kissed him on the cheek. My family's very affectionate and Jayson's like a big brother to me."

"Oh." My stomach twists painfully and I'm afraid I'm going to be sick. Jayson told me the truth, and I didn't believe him.

She doesn't seem to notice my distress because she continues speaking. "I suppose someone could misconstrue my friendliness for flirting. I've been accused of hitting on my friends' boyfriends in the past." Her expression opens when she puts everything together. She grabs my hands in hers, her face creased with concern. "Julie, is that why you and Jayson broke up?"

I press my lips together in a thin line. I'm suddenly horrified that I'm ruining Angelica's party. My mixed-up feelings have me acting out of character. Under normal circumstances, I'd never be so unprofessional as to confront a client at their party. I force my lips up into a smile. "No, not at all. I'm sorry I brought it up. Please forgive me."

She doesn't look convinced. "You sure?"

"Positive. Just ignore this entire conversation and enjoy your party. Congratulations on your future adoption."

I hurry through the kitchen, out the back door, and double over against the building. Jayson didn't cheat on me. He wasn't married. And he'd gone to therapy to move past his childhood fear of dogs. For me. My heart races in my chest. I've messed up *everything*. I finally found someone trustworthy and supportive, and I blew it all up because I'm paranoid. The door beside me opens and Britt peeks her head out.

"Is everything okay? Angelica's concerned about you."

I take a few deep breaths and straighten, placing a hand to my chest and feeling my pulse pound underneath. "Oh, you know. Just realizing how much of an idiot I've been. No big deal."

She comes through the door and it clangs shut behind her. "What are you talking about?"

I swallow, embarrassed to admit how wrong I've been to Jayson's sister. The words come tumbling out before I can stop them. "I thought Angelica was Jayson's wife, and he was using me to cheat on her. That's why I broke up with him."

She takes a few beats, digesting this information. "Did you tell him your reason?"

"I did, but I didn't believe him when he said it wasn't true. I've ruined everything."

My head drops into my hands. How could I have allowed my past to dictate my present? I don't deserve Jayson. He was willing to do the work. What have *I* done to move forward from the betrayal I experienced? Kept myself busy and tried to ignore it all. *Look how well that's worked for me.*

Britt touches my shoulder gently. I meet her gaze, prepared for her rightful judgment. The sympathy I find instead makes me feel even worse.

"You've certainly made a mess, but I don't think it's irreversible."

Her words feel like drops of rain on the parched soil of my hopes. "You don't?"

"No. It's obvious you both really like each other. Jayson's been moping around the house for the past few weeks. He definitely misses you."

"He does?"

"Yes. And you obviously miss him, too."

I nod vigorously. "Do you know how much torture I've been in thinking I would have to see him here with his wife?"

Britt chuckles. "I can't imagine having to take part in one of my ex's celebratory events, and I don't have feelings for any of them anymore."

Obviously, I need to apologize to Jayson, but after everything I've said to him and believed about him, I don't know if that'll be enough. The thought that I won't be able to make it up to him guts me. I don't want it to be too late.

"I..." I pause and take a fortifying breath. It's terrifying to say this out loud, but I need her to know how serious I am. I look her straight in the eye when I say the words. "I love him."

49

Jayson

LOOKING UP FROM the paperwork in front of me, I sigh. It's half-past eight and I haven't stopped for dinner yet. My stomach rumbles in response, but there's still so much work to do. I'll work another thirty minutes and then take the rest of my work home. My stomach argues loudly for dinner. I pat it, hoping to assure it. I'll pick up food when I leave. Maybe sushi from Dragon Sushi. I'm craving a Tipsy Tiger roll. My eyes return to the documents, and I try to refocus.

A knock on the door breaks my concentration. I'm shocked to find an hour has passed.

"Come in," I say, curious to see who else is still here this late. I'm not surprised when my aunt pokes her head through the crack in the door.

"Hey, Jayson. You're obviously busy, but could you spare a moment to help me with something in the conference room?"

"Of course. Give me just a minute."

"Sounds good." She flashes a bright smile, then turns, leaving my door open.

I shuffle all the papers back into their folders and stuff them in my briefcase. I'll help my aunt and then leave. My stomach gurgles in agreement.

When my desk is straightened up, I shut off the light to my office, close the door, and take the stairs up to the conference room. The door is open, so I walk right in.

I expect the table to be littered with papers, but that's not at all what I find. There are two place settings for dinner and several takeout containers. Beyond that is a large metal tray filled with chocolates. I move closer and realize they spell out two words— I'm sorry.

The door shuts softly behind me. When I turn, Julie's standing there. What's she doing here? She takes a step toward me.

"Jayson, I'm so sorry about everything."

There's a tremor in her voice. Is she nervous? Upset. My heart pulses at her distress, but I force myself to stay where I am, rather than wrap her in my arms like I'm itching to do. She obviously has more to say and I want to hear it.

"I'm sorry I didn't believe you when you said there was nothing between you and Angelica. I was just so nervous about opening my heart again and when I saw you at lunch with her after you said you were working, I jumped to the wrong conclusion."

"Julie—"

She holds her hand up. "Please let me finish." When I nod, she continues. "I feel awful that I doubted your integrity and I hope you can forgive me. The truth is, I miss you terribly. I understand if it's too late, but I just had to try because..." She steps closer until we're an arm's length apart.

"I think about you all the time. Every time a customer orders a Sinful or Jitterbug, your face clouds my vision. When I see this building in the distance, I remember the awesome lunch you prepared for us. Blue Goose will never be as good unless I'm sharing it with you. I got an email about Two Left Feet's next show in Greenville and I immediately wanted to call and ask if you'd go with me to see it. I can't turn around without being reminded of all the fun we've had and how wonderful you are. You've been so good to me. Better than I deserve. You went to therapy so we could be together. How much more evidence of your care for me do I need? I'm so sorry for not believing you. Please forgive me. I love you, Jayson."

My whole body freezes at her last words. Did she just say what I think she said? Does she really love me? It's a relief to know she believes me now, but I have to know what convinced her. My blood pounds in my ears from Julie's declaration, but I need to know before anything else can happen.

"What changed your mind?"

A blush creeps up her neck to her cheeks. It might be the cutest thing I've ever seen.

"I, uh, met Angelica's husband, *James,* at their baby shower. She told me you gave her information about the adoption process at your lunch meeting. I'm *really* sorry for rushing judgment. You didn't deserve my suspicions. I promise I'm going to work on my trust issues. I have an appointment with a therapist next week."

Wow. It's a big deal that she's taking steps to grow and change. I know how hard that can be. "It's a relief you know the truth. I hated knowing you thought I was like your ex. Please believe I'd never do that to you."

"I'm sorry for doubting you. Am I too broken for you to give me a second chance?"

My heart tugs in empathy. The anguished look on her face crumbles my last shred of restraint. I reach out and pull her to me, crushing her against my chest. Her arms wrap around my waist, and I breathe in her sweet smell. This just feels right. I kiss the crown of her head.

"You're not broken. Your past hurts have made you understandably wary. I should have given you more details about meeting with Angelica so you wouldn't have had any cause to worry."

She pulls back enough to meet my eyes, her voice barely a whisper. "Do you forgive me?"

I see the uncertainty in her face and answer immediately. "Of course I do."

"I can't believe you went to therapy for me. I'll never forget that, Jayson."

My hand reaches up and moves a stray lock of hair from in front of her eyes to behind her ears. "I don't want there to be any barriers between us. I love you, Julie."

"You do?"

I have to stifle a chuckle when her eyes widen at my confession. "I do."

I bend my head down toward Julie, stopping inches from her face, then raise my eyebrows in question. She responds by grinning and stretching up on tiptoe until our lips touch. Relief, longing, and everything else I've felt during these weeks apart flow through the kiss. She sighs and my lips can't help curving up.

"What was that sigh for?" I say when the kiss ends.

"I've really missed you."

"I've really missed you, too." My stomach growls, breaking the moment.

She takes my hand and pulls me over to the table. "I brought Dragon Sushi."

I wrap her in a tight hug, amazed at how perfectly she gets me. My heart feels full to bursting and I can't help picking her up and swinging her around the room in my arms. She laughs when I set her back down. "What was that for?"

"You're incredible. I've been craving sushi all evening. How did you know?"

She shrugs. "Just lucky, I guess."

I push Julie's chair in for her before taking a seat myself. The only sound in the room is our chopsticks tapping against plates until my hunger is no longer so sharp. I look over at Julie, who's staring at me with a smile on her face. My hand reaches across the table and takes hers.

"What?"

"Nothing really. Just happy to be with you again."

"Me too. So, how's Sadie? Did she like the biscuits?"

Julie looks away, removing her hand from mine and placing it in her lap.

"There's something I have to tell you."

Her serious tone makes my stomach dip.

"What is it? Is Sadie okay?"

"She's fine, but I don't have her anymore."

"What happened?"

She twists her hands, avoiding my eyes, and I know I'm not going to like whatever she says. "When I realized I was falling for you, I resolved to do whatever it took to be one hundred percent in the relationship. So I gave Sadie away."

My heart nearly stops. She gave away her dog for me? The enormity of her action smashes into my heart like a sledgehammer. "Oh, Julie."

A tear hits the table and I'm out of my seat in a flash, wrapping my arms around her and pulling her to standing, kissing her tear-stained face before leaning my cheek against the top of her head. "Is it too late to get her back?"

She sucks in a shaky breath and releases it. "I gave her to my brother and sister-in-law, so probably not."

"Tell them you made a mistake and really didn't mean to let her go. We can go right now and get her."

I loosen my arms, but Julie's hand grips the front of my shirt and pulls me tighter.

"It's actually probably the best for Sadie. I haven't been able to give her as much attention because I work so much, and they have a house with a yard."

"But she's your dog. You love her."

She nods against my chest. "I do, which means I want her to

be happy. Even if it's not with me. I can at least visit her whenever I want."

"Still, that can't be easy for you. She's been yours for four years."

"I appreciate your concern, but I'm committed to my decision."

I stroke a hand down her back, thinking. "Can I still meet her?"

"Of course."

"What about this weekend?"

"If that's what you want."

Julie sacrificed something she loves for me. It's almost impossible to wrap my head around. I'm going to do everything I can to prove I'm worthy of her love. My heart overflows with affection, and I tighten my arms around her. "I love you, Julie."

"I love you, Jayson."

I'll never tire of hearing those words.

Epilogue

FIVE MONTHS LATER

Julie

WHEN I CALL, Sadie comes running from the far end of the yard with a stick. I rub her head lovingly and take the stick from between her teeth.

"You can't take that inside, sweet girl. Rachel's rule."

Sadie wags her tail, apparently unaffected by the decree. I check her paws for mud before opening the door and letting her back into the house, then fill her food and water dishes.

"Okay, Sadie girl, I'm off to shower and get dressed. Enjoy your dinner."

I climb the stairs to the guest bedroom where I've been staying. Rachel and Tom are finally in Costa Rica on vacation. And for book research, as Rachel's been quick to point out. I hope they're having a great time. I've enjoyed house sitting and seeing Sadie every day, though with work busier than ever, she really is better off at my brother's house.

Fresh out of the shower, I spin giddily around the room. Jayson told me to dress up because he's taking me out tonight to celebrate. What we're celebrating, I don't know because he won't tell me. I didn't bring any nice clothes with me, so I went shopping in Rachel's closet and found this sexy little black dress, which should be perfect. I have no clue where we're going, but I don't care. Any place with Jayson is perfect.

In the living room, Sadie is curled up on her bed near the window. Something occupies her attention out in the yard, probably a squirrel.

Jayson should be here any minute. While I wait, I wipe off the counters, then straighten up the throw pillows on the couches in the living room. My body buzzes with excitement and I can't help but be amused that I still feel like an enamored teenager with Jayson. Things just keep getting better with him. He's very comfortable around Sadie now and has even taken her on solo walks when I house sit. I try not to let my imagination run away with thoughts of what it'd be like to have a home with Jayson. Someday, maybe.

The doorbell rings and I drop the pillow in my hands. Sadie's head swivels from the window to the door. She leaps out of her bed and rockets to the door, her tail wagging furiously. I can't help chuckling even as I hurry to the door myself.

"You know who it is, too, huh?"

I grab her collar, just in case, before opening the door. Jayson pulls a dog biscuit from his pocket and a bouquet from behind his back. Sadie takes the treat and I accept the flowers, ushering him inside. When the door's shut, I let go of Sadie's collar, then reach for Jayson's shoulder, drawing him to me for a kiss.

"Hello, handsome. You look very nice," I say when we draw apart.

"You look great, too."

"Thank you for the flowers." I bury my face in them and

inhale deeply.

"You're welcome. Are you ready to go?"

"Let me put these in water first. Would you let Sadie out one last time? I don't want to worry about getting back early from our date."

We stroll leisurely along Patton Avenue, hand in hand, chatting about the day. I pause when Jayson's office building comes into view. Is it another dinner on the roof or does he just need to pick something up? He holds the door open for me and I need to know, so I won't be disappointed if it's just a pit stop.

"Dinner on the roof?"

He chuckles and shakes his head. "Not quite the surprise I hoped it'd be."

"It's still surprising. And exciting. I really enjoyed the last time we were up there. Maybe we can do a little recreating of that scene, if you know what I mean."

I wiggle my eyebrows and Jayson laughs.

"I'm counting on it," he says.

It's quiet on the elevator ride up to the top floor and in the stairwell that leads to the rooftop access. My mind is wondering if it's tacos again and, if so, which one I want to eat first. Lamb? Chicken BLT? Ooh, fish! Jayson opens the door and motions me through ahead of him. My jaw drops as my eyes drink in the scene.

Jayson has strung small white lights along the rooftop and there's music playing from a speaker near the table. It's faint, but it sounds like an instrumental version of "Just the Way You Are." There's a crisp white tablecloth on the table and cushions on the chairs. A bottle of champagne rests in a tub of ice. I'm quite impressed by the romantic atmosphere Jayson created.

His arms wrap around my waist and I lean back against his

chest, feeling the kiss he presses to my hair.

"This is perfect, Jayson."

"Just wait. Sunset is in about twenty minutes."

"I bet that'll be amazing."

A memory wiggles its way to the forefront of my mind and I turn in his arms so I can see his face. "Jayson? Is this because of what I said the last time we were up here?"

He smiles. "Of course. You know I want to make you happy."

"You're very good at it."

"So are you."

Jayson ushers me into a chair, scooting it into the table when I sit. He removes two containers from a cooler next to the table. He opens the first one and divides it between our two plates. Then he opens the second and sets it in the middle of the table. I smile up at him.

"Caprese salad and garlic knots. This looks familiar."

He grins and sits down across from me. "I hope you're up for Italian tonight."

"I never turn down delicious food of any kind."

"I ordered the pasta carbonara for you because I wasn't sure what else you might like."

"Perfect. What did you order for yourself?"

Jayson catches the tease in my voice and grins. "Just the chicken parmesan tonight. I want to eat dessert."

"There's dessert? Can't wait!"

The sun sets while we eat; the sky turning from orange to blue to black. Finally, the stars poke through the darkness and it's just as beautiful as I imagined. Jayson clears our plates.

"Are you ready for dessert?"

"Always."

He places a container of chocolate-covered strawberries on the table.

"I thought this would go well with champagne."

"I agree. Though you haven't yet told me what we're

celebrating."

"Yes, I know."

Jayson stands from his chair and walks to my side of the table. He takes my hand in his, then lowers to one knee. I suck in a breath, my body flooding with excitement. A small, black velvet box appears in his other hand. When I meet his eyes, love is written all over his face.

"Julie, I love every moment I get to spend with you. Your love and support have meant so much to me. You are an intelligent, savvy, incredible woman. I can't imagine anyone more amazing than you and I'd love the opportunity to spend the rest of my life learning more about you. Julie Marie Quinn, will you marry me?"

Like there's any doubt. "Yes, Jayson! Of course I'll marry you!"

He opens the box, removes a gorgeous diamond solitaire ring, and slips it onto my finger. I admire it for a few seconds before grabbing Jayson's face with my hands and kissing him with everything I have.

When we break apart, Jayson's smile is the biggest I've ever seen.

"I can't believe I get to kiss you forever."

"Well, believe it, Jayse. Now, pop the champagne and let's celebrate!"

I catch the mischievous glint in his eye. "Whatever you say, Jujubee."

Thank you for reading *One Sweet Love*! If you enjoyed it, please consider leaving a review online.

Want to stay in the know about future books? Sign up for my newsletter at MeganByrd.net/newsletter

Find additional *One Sweet Love* content including a bonus scene at MeganByrd.net/OSL

ACKNOWLEDGEMENTS

There was a wonderful group of people involved in the process of creating and publishing this book.

Heather Gerwing, once again thank you for your wonderful insights and comments throughout the process. I appreciate being able to run myriad of things by you—storyline, cover design, title. I appreciate your friendship and sage advice.

Susan Ward, thank you for sitting on my porch with me to talk about the EMDR process and providing helpful feedback on the scenes to make them as accurate as possible.

Quinton Sawyer, thank you for reading the book and providing helpful suggestions about the characters and story.

Eleanor Vaughn, your perspective and comments made this a better book. Thank you!

Thank you to my Beta readers who helped shape this story: Cali, Kristina, Anna, Patti, Kara, Kristina, and Jodi.

Wigo_wiggles, thanks for the awesome character illustrations.

Special thanks to The Chocolate Fetish for making delicious truffles and chocolate creations that spark (and reward) my creativity.

Devereux and Banzhoff, PLLC, thanks for letting a strange woman look around your office in the Jackson Building and take lots of pictures.

My wonderful family—thanks for kicking around ideas with me on drives and at dinner. It's fun talking about the book with you and having your hand in the final product.

ABOUT THE AUTHOR

Megan Byrd lives in Asheville, North Carolina with her husband and two kids. She hates running, but loves hiking in the mountains toward a waterfall or scenic view and taking kickboxing, HIIT, yoga, and Zumba classes. When she's not reading, writing, or chasing waterfalls, she enjoys visiting local bookstores, wandering through thrift shops in search of special gems, listening to live music, and catching up with friends.

Want to be first to know when the next book is available? Sign up for her e-newsletter on her website to receive behind-the-scenes sneak peeks at her current work-in-progress, book recommendations, and other fun things. You can also visit MeganByrd.net/OSL for a bonus scene and to read about the inspiration behind this book.

MeganByrd.net
Instagram: @megan.e.byrd
Facebook Reader Group:
Facebook.com/groups/meganbyrdsweetreaders